Praise for

The Stone Road

Winner, Aurealis Award for Best Horror Novel, 2022
Finalist, Aurealis Award for Best Fantasy Novel, 2022
Finalist, Australian Shadow Awards for Best
Novel, 2022

"A coming-of-age story with a dreamlike quality. . . . Those who appreciate fantasy that leans toward fable will gladly follow along on Jean's journey."

—***Booklist***

"*The Stone Road* is lovely, hypnotic. I want to drink this book."
—H. A. Clarke, author of The Scapegracers trilogy

"Trent Jamieson's *The Stone Road* is a heart wrapped in thorns. Its world, even as it unpicks itself at the seams, is shot through with bright mysteries. . . . To read *The Stone Road* is to enter a lyrical, wavering world, a landscape wearied by time but vibrant with monsters grown out of history, watched over by clever birds, whispered beneath by the dead, where a girl strives to hold one town safe even as time and the long shadow of other people's choices erode what she knows to be true."
—Kathleen Jennings, author of *Flyaway*

Also by Trent Jamieson

Day Boy

Death Works
Death Most Definite
Managing Death
The Business of Death

Nightbound Land
Roil
Night's Engines

THE STONE ROAD

TRENT JAMIESON

EREWHON

an imprint of Kensington Publishing Corp.

www.erewhonbooks.com

EREWHON BOOKS are published by:

Kensington Publishing Corp.
900 Third Avenue
New York, NY 10022
www.erewhonbooks.com

First published in 2022 by Brio Books (Sydney, Australia)
First published in North America and Canada, the UK, and the Open Market by Erewhon
Books, LLC, in 2022

All Kensington titles, imprints, and distributed lines are available at special quantity
discounts for bulk purchases for sales promotions, premiums, fundraising, educational, or
institutional use.

Special book excerpts or customized printings can also be created to fit specific needs.
For details, write or phone the office of the Kensington sales manager: Kensington
Publishing Corp., 900 Third Avenue, New York, NY 10022, attn: Sales Department; phone
1-800-221-2647.

Erewhon and the Erewhon logo Reg. US Pat. & TM Off.

978-1-64566-070-5 (paperback)

First Erewhon hardcover printing: July 2022
First Erewhon trade paperback printing: May 2024

10 9 8 7 6 5 4 3 2 1

Printed in the United States of America

Library of Congress Control Number: 2021935355 (hardcover edition)

Electronic edition: ISBN 978-1-64566-036-1 (ebook)

Edited by Liz Gorinksy and Mandy Brett
Cover art by Qistina Khalidah
Cover type design by Samira Iravani
Interior design by Cassandra Farrin
Author photograph by Olivia Pratt, Hannah Photography

For Alex Adsett, who carried this book
all the way through storms and plagues
and tumults. Thank you.

The roads are poor
and the troubles many.

Part One

Huskling Eat Your Bones

Furnace woke the day I was born. The earth shook, birds clotted the skies, and the dead, suddenly blinded, howled low and loud enough that almost everyone in Casement Rise heard them. Afterwards, a thin scratch of black smoke rose from behind the Slouches, the low hills west of town.

Furnace had been lit, and soon it began to call: a deep humming in the earth and the air. A deep humming that burned right through the body.

Nan sent three men that way to find out what caused the smoke, what it meant. Good men; strong and trustworthy. They did not come back for weeks, and when they did, they were changed. Quieter, sullen, whispering of a promised land. They called it Furnace—so did everyone, after that—and they soon left again, going back to Furnace. Three others went with them. Those six were not the last to be called, but no one else came back.

My life was bound with Furnace, and that was a bleak and thorny tangle of a thing, worse than the angry mysteries of my mother.

I was born mad, she said. Born with teeth, and I bit Dr. Millison's hand as he cut my cord, tasting blood before milk. Suckled hard, and gave pain before I shed any tears. That was her version, anyway. I was a baby. It was all heat and light and touch in my infant mind. I knew nothing of my own ragged birth or the earth's agitation. Didn't know when Furnace called my dad, and drew him away from my mother, who took to drink and nights of crying not long after.

I knew nothing about all this until the dead man spoke, and I was older by then. Before that I was walking, talking, singing, and crying, always with Nan, thinking the whole world was all about me, the way children do.

The dead man grabbed my leg, as hard as you could imagine, his fingers digging deep into my skin. He pulled me down to the black earth, and whispered, "Finally! I gotcha! The light burns down here, but you I could see. Listen. There's a hungry fella coming for you. Listen to me. Listen." His breath was hot, his eyes white, the pupils pinpoints scratching for sight.

I didn't listen; I howled.

I don't remember what else he told me, but I will never forget Nan's response: the sudden sourness of her sweat mingled with tobacco, like it had turned all at once to fear; the way she yanked me from his dead grip, swift but gentle (and she could be anything but gentle). There was a part of me that watched, distant and cold, oddly satisfied as she struck the dead man hard with her walking stick. Then he was gone, like he had never been there at all.

But my leg stung, and his fingerprints would mark me for days. The first touch is like that.

"Keep your feet clear of the earth, Jean! You must keep your legs up. Higher, now. Higher, Furnace take you! You're not ready."

I cried, and she held me steady, and stared hard into my eyes. I stared back—I was never one to look away—and she smiled at that a little. Nan always respected strength, even as she hunted out weakness. I sniffed and snuffled, and the tears came. She rubbed her thumbs across my cheeks.

"This has started too soon. The dead are always talking, and there are so many of them now, but you shouldn't hear them. Not yet. I'm so sorry, child."

She didn't sound sorry; she sounded angry, perplexed. Maybe other things as well, but what do children know? She held me up from the earth, hard on her hip, her other hand tight around her walking stick, until we were home. I wasn't a baby anymore, and Nan wasn't a young woman, but she carried me all the way, and she didn't falter.

From then, until I was much older, I was forbidden to walk barefoot outside. Even in boots, Nan told me, I had to be careful wherever the earth was clear of grass. Because that's how the dead speak. That was how Nan and I heard them: up through the earth and the soles of our feet.

That is the first thing I distinctly remember, that dead man's touch. From that point on, memory came to me clear and true, at least with most things.

Furnace called others in our town, but even then I was heading to the Stone Road. I was called to death. Nan did her best to keep me from it—keep me from the town, too—and saw to my education. I learnt more from her tales of the town than I ever did from walking through it. I rarely walked outside without her company, and hardly saw anyone on my own. And I guess it worked, for a while.

Then it didn't.

On my twelfth birthday, a man came to visit, uninvited.

Twelve is a lucky number, though it didn't turn out so lucky for me. I suppose that's no surprise; it was my birthday, after all.

There was a party. There had been cake, and fairy floss made from an old hand-wound machine that Aunty Phoebe brought out with great delight every time someone in town had a birthday, whether they had a sweet tooth or not. Nan's friend Jacob had come over with his placid pony, May, both pony and man possessed of infinite patience. He let me and the other children ride her even though I was a bit old for such things. I'd received from my aunts, who were generous that way, exactly three books, all of them printed by publishers in the Red City, all of them adventures. I liked that kind of book a lot. In truth, I'd rather have been reading them than playing party games.

I was the only one who saw the man, at first.

He came up from the creek, dressed in a cloak of leaves, walking daintily, like a cat crossing a puddle. He moved so gracefully that it was hard not to be captivated. I held my breath, watching him. It was the sort of grace that threatened to become chaos, but never did.

I might have run if I had more sense. Instead, I watched, waiting for it all to come undone. He was the most interesting thing I had seen that day. Which was why it was all the odder that no one else seemed to see him.

However, they did move to let him pass, with troubled looks on their faces that rippled out from his passage. Soon enough, everyone was frowning like someone had been sick in front of them, but no one was ill. Lolly Robson *had* thrown up on himself from all that fairy floss, but that was hours ago, and his mother had taken him and his brothers home—much to their horror, and his shame.

Even though it was my party, the guests were happy to leave me alone. My birthdays had a reputation for hazard. I was different. The other children weren't grabbed by the dead when they walked barefoot. Their nans didn't get up before dawn, and go out into the dark doing whatever it was that mine did. Seeing to problems, she called it. I just saw it as a secret. But I didn't ask. I'd given up on asking. I never got an answer, just reproach.

I stood alone, a bit distant from everyone, watching the adults and their reactions to that graceful man's approach.

He was swift, though he didn't hurry, just walked right up to me. "Miss March," he said. His voice had a chill to it. "I believe it's time we met."

He smelled of rot and river water, with a deeper scent of smoke. That last one was familiar: It filled the town whenever the wind blew in from the west over the Slouches, carrying the smell of Furnace with it, and giving me migraines. One was already coming on. Why did he smell like that? It brought back memories, things I thought I'd forgotten from my most babyish years. That smell. A chair. My nan holding me.

I was frightened, but he positively beamed at me, as though I was the cleverest, most enchanting thing he had ever seen. "I came to say happy birthday. Why, it's my birthday, too, don't you know?"

"Happy birthday," I said, and he clapped his hands.

"She speaks!" He touched my face. I flinched—his fingers were clammy, the smell of smoke rising harder against the rot. I moved to step back, but he grabbed my wrist. "Thank you for the birthday wishes. They're much appreciated, Miss March. I was beginning to think you were a mute." He glanced at my boots. "You're half-deaf as it is, wearing those. What's your grandmother doing? You take those heavy boots off sometimes, I bet? Don't you? You're not *all* timid."

He crouched down, and peered into my eyes. I tried to shut them, but I couldn't. I tried to yank my hand from his, but he held it, steadily. He kept up his study of me. "Right. Don't talk too much, now. It's better if you keep your mouth shut, and listen."

His eyes shone gold. They were quite beautiful, but there was something wrong in them: a shadow, and a hunger of sorts. How did he know my nan? He certainly thought little of her when it came to me.

"Don't you want to know how old I am?" he asked.

When I shook my head, he seemed ready to slap me. I knew that look, though I mostly saw it on my mother's face. I flinched.

Instead, he smiled. "I'm twelve," he said. "How am I twelve when I'm a man? Do you know?" His grip tightened, and his mouth unhinged. His teeth were dark and sharp, his breath smelling of ash. "How am I twelve when I feel so old?"

I shrugged. How could I possibly know the answer? He came even closer, close enough that our lips almost touched. The world buzzed and popped, and my heart lost its rhythm, turning into a painful clenching. All I could smell was smoke. Time stilled. His hands that threatened violence lifted, and he reached up and pulled a golden coin out of my left ear. I swear, I'd felt it swell there.

There was a cruel delight in his eyes, almost as though he hadn't expected that to happen. He winked. "Birthday magic," he said. He pressed the coin into my palm. "This is my gift to you. If you want it."

I nodded, clenched my fist around it. He smiled like he was truly happy. "I'm so very pleased," he said. "Magic is the key to a good friendship, they say."

"Get away from her." And there was Nan. Face bloodless, full of fury. "Away."

"I only came to wish her happy birthday." He sounded surprised, almost offended.

"You weren't invited."

"I should have been."

Nan held her walking stick like a club. "Get away from her." She didn't shout it, just said it cold and calm. In that moment, I was more scared of her than him. I'd not seen her like this before. A little moan passed my lips.

The man laughed. "You've coddled her, Nancy. Why? You weren't treated so gently. She's a mouse; a tiny, frightened mouse. Look at her, not a single bruise. At least, not from you. And there you are, weakening, weakening, and she's never been tested. Doesn't even suspect the troubles coming her way."

I looked from him to her. What troubles? But Nan wasn't looking at me.

"Get!" She swung her stick, and somehow missed.

"You shouldn't do this," he said. "You should have invited me. We've had our chats, but she's my concern now."

"Go," Nan said, and swung again.

He danced backwards, out of reach.

"Happy birthday, Jean," he said. "It's going to be an interesting year."

Then, without a hint of hesitation, he turned, so gracefully, and dived at my grandmother. What she did next was not at all graceful, but it was precise. She swung her stick, and there was such a loud crack that my ears rang. The world stopped buzzing, and the graceful man was gone, with nothing left of him except a pile of leaves that Nan quickly threw a match into.

She grabbed my shoulders, looked in my eyes like she was hunting something there. I wanted to turn my head, but that gaze held me. What was she looking for?

"You still in there?"

"Yes," I said.

Something loosened in her. "Did he hurt you?"

I realised I had pissed myself, and I started to cry, full of shame. I knew that he had wanted to hurt me, though I didn't know why.

I shook my head. Behind her, far too many people were staring at me. The children had stopped playing. Some folks were leaving, herding their children before them. I couldn't see my mum. Later she'd come home, smelling of liquor, and she'd hold me, her eyes hard, like it was all my fault, like I'd called trouble down on me, and she was comforting me despite herself. But she'd hold me anyway, and I'd let her.

Nan leant down by the burning leaves, not much more than ash now. She jabbed at them with her walking stick, and they fell apart.

"Go clean yourself up," she said, tapping her stick against her heel. "You're safe now."

I didn't believe her. I didn't know what to believe, but I knew I wasn't safe. Troubles were coming, no matter what Nan said.

I suppose I shouldn't have been surprised. Every birthday of mine was a challenge. Mum and Nan would grow tense the day before; they'd start whispering, stopping before I entered the room. Who could blame them for being so anxious?

When I turned one, the townsfolk say, a big grey bird the size of a dog with a beak like a hawk came, and sat on my window. When I reached for it, it tried to peck out my eyes. But I was quick, and I laughed and swatted it away. That bird went and ate Mrs. Card's tiny dog, Beatrix; so I heard. Nan never spoke of it, but my Aunty Liz told me.

On my second birthday, a column of fire burned right in the heart of town. It died away as soon as Nan went to it. No one else could have banished such a thing, or so Jacob whispered to me one evening when I asked him about my birthdays. "Your nan's special. So are you."

"What about my mum?"

"Of course. She is, too." But he made the circle of the Sun upon his palm, and people don't do that unless they've said something bad. Then the conversation stopped, and I didn't learn what that special thing was.

On my third birthday, there was a storm so hard-edged that buildings fell right over, and four people went missing, blown out of town like that girl and her dog and the twister in the storybooks (though some say that all they did was go to Furnace). I never thought it odd that the world could, on a whim, just yank people away. That's what I grew up with.

When I turned four, the sun was sealed up by the moon, and there was a distant howling, like a hundred wolves had been set loose upon the land. The howling didn't last long, falling away to a silence that was, somehow, far worse. That one I remember: The land grew so still it made me cry. Nan held me until the sun returned. The memory remains so clear to me.

My fifth birthday was marked by a cloud of locusts that ate most of that year's crop. They called that year Jean's Famine, though no one would say that to my face. Nan discouraged it, but I still heard it when no one thought I was around.

On my sixth, three people were found dead in their homes. Whispers of a man without skin, a monster, went around town.

On my seventh, there was a distant ringing, and a rope appeared, hanging from the sky. The farmer, David Preston, decided to climb it, despite Nan warning him not to. Soon after, the ringing stopped, and we watched David's head fall to the earth. People blamed us, particularly his brother Myles, who has been punishing us ever since.

When I turned eight, a tall tree in the park flowered with sweet-smelling stone fruit that made anyone who took the smallest bite sick for weeks. Somehow that fruit ended up finding its way into every kitchen, lurking in every pantry. Myles came at the tree with an axe, but Nan wouldn't let him chop it down. She consumed the fruit herself, staying at its base throughout her sickness. From that point on, the tree stopped producing fruit, and instead shone white and ghostly. Townsfolk called it White Tree, and were banned from going near her.

Nine, and something stole the Robsons' best cattle. Took all Nan's skill to stop a war.

On my tenth, there was a fire upon the river, a twining flame that raised itself high, like a demon, or a twister. It didn't make a sound, but it set the birds restless. No one was stupid enough to swim to it, which pleased Nan, so we stood upon the banks, and watched it burn, town on one side, birds on the other.

On my eleventh birthday, nothing happened, but a few weeks later Jim, the trader, arrived, and said that there had been an insurrection in the Red City, and five Masters had been dragged out into the day. A terrible death for them: The sun set them alight and screaming at once.

The Council of Teeth, the rulers of the Red City, were swift in retribution. They feared a loss of face almost as much as open rebellion. I remember Nan demanding that Jim be specific about the date, then looking at me with a grim horror, a look that I'd never seen her give me before. It went away quick, but I didn't forget. Since that dead man's touch, I'd not forgotten anything.

All these things happened, and the town saw me at the heart of them.

Nan said that there were bad occurrences every day, some you needed to look for, others you didn't, and my birthdays weren't that special. I didn't quite believe her, but felt lucky that, except for the bird, none of these things really happened to *me*, until the graceful man and his golden coin.

My coin, now. I didn't tell Nan about it. Something stopped my mouth. I took it to my room, and hid it beneath my bed.

Every night I'd look at it, and I'd smell smoke, and the hint of a headache would drift behind my eyes. Sometimes the coin would burn hot in my hands, and the next day I would hear of so and so, gone west, gone to Furnace. Despite the horrible prick of my guilt, I never told anyone about that coin. Not when I was twelve, or for a long time after.

Well, I told *someone*.

There was one person I could talk to about that coin, though he wasn't really a person anymore.

That evening, while Nan and Mum held a whispered conference in the kitchen, I snuck outside, sat on the edge of the stairs to the verandah, slipped off a shoe, and touched a single toe to the earth.

The dead boy was there. Sometimes he wasn't, and I'd lift my foot up straight away, lest an angry man start talking or moaning about the blinding light, and the closed gate. I had no patience for the other dead; they scared me. But I liked to talk to the little dead boy.

The dead below couldn't see where they were, but they could see me, and Nan. The boy had forgotten his name, but he remembered other things.

"Jean?"

"Yes, it's me."

"Good. Your nan, she's a terror!"

"I was nearly killed today."

"Don't you horrify me so, Jean! Nearly killed on your birthday? Your birthday, it's always your birthday!"

"I'm all right now."

"What happened?"

"There was a man, a graceful man."

"Oh, the one that treads so lightly out of the west! The one that catches us like fish. I don't like him. Keep away from him, Jean."

"I will," I said, wondering why he'd never mentioned him before. "But he gave me a coin."

"I wouldn't take a gift from him."

"Too late."

"I suppose you must keep it, then."

"He reminded me of the chair," I said.

"Oh, that was a ghastly thing."

"Yes," I said, and shuddered. Not wanting to think on it.

"Did you have a good birthday?"

I thought about that instead. "Until then, yes. I think."

"Was there fairy floss?"

"Yes."

The dead boy sighed, the sort of sound that could break your heart with sadness. "Was there cake?"

"Yes."

"What was it?"

"Chocolate, of course!"

"Oh!"

"Do you remember chocolate?"

"I've forgotten so much down here," he said. "It seems so long ago, all those foods and sweets. But I'll never forget chocolate."

That made me sadder than I cared to admit. "Would you like a story?"

"Yes, for a little while. If you don't mind."

I looked around; no one was about, so I opened one of those adventure books, and started to read to him. There were pirates and everything. The dead boy helped me with the difficult words, and I forgot about the graceful man.

But Nan didn't.

It started raining that night, and kept raining for five days straight. Nan would leave before dawn, and come home, cursing, around midday. She'd be drenched to the bone, feet covered in pale mud. She took it out on me and Mum. Stared like a trapped hound out at the rain. Our dog Elic, who *was* a trapped hound, stared with her. We all got that way. Everyone in a mood. The house damp, the only dry spot the kitchen, where the stove burned day and night.

Maybe it wasn't the rain that bothered her, though.

Finally, Nan brought out a long length of fine-woven cord, slender and pale, and then she cut my hair, which had never been cut before. She hacked at it with scissors until it was little more than a finger length, me howling and moaning all the way. Once she was done, she sat down, and started tying little knots in the cord, each pulled tight around a strand of my hair, daubed in her blood. She sang as she worked, a low and mumbling melody.

I asked her why she'd done something so cruel. She scowled at me, and said that a woman had to have a hobby, a busy woman even more so, and there wasn't a person in town as busy as her, and I should be happy that it wasn't my blood that she was using, and that if I didn't stop asking stupid questions, she might just start using mine instead.

There were metres of that cord, and she worked for hours, hardly making any progress at all. But it kept the ill humours from her, mostly, and it kept me free to go read my books. I'd check on her, from time to time, and she'd look up at me. "Find something better to do," she'd say. "Can't you see I'm concentrating?"

There was no talk of the graceful man. We hardly talked at all except to snap at each other. But every so often, Nan might put down her knotting, and say something like, "The rivers north will be rising."

Mum would nod. "People will be drowning."

Hardly inconsequential talk!

I couldn't help but think of those poor souls caught up in the river struggling at first, then growing still from the inside out, except for the motion of the brown water itself, tossing them this way and that.

The rain fell, and my dreams filled with dead folk floating, rolling in the current. When they came face up, they'd stare at me, flesh swollen and angry, as though it was all my fault. There was a splash, and on the opposite shore, I'd see the graceful man, sitting in a chair, fishing rod in his hands. He'd wink at me, flick the rod up, and a corpse would tumble from the water and onto the riverbank. He'd smirk down at it, and open his mouth, wider, and wider.

I'd wake and find my hands cupped around the golden coin, and it'd be warmer than my touch could account for, almost hot enough to burn. I'd slip the coin under my pillow, and fall back into the turbulence of dreams, but he was no longer there. Until he was. Over and over.

No wonder my days were full of such grump and grumble. I was half asleep on my feet.

One day, Jacob came over, and Nan left with him. Myles Preston's farm was flooding, and they had to get their sheep to higher ground. I knew Myles didn't like us, but he was happy to ask for our help.

"You stay here," Nan snapped at me. "Ella?"

Mum shook her head. "I'm not going there. Why would you ask that?"

Nan nodded. "Very well."

When they were gone, I looked at Mum. "Why aren't you going?"

"Me and the Prestons," Mum said, turning to look towards the kitchen, where I knew her bottle was. "We have history, that's all I'll tell you. No one likes the Prestons."

"But Nan—"

"Your nan's a better woman than I am, Jean."

That was all I could get out of her. A little later, she poured herself a drink.

The creek on our land started to rise. It came in from under the levee, and went out under it, too. I'd never seen it much larger than a trickle before. Nan told me to give it a wide berth, said she was worried enough that it might flood the whole town without worrying about me being swept up by it.

Still, I walked out there under a big red umbrella to watch the water churn. There was an old me inside the young me, not of the future, but of the past. I'm the churning of the waters, she's the current. I didn't feel her often, but she was full of defiance. And she had interest in the creek.

I didn't see any bodies, though I kept my distance, the water brown as mud, raging like some wild beast.

But there was one spot that was calm.

I walked down to the edge of the bank nearest it, and peered into the water. It was like looking at brown glass. The creek roared, and hissed, but this bit was perfectly calm, like a bath before you dip that first toe. I wanted to touch it as much as I didn't.

I hesitated, and it waited for me. Somewhere nearby a tree fell, cracked and crashed into the froth. I jumped, but the water stayed perfectly still, and the fallen tree rolled past, throwing up waves, none of them striking this bit of shore.

I stood there, staring down.

She's a mouse. Look at her. A frightened mouse.

I reached my hand in, felt around; the water was warm and soft. I held my hand beneath the surface for a full ten counts before starting to pull it up, when something grabbed my wrist.

I hung there unbalanced, and the water began to churn.

I wrenched my arm free, so hard it hurt. I fell on my bum, and scrambled backwards up the muddy bank. There were leaves pressed into the palm of my hand.

I brought them to my face. They smelled of smoke. And then the creek edge where I had just been standing fell away into the torrent. I almost jumped out of my skin.

Nan was knotting when I came in with mud all over my clothes. I choked back tears, but my face must have been so wet you could hardly tell.

"You go down to the creek?" she said, looking at me.

I nodded.

"What did I say about going there? Do you want to drown?" She didn't wait for an answer. "Draw the bath, and don't waste time heating the water. Then you're off to bed."

I didn't argue, just filled the bath from the tank, then soaped down my clothes and my skin. By the time I was done, the water was brown, and I was shivering, but nothing grabbed me. I went to bed without any supper.

When I slept at last, the river had grown indistinguishable from my dreams. Churning and calm, churning and calm. Then grab, grab, grab.

You can't call that sleeping!

Finally, the rain stopped.

The day after that, Nan put on her big, blue felt hat, and took me over the white dirt hump of the levee that circled the town.

I'd never left Casement Rise, and while I knew there was a world beyond the levee and the Summer Gate, I'd not given it much thought. The Council of Teeth ruled the Red City and the north, and Furnace burned in the west. All I really knew of the outside was that it pushed against my home. There was the town, there was Nan, and my mother who made pots, and that had been enough.

Nan held my hand. I hadn't been expecting to come this way, but then that's how most of her walks went, to unexpected places. I thought we might be off on an errand, which she'd started taking me on of late, watching me when she thought I wasn't looking. I didn't like that at all, so I'd started watching her, too.

It's remarkable, the things you learn about someone when you really look. The anger that seemed to edge everything Nan did. The resentments just beneath the surface. What was she learning about me? I guess I'd never know the answer.

Today we'd not gone to the gardens or made a delivery of pots; she'd not held someone as they wept, and begged her to talk to the dead: their dead. The one they had lost, the one they wanted comfort from.

I knew she was serious because she hadn't rolled a smoke, nor gotten me to roll her one. She wasn't singing, either, and Nan always sang under her breath, unless you were in trouble.

We walked up the levee. She stopped at the top, examined a marking on a tree, frowned, made the mark larger with the burnt tip of her walking stick (though I couldn't tell you why); then we walked down the other side. The levee wasn't that steep; it was still muddy with all the rain, and it stuck to my boots.

"Watch your step," she said, as we descended. "Don't tread on any of the markings."

"Worse than stepping on a crack?" I asked.

Nan rolled her eyes. "When has a crack ever done you harm? What nonsense! These markings are powerful, and you mustn't damage them. The rain's done enough of that."

I walked carefully then: one sucking step after another, until we were all the way down.

"Where we going?"

She didn't answer, and I didn't press her. I felt lucky that she'd taken me along with her. Nan was always busy, even if I didn't always know with what. It was nice to be part of it. And sometimes I didn't really understand when she answered anyway.

Besides, here we were at the bottom of the levee. The whole wide world about us. It was dizzying. The summer sun lashed down through the blue; insects creaked, and scratched.

Nan didn't slacken her pace for me. We hurried from the levee. Nan flattened a path with her walking stick through nettles and low scrub, around thickets of warpweed, gagweed, and dogstail. The air was humid and thick. Cows, shimmering with steam, moved in a field north of us, flicking their tails at flies.

She stopped at the edge of a road, and studied it. Concrete, cracked and dirty, and edged with weeds. It gave off a heat in the sun that made me wince even in all that wet air.

"Roads are fickle things," she said.

"What?"

"You need to be careful around them. They take you places, but not always where you think they will. They can lie, and some can make you sicken."

Then we were off again, before I had time to make sense of that.

"Where we going?"

"To visit a tree."

"I've seen trees," I said. I stopped all at once, still holding Nan's hand, and she did, too, stopped by the dead weight of me. A prickle was digging in my shin through my sock.

"Ah, but you're a lump of a thing," Nan said. She had hard, dark eyes that could cut into you. There was a bit of an edge to them right then, but she softened it with a smile. I pulled out the prickle, showed it to her. Nan sighed. "Need to toughen you up," she said.

I flicked the prickle away.

"I've seen trees," I said, again, and spat on my fingers to rub my shin.

"Yes, but there's trees and then there's trees. Ones that're silent. Ones that aren't. Some that're friendly, some that hate. This tree takes an interest in the world, and sometimes forcefully, like White Tree, only older and bigger, and less cruel. This tree is a friend, if she likes you."

"Will she like me?"

"That's what we're going to find out. Amongst other things. There's trouble coming. He's taken a serious interest in you."

"Who has?"

"You know," Nan said.

"He smelled like the chair," I said.

She nodded. "Yes, the chair. I remember."

There was a time when I was much younger when a chair in the kitchen took on a sinister air. I'd see it, and I'd shiver. I didn't like sitting in it; my nose would fill with smoke, and my head would start aching.

Nan told me not to be foolish, but it only got worse.

I'd fall asleep thinking of it. I'd dream dark dreams where there was nothing else in the house except that chair, and I'd wake screaming. I stopped eating. I could hardly walk into the kitchen.

Finally, Nan took notice. She started to watch the chair closely. Sometimes I'd catch her talking to no one, just looking at the chair.

Then one day there was a fire in the garden. Four rose bushes went up, and four men went west all at once, and after that, the chair lost its menace, though I still didn't like sitting in it.

"Now, hurry."

The road turned north, and Nan used her stick to point things out.

"See that hill?"

"The one with the tower?"

"Yes, though that isn't a tower, that's an old power pylon from before the Years of Heat and Sadness—those things made the land thick with electricities. Beyond that tower is Huskling land. They're friends, too, in a way. Dangerous friends."

"Husklings are monsters," I said. I'd heard enough about them. It was all, *Furnace take you, girl*, or *Huskling eat your bones*, if I was making trouble.

"Oh, they're monstrous, all right, but we've a treaty with them. And before you ask me what a treaty is, we live and let live, and sometimes we help them, and other times they help us. They're monsters that can be dealt with."

I nodded, tried to take it in. Nan squeezed my hand.

"It's time I started teaching you properly. You're getting older, and I'm getting ancient. We've responsibilities, and I've kept them from you long enough." She shook her head, mumbled to herself, "She doesn't need your justifications, Nancy."

I looked at her as she came to some conclusion. I felt as though a door had opened a little, that she'd let me in somewhere.

"Yes. To the west of that hill is the Prestons' place. They manage sheep. East of it, the Robsons' land: cattle country."

I scrunched my nose up at that, and Nan tapped my wrist. "Don't you be too harsh, no matter what I say. It's a hardscrabble life out here. They're farmers; they keep us from starving. Can't grow everything within the levee, and trade's too sporadic with the north. That thicket beyond the station house is their ceremonial place. They're heathens one and all; you have to admire that. You know young Lolly Robson, don't you?"

I nodded. "Of course I do," I said. "He spewed at my party."

"Oh, I'd forgotten about that. That party proved more memorable than it should have. He's quite the foolish child. You have considerably more sense than him."

The road took a turn to the east, and up a rise. Nan stopped talking, and we sweated our way up that hill, the town behind us. When we reached the top, we stood there to catch our breath. Down below was a field of the sort that tended to brown, but was green after all that rain. In the middle of that field, rising high, was a solitary eucalyptus, its limbs bone pale. Shapes circled it, thousands of white birds.

Nan gave my hand another squeeze. "Down we go," she said.

The tree grew bigger, more solid as we approached.

"Watch," Nan said. "Give her close attention."

I wanted to ask why, but I did what I was told.

She had once been higher, you could tell, but lightning had turned the top third of her to charcoal, the kind of damage that would destroy a lesser tree. Her trunk was scarred, and where it had been cut, she bled a thick red sap. She rose defiant from the earth. My heart beat faster, and I couldn't decide if it was from fear or fascination.

A little closer, and I realised that those cuts were writing. Not words as I understood them, but something else, sharp lines that slashed across each other. I wanted to read them, but whatever meaning they expressed slipped away from me faster than I could gather it.

The white birds had eyes as red as the tree's sap, their beaks darker than the burnt crown of the tree. Round and round they flapped, and rushed and cackled.

"They're clever birds," Nan said. "They're the tree's eyes and ears and voice. Watch them spin up there. They scratch their stories into the trunk. It keeps them smart."

How did stories keep creatures smart? I wanted to know, but you can't ask questions when your mouth's gaping open in wonder and delight.

Round and round and raucous. I could have stared at them all day. There was so much motion. Then, out of that chaos, a single bird flew, down and straight at us. Nan's grip on my hand tightened. "Be ready," she said.

I didn't have time to ask her *Be ready for what* because the clever bird was already there.

Wings beating hard, I could feel the wind of them, like air searching my skin. Its eyes examined me, first one then the other, as it looped to the right, and then the left. Then, with a snap of wings it landed on Nan's arm, and walked its way up her shoulder, where it stopped to get a better look at me.

"Welcome," the bird said, dipping its head. A talking bird, now that was something, though there wasn't much welcome in its raw voice.

"You a bird or a tree?" I asked.

Nan shushed me, but the bird laughed. "I'm both, and neither. Just a clever bird for my tree." The bird pressed its beak against Nan's ear. "Nancy, she's growing so fast."

"Yes, she is," Nan said. "She's a treasure."

My ears burned. Nan didn't give out compliments often. She'd certainly never called me a treasure before.

"Things have come on faster than I would like. He visited her."

"Yes, she smells of him. He's already so brazen."

I knew whom they meant. Those golden eyes, that sharp smile. I felt observed from a distance, like they had called his gaze down upon us. I turned my head, but couldn't see anyone watching.

Nan squeezed my hand. "So is she."

"Yet she still wears boots."

"I can take 'em off," I said.

Nan frowned at me.

"You want to protect her, but this only stunts her growth. She has challenges that are hers to face, not yours."

"She's my granddaughter."

"How'll you protect her when you're down amongst the dead?"

I looked at Nan. She wasn't going to die, not yet. She couldn't!

"She'll be ready," Nan said.

I didn't like the way they spoke about me. I was right there. I opened my mouth to say something, but Nan shook her head.

"We'll see," the bird said. "Let us see."

Nan stepped back, let my hand go, kept walking away from me. I wanted to follow—there was a dread rising in me—but she shook her head again. "Keep calm, girl. Stay right there."

I stood still. I didn't feel calm.

"Good," Nan said. "She's ready."

The clever bird launched itself from Nan's shoulder, cried low and sharp. In a burst of wings, the other birds flew from the tree, and went all a-gyre around me: a surging whirlwind of furious white that tightened and turned faster, the sun blotted out by feather and claw and sanguine eye. I stood in the heart of that storm, still and curious, bursting with the wonder of it. This was magic, pure and simple, and Nan had taken me to it.

I giggled, raised up my hands.

And then the circle closed upon me all at once, and fell upon my flesh.

The weight of them, the dry dust-heat of them. Their claws scratched, their beaks pricked and raked. I tried to stay steady, but there was such a terror in me. Those scratches stung like little daggers in my skin.

"Open your eyes."

I didn't.

"Open your eyes! We can scratch them out whether they're shut or not."

So I did, and they looked deep into me with those bloody red-stone eyes; a hundred pairs of eyes, a single consciousness. I fell into that gaze, and for a moment I was both in and out of myself. I was a girl swarmed by birds, I was a bird clambering over trembling flesh, I was a tree watching it all, and thinking ancient thoughts, of kindred burnt or hacked down, of the river changing its shape, of deep roots to chase the water. There were memories of monsters, too, misshapen things, and things as graceful as my graceful man, and I even saw Mum and Nan. Both of them swarmed, both of them struggling. There was a knife that slid along a throat. And then there was Furnace, burning, smoke rising, a golden-eyed man snatching the dead right out of the earth.

All of this, and then I fell straight back into my body, smothered and scratched, and every bit of me burning. I flung out my hands, but they didn't stop. I couldn't breathe. I opened my mouth, and tasted feather and beak. I swayed in that tumult of wings and eyes. Enough. Enough. Enough! I dropped to the ground, and curled into a ball, and they flew from me, except one bird that had been caught in my dress. It flapped and beat at the air.

I opened an eye, and then the other. I reached for its caught claw, and freed it.

The bird didn't fly away; it settled on the ground beside me.

"I won't forget this kindness," it said, and scrambled through the air back to its kin and the story-marked tree.

I lay there, curled up. Nan stared at me, and I couldn't tell if she was angry or disappointed.

"Stand," she said.

I was raw all over. I could taste blood on my lip. I got up, and ran to her like I was a baby. A bird had landed on her shoulder again—not the bird I had freed, I didn't think. It looked down at me imperiously, and I stopped in my tracks.

"You've been too kind. You've ruined her."

"Ruthlessness isn't the answer," Nan said. "Look at Ella."

"Tell that to the fire," the bird said. "You've not even taken her to the road."

What road? I looked up at Nan, but she waved me to silence before I could even voice the question.

"She isn't ready."

"No one's ready," the bird said with absolute authority. "Take her. Or she will never meet the measure of her challenge."

Nan's lip thinned. She brushed the bird away, and came to me.

"It's all right, my darling," she said.

"I want to go," I said.

"Yes," Nan said. "I'm sorry to visit these horrors on you; I know how clear your memory is."

I snuffled. When I closed my eyes, I was oppressed by my memory, everything so vivid I could taste it. I stared at the levee ahead, and Nan held my hand all the way home.

Soon as we were there, she made me a cup of tea, sat me down, went back to that cord, and tied her knots. Tiny, delicate knots. One after the other, so close they touched.

I heard Nan and Mum talking low and quiet after I had gone to bed. I'd gotten up to have a drink of water. My skin itched from all those scratches. When I closed my eyes, the birds were all I could see: white wings, red eyes, thorny beaks.

I stayed in the shadows of the hallway, curious at their soft voices. They usually spoke as if I wasn't there, even when I was.

Firstly, it was of this and that, and of the birds, but then Nan sighed, and her voice lowered even more. "She's too timid, Ella. For the trouble ahead. For all of it."

"Yes, but that's how you raised her. To keep her safe."

"She soiled herself when he visited. I've made a rabbit when I should have made a wolf."

My face burned.

"I wasn't timid," Mum said. "I was all rage, and look what happened. Maybe you should send her away."

My gut tightened. I almost ran in, but my legs turned cold and shaky instead.

"Jim's always at you to—"

"Enough of that! Jim doesn't want a child on the road. I thought I made the right decision, after what happened."

"Don't blame yourself," Mum said, though there was plenty of blame in her voice. I heard her pour a drink.

"I'm scared she won't ever be ready. He's right, that graceful man of hers; the Tree, too. My strength runs from me, the waves crash in, but the tide's on the ebb. I can feel it."

"You've a long time with us yet," Mum said, but there wasn't much force to it. Sometimes I think she wished Nan dead. "A long time."

Nan was in silence a while, and I knew she was rolling a smoke. She would walk past my room, and smoke it out on the back verandah. "And she'll have a longer time after I'm gone."

A chair scraped back along the floor, and I bolted to my bed. I lay there as she walked down the hall, and looked in at me. I kept my eyes shut, and she didn't come in. How could they think about sending me away? What trouble wasn't I ready for? A red anger rose inside me. I wasn't timid. I wasn't a rabbit.

I knew what I had to do to prove them wrong. Something wild, something a wolf might do.

I didn't sleep much that night, just thought on it. When I did, the graceful man was there, flipping a golden coin up and onto the back of his hand, not saying a word.

"What're you waiting for?" I demanded.

He flipped the coin again, slapped his hand over it, then snuck a peak.

"You," he said.

I woke with my hands around that coin, squeezing it so tight that it hurt.

I didn't get up early. Those hours around sunrise were Nan's time.

I waited in bed, reading. The characters in my adventures were always brave, even when they were scared, and they had some true calamities. The Red City up north, where my books were written by authors who wrote them to keep pots boiling, was a violent place full of cruel Masters that'd drink your blood like a tick, and Day Boys who'd stab you if you looked at them wrong. I didn't have that to toughen me up; all I had was Nan and Mum. How was I to be brave with such examples?

Jim, who came down from the north every few months to trade, and who visited Nan every time, said the Red City was a wild place, even if it was civilised by its Masters and the Council of Teeth. There were rules, and if you broke them, you'd be thrown in a cage. He said that though the roads in the south were poor, and the troubles many, at least we were free.

I never felt free.

But I could be brave. That seemed to me a very deliberate act. You became brave by doing brave things. I was itching to prove that. Enough that my fear was pushed away. All I wanted was to get it done. But I had to be patient.

At about nine, I got out of bed, tiptoed past my mum's room—she was sleeping—and went into the kitchen. There was a nearly empty bottle of bourbon in there; it had been full the last time I saw it. I unscrewed the cap, and had a whiff. It made my eyes water.

I made a quick black tea, ate some oats, packed myself a sandwich and a handful of dried fruit. Got myself ready, and headed out of Casement Rise.

The town was busy; people didn't pay me much mind. There was always work to be done. A hundred little things, maybe more, that kept the place alive. Nan said a town like Casement Rise was dead unless we all worked together, grew stuff to eat, made things to trade with the travellers, like Jim. We weren't like the north, where it was warmer, and there were so many people that you could spend your days reading or singing or whatever, and where a word like leisure was possible.

I didn't imagine Mum would notice me gone until midday. Hopefully I'd be back by then. Nan would be mad, but she'd know I wasn't any rabbit. Hopefully.

On my way to the levee, I saw Aunty Phoebe, and she waved me over. I told her I was off to play in the park, which was a mistake. As my mum said, never give Phoebe an opening or she'll walk right in, and set up a shop there.

"School's on," she said. "Won't be anyone but babies and their mums in the park. Don't you get bored, not being at school?"

I shook my head furiously. "I get an education from Nan," I said. "I can already read, and I can spell."

Phoebe nodded. "Don't you get lonely? A child needs to be socialised!"

"Not a bit," I said. Well, maybe I did, but I wanted to get on before someone else saw me. I didn't understand children. They talked too fast; they had weird games and imaginary friends. And they certainly didn't understand me. At least I had my dead boy. He didn't see my being raised by a drunk mum and a grumpy nan as anything odd.

Aunty Phoebe gave me a hug. "I miss your dad sometimes," she said, all wistful. Here we go.

I nodded. It was getting late. I knew next to nothing about him, except he'd gone soon after I was born, over the levee, west to the Slouches and beyond, into Furnace. Left me behind.

I patted Aunty's hand. I must have looked so anxious to go that she nodded. "Off to the park with you, then. Tell your mother I'll come visiting tomorrow."

"I will," I said, already walking. Mum wouldn't be happy with that. She and Aunty Phoebe didn't get along. Mum said she was as draining as a bag of anxious cats.

I laughed thinking about it. As if you could get cats in a bag, let alone anxious ones.

A few blocks down, Mrs. Card was holding some heavy cotton bags, her face red. She'd been at the markets. "You look in a hurry," she said.

"Yes, Mrs. Card," I said. "I need to get to the park."

"The park, yes. It's a nice day. Hot, though, when you're carrying bags. I'd like to sit in the park, maybe read a book. You can read, can't you?"

"Of course," I said. I was almost hopping from foot to foot.

"Books about flower people and pretty things, I suppose?"

I made a face. "Pirates and fighters."

Mrs. Card shook her head. "You look as strong as a pirate."

I flexed my arms for her.

"Yes, very strong." She hesitated. "I don't suppose you would carry these bags for me?"

I looked at the bags, then her red and sweating face. I looked in the direction of the park. "I can carry the bags, if we're quick."

Mrs. Card looked as happy as a bug. "I don't want to slow you down if you have park business."

"It won't slow me down . . . much," I said.

"Good. You're a good child, for a pirate," Mrs. Card said.

I took her bags, and swung them over my shoulders. "What's in these bags? Bricks?"

Mrs. Card laughed. "Oh, odds and ends. Not too heavy, are they?"

"No. Not at all."

I lugged them slowly to Mrs. Card's house on Coopers Lane, and helped her unpack the bags. There were sacks of flour and boiled fruit and jam. Mrs. Card gave me a slice of pie and some cream, and insisted that I have a quick cup of tea.

"I've got to go," I said.

Mrs. Card nodded. "Absolutely. Two sugars? Milk?"

"One, and yes." I said, and we waited for the tea to steep. Why had I decided to walk that way?

But Mrs. Card was truly grateful. She had lost her husband, Matt, in some accident that Nan never talked about, except to call it an accident. Her son had gone to Furnace, and not come back, like the rest of them. It hadn't been that long ago—I could remember him a bit. Nan always said that loss needed company, and that her job was sometimes just that. I let her tell me about her day and the shops and the weather. I tried not to look like I didn't want to be there. After all, the kitchen was bright, and smelled of spices and baking. All the things I would have loved, if I wasn't hunting danger.

I drank my tea, had a second slice of pie, and Mrs. Card wrapped another one in paper, for my adventures in the park. If only she knew.

I ran directly to the park, then past it. Aunty Phoebe had been right: babies and mothers! None of them would have wanted much to do with me. I gave mothers and babies the frights, or something. Maybe I needed to comb my hair.

I found a spot where the levee was deserted, and there were a few trees that hid part of the climb from the town. I took a deep breath, and clambered up as quick as I could, hoping no one had seen me.

I got to the top without looking back, and hurried down the other side before anyone might wonder what a girl was doing climbing out of town. I thought of Nan coming after me, and was filled with the worst horror. This bit of the levee was steep, and I tripped, rolled, and ended up winded at the bottom of it, right on an anthill. They came out in a fury. I scrambled away, slapping and cursing, bad as a pirate. Right into nettles.

I cursed again, and spat on my itchy skin.

I looked back up the levee bank. I'd knocked a few markings on my tumble down, and I could clearly see where I had fallen. I knew Nan would see them; I just hoped she wouldn't blame me.

What were a few old scratches in the dirt, anyway?

The pepper trees that lined the river to the north prickled my nose, and burned my throat. Cicadas buzzed and hissed, louder and louder, until they stopped, only to start all over again. I was sweaty and itchy, and the day was getting later, but I had something to prove. Nan and Mum's disappointment had been palpable; it stung me still. I was always getting into trouble, but this was a disappointment that they had hidden from me. I'm not sure if I'd ever understood that people could hide things, and that those hidden things could be worse than anything else.

I stood beneath the pepper trees, trying to gather my bearings. I knew the town within the levee like it was painted behind my eyes, but this was a different world. It went on and on, in all directions. There was more than just a tame little creek: There were rivers and mountains and plains, and somewhere a sea—not just a sea, but seven of them, maybe more; I'd never had the opportunity to count them. I was such an insignificance!

Perhaps Nan and Mum were right. A little niggle of doubt began to work at me.

"Do you consider this to be a wise endeavour?" I looked up. Red eyes studied me from the nearest branch. White wings stretched open and shut.

I shrugged. Nothing like that sort of question to get your back up.

"That's hardly an answer."

"I know what I'm doing," I said.

Its eyes were full of laughter, but it was not quite mockery, or delight. "May I accompany you?"

I wanted to say no, just to be contrary, but an extra set of eyes could be good. I thought about it a while longer. "You may," I said, finally.

"And where are we going, alone?"

"I'm not alone, I'm with you. And we're going to see the Huskling King."

"I cannot protect you there."

I puffed up my chest. "I can protect myself."

The bird laughed in the way birds do, rough as an old saw, the mimic of a laugh. "Oh, child," it said, and launched itself from the branch and onto my shoulder. Its dark claws dug in. "Why would you go there?"

"I have my reasons."

The bird looked at me, first with one eye, then the other.

"Do you know the way?" I asked, sick of tilting my head so I could look at it.

"It's not whether I know the way that is the question," the bird said, "but if I should tell you."

"Please," I said.

"I cannot protect you there."

"Please."

The bird shuffled, and fluffed up, and shuffled again. "Very well," it said. "Keep walking, with the sun to your right. There's a trail up ahead."

We walked through the grove of trees, across a paddock, then another.

We came across a wide space fringed with wood.

Something stopped me on the edge of that clearing. "What is this place?"

The bird was still. "Not a good place. Something awful happened here."

"What?"

"It won't tell me. Places speak, but this one, it's silent in all the wrong ways."

I knew what it meant, though. The clearing was quiet, but it felt like it shouldn't be.

"I don't like it."

"Neither do I," the bird said.

I squeezed my hands to fists. I was here to be brave. I walked out into the space. I felt a rising panic, like I had been here before. Like I was walking over something that might at any moment fall away beneath my feet. The clearing was thick with warpweed. There was an old stack of half-burned wood in the middle. Something about it made me queasy, an almost memory, but I knew I had never been here before.

"Hurry. Don't linger."

The clearing filled my head. It was as though the space was screaming silently, that the earth was roiling and still all at once. It made me run faster, and I was through it quick. On the other side stood a high gum tree. Ten circles were cut deep into its trunk, a rotten blanket at its base.

"What happened here?" I asked, pointing at the marks in the wood. "That something you can read?"

"I don't need to read it. It isn't my language. Nor my memory. Bad things happened here," the bird said. "Please, we must leave."

I looked back at that clearing. I didn't like it, no matter how wolfish I might be. I hurried on. But I felt that space in me, and it was unsettling. A sickly clarity that was too clear to see, like a migraine.

"It's all right," the bird said. "You're free of it."

We came to a creek, and I had to scramble from river rock to river rock, some of them slippery with weed.

On the other side was a barbed wire fence that zigzagged all over the place. I was small enough to push through a gap. The bird flew up into the air, and landed again on my shoulder.

A little later, I spotted a face. A boy, hiding in the scrub, watching us. I knew that face: I'd last seen it spewing up fairy floss at my party.

"Lolly Robson," I shouted. The boy looked to be as disappointed at being discovered as I had been when the bird got curious about where I was going—though now I rather liked its weight on my shoulder. "Lolly, quit your hiding, and your sneaking. You're older than me. You should know better."

Lolly crawled out of his hiding place. There were sticks in his hair and his smile was as crooked as the Robsons' fence line. "Why, good afternoon, Jean. Oh, and good afternoon, clever bird. It's not sneaking when it's your own farm."

"Not your farm. You're a child, and a liar." He had a bruise on one eye, clear now that he was out from the shade of his hiding place, and I could see he was snotty from crying. He had older brothers, and they were a wild lot.

"It's Mum's farm, and it'll be mine one day—well, maybe. What're you doing on it?"

"I'm off to see the Huskling King."

Lolly frowned. "Why would you want to do that?"

"Why not?" I didn't want to tell him I was doing it to prove a point. If Nan thought I was a rabbit, I was going to show her I was a brave one.

"He's no monster, true, but he's a dangerous fellow. I know that much."

"So do I," I said.

"Well, you're not too clever. This isn't the way to the king. Why, you couldn't have picked a more wrong way. You'd have spent all day wandering between our farm and the Prestons'."

I swung my head to glare at the bird. "What?"

If the bird could kill with a look, Lolly would have been dead. "I may have gotten lost," it said, dryly.

"I've been meaning to see the king myself," Lolly said. "Perhaps I can guide you."

"Are you going to guide me to the king, or are you going to take me home?"

Lolly blinked. "Why would you want to go home?"

The bird was giving off more death stares. "It *is* getting late," it said.

Lolly shook his head. "It's hours until sundown. We can be there and back in an hour." Lolly looked at me. "All you want is to have a peek at the hall, isn't it? No audiences or anything?"

I had both his and the bird's attention now; I thought this was the most important question I would be asked that day. "A peek is all I want," I said.

"Then we should hurry."

And we were off, Lolly jabbering, me hardly listening, and the bird squeezing its claws into my shoulder.

"What's your name, bird?" Lolly asked, and the bird hissed at him. I was a bit angry that I hadn't thought to ask that question.

"Mr. Hiss, is it?"

"I have no name, and I am not a 'mister' anything."

"That's okay, Miss Hiss."

"I am bird, and I am tree, neither he nor she."

"Bird it is."

Bird sighed. "That is acceptable."

There was no winding path now, no creek crossing. We followed a gully, muddy in its bed with the recent rain, then went up and over the hill Nan had pointed out the day before. The other side of the hill had been gouged into, down to the rock beneath. Here and there were deep furrows in the earth that ran all the way to the foot of the hill.

We passed broken tools, shovels and picks and discarded lengths of rope.

Down near the bottom of the hill, there was a whole grove of gum trees. We stopped there.

"You know about the art, don't you?"

To be honest, I didn't.

"Oh, Dad told me this one, before he . . . you know," Lolly shook his head. "I never seen it, but the Husklings are great artists. They've got a monstrous nature, but a creative one. They don't just scowl and grumble, they make art, sculptures. Like the Defiant, far down south." He looked at me. "You've heard of them, haven't ya?"

"I might have," I said.

"It's all right. You're younger. You don't know what you don't know."

My face was burning, but there was no harm in his words. Lolly didn't have a bit of cruelty in him.

"The Defiant," he said. "They're these huge statues of Masters, made back when the Years of Heat and Sadness were burning out. Higher than the clock tower, I've been told. Higher than your tree, Bird. There's seven of them, one for each day of the week. They look south to the coldest sea, and their hands are raised to the sun, except for one that's crouched low, like it's frightened."

"How do you know so much?"

"People come visiting. Was an old auditor—a lawman—that saw them. Showed me his guns, said he killed a bloke down that way. Anyway, there's sculptures here, on the other side of this grove; that's how you know you're in their lands. You ready?" I nodded. "We better be quiet."

We walked without a word, through the grove of trees and into a clearing, and there were the sculptures, placed in great sweeping circles about the clearing. They were so cleverly made that they looked alive. If stone could breathe and dance, then these sculptures would have.

And nearest to me was a face I recognised at once.

My own.

I didn't like it. This was no reflection; it was far too intimate. This said things!

Her lip was curled in a way I could feel my lip curling now, her arms crossed against her chest. I uncrossed mine at once.

"Storm in the Holy Sun!" Lolly said. "Look at you! Sure you haven't been here before?"

I shook my head. "Not even in a dream," I said.

Why was there a statue of me here?

I had to find out. "Which way's the king's hall?"

Lolly pointed west. "That way, through those trees. And no, you—"

But I was already stomping there.

"This isn't wise," Bird said.

"You can fly off if you want."

"I can't protect you."

I ignored them as I hurried past statues of bulls and men and women, some of them doing things that I'm sure would have fascinated me if I wasn't getting so hot and angry in the head. Not even sure why, other than I felt something had been stolen, and I hadn't even been asked. Like I hadn't been told by Nan and Mum that I was lacking.

Lolly was behind me through the trees, shouting softly at me to stop.

There was the Huskling hall. The king's hall, and it was no more than an old tin-roofed shearing shed covered in skins.

I hesitated, then, but only until Lolly ran into me. I thought of my mum and Nan worrying that I was such a timid rabbit. I thought of that statue, and I stomped on until I was but a few meters from the hall. I walked around it once, hunting for a door.

Lolly stood a ways back, his face drained of colour. "It's not too late," he hissed, low. "They're not awake."

"How can you tell through these walls?"

"Because—"

I glared at him. Had I looked that scared when the graceful man came visiting? Of course I had!

I cupped my hands around my mouth, and shouted, "Wake up! You've visitors. Wake up!"

I heard a noise behind me, turned. Lolly was sprinting back the way we had come. Bird looked at me, then flew up and away, leaving a streak of white shit on my shoulder.

Something gave a low chuckle. I turned. The hall rippled. Those skins billowed, and dropped from the walls of the shed (*they* were the walls), lifted little narrow heads, and stared at me.

I could see beyond them now, into the space of the hall, and there sat the largest of the creatures, dark beard beneath its chin, thin hands clapping.

"Visitors?" the king questioned, in a sharp wet voice, the sort that might drown you, or stab you, or both. "I see only one visitant. One rude child, lacking in dignity and eloquence."

The Husklings shuffled towards me. There was something horrible and wonderful about them all at once. They were almost human, except they walked on all four limbs, and were draped in folds of flesh. Their hands were long and delicate. They were bats, if bats scurried instead of flew. But then, that's what some of them did: madly flapped their limbs, and the flesh between hands and belly billowed and rippled, and they were up in the air, flying. Huge bats, pale, stinking of carrion. Big wide eyes that were troubled by the brilliance of the late afternoon. They landed in the high trees that surrounded the hall. Tree branches creaked and groaned. Some of them tussled and shrieked, like flying foxes might if they were given the voice of men. Some of them stared down at me. I could feel the prickling intensity of their gaze.

"We've a treaty," I said.

"Yes, one that says, most explicitly: Keep out. And, yet, here we are, and you have not kept out, have you?" The king yawned, but he did not look at me with sleepy eyes. There was something else there. I couldn't tell if he wanted to laugh at me or if I was his dinner. He pulled himself down from his throne, moved in a great flexing, folding, gathering of flesh, and he was next to me before I could even think of running.

He bent down so that his face was close to mine. His eyes widened. "Oh, but I am familiar with you."

"Why am I back there?" I jabbed a hand behind me in the direction of the grove.

"Oh, you saw. How delightful. We've an interest in you, and your family."

"Why's everyone got an interest in us?"

The king rocked back on his hind legs. He bunched his wings around his belly, perhaps to hide his nakedness. "You really don't know? Your nan has kept so much from you. What instruction has she provided you?"

"I know words and numbers. I can read."

"Yes. Yes, hardly a surprise at your age. I'm sure you know the eight planets, too, and that the earth circles around the sun, or some such. But what else? What has she told you about what she does? What has she told you about the other thing, your . . . trouble?"

I opened my mouth to speak. But all at once the Husklings in the trees were hooting and shrieking. The king's eyes widened, and he looked back over my shoulder.

"That's enough, Bartlett," Nan said.

The king winced. "You know how much I despise that name."

"Yes. Now, what have you done to my granddaughter?"

"It's not what I've done, is it, but what you haven't. She has an absence in her. Why? Why have you done nothing to fill it, while Furnace burns?"

Nan didn't answer him. She crouched down, stick across her knees. In one hand she gripped a big bone needle. She touched my face with the other, looked deep in my eyes. "He hurt you?"

I shook my head.

"Get behind me," she said. And I did. "See this needle, Bartlett? You know what it is."

The king's eyes narrowed, but he raised his hands. "I am cognizant of its puissance. Didn't I give it to you?"

"Yes. It cost me, though. It wasn't a gift."

"And what will your granddaughter cost you?"

"There will be no transaction, Bartlett," Nan said.

"Everything is a transaction, Nancy. She came here of her own free will. She is your kin; she should have known what that means."

Nan touched my arm. "Go home now, Jean."

"I want to stay." I clenched my fists. Nan glared at me.

"See?" The king said.

"Go." Nan said, in a voice that brooked no argument whatsoever.

I walked beneath those trees with the Husklings looking down. Any one of them could have dived, and devoured me, but I was stubborn; I didn't hurry. I stopped at my statue. This time I noticed another near it, one of Nan, its face like I had seen moments before, resolute and hard, a face you couldn't argue with.

Standing by her was a sculpture of my mother. I recognised her even though she was much younger; she'd have been no mother then. Her smile was wicked, her eyes a challenge. There was a knife held loosely in one hand, like she knew how to snap it up, and strike at anything. Like she was daring the world to try and fight her. It wasn't the mum I knew.

And there was me, looking uncertain. No knife, no challenge. My arms crossed. I might have been about to cry, that curled lip a quivering one instead.

Bird came, and landed on my shoulder. "I found Nancy," Bird said. "She was already on her way. I suspect she's angry."

"I'm in so much trouble," I said. "Will you show me the way home?"

"Yes," Bird said.

Turned out, I knew the way back. The world was already becoming familiar. At the gully, I came upon Lolly. He was carrying a big stick.

"What are you doing, Lolly Robson?"

"Coming to rescue you."

"I don't need rescuing," I said. "Nan's already done that."

"Where is she, then?" Lolly said.

"Back talking to the Huskling King. She told me to leave."

"She's going to kill you. If the king doesn't eat her. Maybe you'll be lucky, and he'll eat her."

I slapped the back of his head. "Don't be so foolish!"

He rubbed his skull, and looked at me with such hurt in his eyes that I apologised at once.

He walked with me back to the levee, holding that stick tight. Watched until I climbed to the top, then dropped the stick, and ran back towards the farm.

I was in so much trouble. I didn't even think how much trouble Nan was in, alone with a needle for protection, and the Husklings all around her. I walked home, and Bird left me there.

Mum was in the kitchen. "Where have you been?"

I told her, shamefaced. She took it well, though her face darkened somewhat. "What on earth goes on in your head?"

"I wanted to be brave."

"Oh, Jean, there's bravery, and then there's stupidity." She touched my face with her hand, softly. Her eyes were troubled, though she tried to hide it with a smile. "Mum's still there?"

"That's where I left her."

Mum shook her head. "If she's not back in an hour, I'll walk out there myself, and talk to old Bartlett."

"Why does he hate that name?"

"The reason most people hate things. It reminds him of what he was, what he can't come back to." Mum poured herself a drink. I could see her hands were shaking. What had she been? What had she lost?

"Clean, and chop those vegetables," she said, gesturing to the table. "Make yourself useful."

When Nan came home, she looked me up and down, snapped at me, and told me what a fool I was. And that I'd have my chores doubled, wouldn't just be chopping vegetables.

But there was no fury to it. I wasn't sent to bed without dinner. I sat with Mum and her, and ate in silence. It wasn't pleasant, stuck between those two storms, but I was starving. Afterwards, when I was reading in the living room, I'd catch Nan looking at me when she wasn't tying knots in her cord, and it was a strange look. If I didn't know how much trouble I was in, I would have taken it for pride.

For the first time, I think I had surprised her. But if I thought that was going to make my life easier, I couldn't have been more wrong.

Part Two

Education

The next morning, Nan shook me awake. Well, calling it morning was an exaggeration. It was still dark.

"Up, Jean," Nan said. "You're coming with me."

I moaned my displeasure, and she clicked her tongue.

"You're twelve. It's past time you learnt a few things."

"Can't I learn them tomorrow?" My voice was hoarse with sleep.

"Don't try my patience. You could have died yesterday. And you're young enough yet for a thrashing."

I squeezed my eyes shut.

"Get yourself up, now, Jean, or I swear you'll never leave that bed again. I'll bury you in it, and you can moan about how cruel I was as you crawl around in the blinding light of the world beneath."

I got up quick. Wiped at my eyes.

Nan gave me a thin little smile. "Get dressed. Put on your boots. I'll be in the kitchen."

Mum snored gently in her room. I looked in enviously, then hurried into the kitchen.

Nan pressed a cup into my hands. "Drink."

It was coffee, black. I sipped it.

"Don't be dainty. We've no time for that. I've sweetened it, two heaped teaspoons, which is enough of a concession to your youth, and a threat to your teeth."

Down it went with a grimace.

"Now, time to go, and quick," Nan said.

There were a few stubborn stars in the sky. Bats were making their way home, and birds were waking. We walked through a town coming to life, some people already up, working in the groves to beat the heat of the day. The butcher's lights burned, and Rachael was laughing in the bakery. I could smell fresh bread baking.

Nan held my hand, singing under her breath, like she did.

Jacob was in the town square outside the barracks. I hadn't seen him since he'd taken Nan to help Myles Preston in the rains. He was brushing down his pony, May; there was rifle in a bag against her saddle.

"Nancy," he said, "and young Jean."

"Taking her to the levee," Nan said.

Jacob nodded. There was something in his face that said, *It's about time.*

"Beautiful morning for it. Quiet, though the day'll be hot. I spotted a couple of fires burning in the north. Think we'll have new folk this afternoon. I better see that the Summer Gate's hinges are oiled. Don't want them seizing up on us."

"Yes," Nan said. "We've been lax of late."

"Not as many of us as there used to be. Things get missed when there are fewer eyes on them."

Nan nodded. "We'll need to work harder. And Jacob?"

"Yes, Nancy?"

"I'll need you to teach Jean a few things. You know, what we've been talking about."

I looked between them. Just what had they been discussing?

Jacob pulled his hat from his head, scratched his scalp. "Yes, though I still think Ella might be a better—"

"My daughter can't teach what she knows. You can."

Jacob grinned at her in assent. May shuddered, and he stroked her neck. "Walk well," he said.

"You, too."

We were off again, and Nan set an even faster pace.

"What's Jacob going to teach me?"

"How to fight. Something I should have started years ago, but what's done is done. I thought waiting was the wise choice under the circumstances," Nan said.

"What circumstances?"

"You've all sorts of education ahead. Let's not muddy it any further with my mistakes. Put your back to the past, keep your front to the levee."

We followed Main Street to the Summer Gate, then climbed the levee. Nan stared north.

"There," she said, and pointed at the fires. "It's dangerous to announce yourself. Dangerous or desperate." A quick shake of her head. "Well, there's nothing we can do about that. We best hurry. The dawn doesn't wait for anyone."

We followed the levee around. I could see lights flickering in the Robsons' farm. I could see the hill that hid the Huskling hall and their sculptures from sight. Up here, the world was hushed. We were neither in the town nor properly outside it, but somewhere in between. When we reached the western edge of the town, we stopped. There stood a big black rock. A ragged white arrow, pointing west, had been painted on it.

"The days are longest now," Nan said. "The nights are short. It's the proper season to start your education. Your memory will be a gift, but it will still take time."

A cool wind blew up from the south. Like the old folks say, the mountains breathed on us.

The wind died. The world held its breath.

Nan squeezed my hand. "Do you know what I do?" Nan asked.

"You walk around the levee," I said. "You talk to the dead, and that."

"Yes, yes, but that is only a consequence of the other thing I do. I fight monsters, Jean. I keep this town safe. By my wits, and by my wisdom, and sometimes—but rarely, thank the Sun—by my brawn. I'm the Walker of this town. I make the boundaries that keep it safe. I fight monsters, and you will, too."

The sun rose over the hills to the east, and spilled into the valley, and it was like the first day of a new life. Which, I suppose it was.

I thought of Nan, fighting monsters. She'd always been strong, but there was strength, and then there was action, and the Nan I knew was not a warrior.

Nan touched the stone. "Here's where we greet the sun, and start our circle."

She crouched down beside it, resting a hand on her walking stick.

I looked out. "Where are the monsters?"

"There's never a lot of them. I've made the town's defences strong; built on the work of my mother as she built on the work of hers, and so on, back to the Years of Heat and Sadness. Those that might seek entrance know that the levee is strong, that, like our line, the defences have yet to be truly broken, but that doesn't stop some from trying."

She grabbed my hand, and placed it palm down on the stone. It thrummed like a living thing. I wanted to pull my hand away—there was something angry to the rhythm, like it wanted to bite—but she held me there.

"Feel that. Feel how steady it is. This is a signal stone, and that's the rhythm of the protections I've laid down. When it's steady and strong, it means that the town is well guarded. That everything is working."

"And if it isn't beating?"

Nan smacked her walking stick against the stone. "If it isn't beating, then something horrible, end-of-town bad, has happened. I've never felt it stop. If it isn't beating, then the town is truly in trouble. That beat, that strength . . . I draw it from myself, and the townsfolk, too, a tiny breath from each. Those breaths are given to you as well, even if you don't realise it. I could take more, perhaps close the whole town in a great silver wall of force, but it wouldn't last. We'd all burn out within a few days. What I look for, and what you'll look for, too, is an absence, a flutter, something not quite right. How does it feel right now?"

"Strong."

"Yes. But there is something wrong there, too."

"You said it was steady and well protected."

"Most of it, but something's been disturbed."

I took a deep breath. "When I crossed over the levee, I fell. Could that be it?"

Nan frowned. "It could be. Show me where."

I led her to the place I had fallen. Nan ran her fingers over the dirt. "Yes," she said. "Yes, that might do it." Then she paused, and pointed at the levee near my feet. There were scratches. The imprint of a heel.

"Something got through last night," Nan said. "Tiny, but it won't stay that way for long."

She pulled a stick from her bag, and a small mallet. She hammered three-quarters of the stick's length into the earth. "That will help, until I can fix this properly."

My gut was cold. Something had gotten into the town, and it was my fault.

Nan didn't seem as concerned. "See its footprints? They are almost matched with yours. It's following your steps back. What a clever creature. A path once walked is easier walked again." Nan looked at my trail down the levee towards the park. "Now, it didn't come to our house—no surprise, it would have found that difficult. Tell me, Jean, where did you walk yesterday, before you crossed the levee?"

There was a sudden, awful tightness in my chest.

"Mrs. Card," I said. "I helped her take her bags home."

Nan nodded. "We had better hurry, then." And we did, all the way to Coopers Lane, and Mrs. Card's house.

Mrs. Card's door was open a crack. Nan looked at it, touched the frame. Wood had been scratched at, the lock broken.

I was all for rushing through, but Nan stopped me. "Careful. You weren't before, but you must be now," she said, and took me back down the stairs from the verandah. I could feel tears welling in my eyes. Nan brushed them with her thumb. Her eyes were gentler than I deserved. "No time for tears; tears will obscure. Here. Look. What do you see?"

I sniffled, wiped my nose, and cast my eye over the house.

"The blinds are shut," I said. "All of them."

"Were they shut yesterday?"

I thought back. Mrs. Card's place was airy, well lit. The house I was looking at seethed, closed and angry. I shook my head. "It feels wrong. Like the house is waiting." This didn't feel like Mrs. Card's house at all; it felt more like that clearing Bird and I had passed through.

What had I done?

Nan nodded. "Jean, we need to be careful. This is a hard way to begin an education, a true education, but this is hard work."

She passed me a little knife. Showed me how to hold it. "Should you need to strike, strike upwards; down, you're scraping nothing but bone, if you don't stab yourself by mistake."

"Is Mrs. Card all right?"

"I hope so. But it's not just Mrs. Card we need concern ourselves with. We've the town's safety to consider." There was that needle in her hand again, its long bone point gleaming. "We best go in."

Nan opened the door, slowly, quietly.

That sense of wrongness and rage was worse in here.

There was a sweet smell, not the sweetness of spice and baking—this was sickly, it stuck in your throat. We walked around the living room. The table had been tipped up, but Mrs. Card wasn't there, nor in the kitchen, though a bottle of milk was spilt. There were tiny, milky footprints all over the chair where I had sat, and talked to Mrs. Card.

Down the hall a vase had been broken, a small sideboard upturned. The bedroom was dark, almost night dark, though light made it through cracks in the window. It was as though something was stopping it by force of will.

Nan squeezed my hand. There was a big lump on the bed. Nan slipped past it, and cut open the window blind.

What I saw was not meant to be seen in daylight. It hissed and groaned and spat.

The creature had wrapped around Mrs. Card like a giant tick. It was sucking, even now, even as its little legs flexed. Mrs. Card was shrunken, the tick grown fat, almost as big as her. With a wet sound, it pulled its mouth parts free, turned to get a look at us, and I could see, a few inches beneath its throat, a new face forming. Mrs. Card's face. It winked at me.

"Why, Jean, what a pleasure. Come a little closer, if you don't mind."

I waved my knife at it. Mrs. Card's face chuckled. "Let me give you a hug." I stepped back, and it turned its gaze on Nan. "Oh, Nancy, I certainly have need of you."

Nan pushed past me, striking out with her needle, but the creature caught her wrist in a claw. Nan's face darkened; I could see the pain of that touch. The thought that anything could hurt her was beyond me.

"How will she live without you?" the creature said. "But I have need—"

"Quiet," Nan said, and she swung down with her walking stick. "You've need of nothing but silence." She struck again, and the creature howled, and burst with a wet plop. Mrs. Card's face went with it. Now we had two dead things on the bed, and it was all my fault. I started sobbing proper.

"That's why you need Jacob to teach you," Nan said, then grabbed my hand. "You may cry, if you must, but the crying won't bring her back."

Nan led me out of the room once she had opened the other blind. The light did its best to wash away the nightmare. The house had lost its unwholesome air. I could breathe again, despite my horror.

"This is my fault, girl. If we'd started your education sooner, I'd . . . but you didn't know. The simplest things, and I've denied you them," Nan said, as she passed me a handkerchief to sop my tears. I'd never heard such contrition. "I didn't prepare you for this. But that ends now. Whether you're ready or not."

I wiped at my eyes. I don't know if I had ever felt so bad. All my sadnesses before seemed so trivial. I needed to know. I needed to know so I didn't do this again. "Why did it have Mrs. Card's face?"

"These monsters want to be us. They want to live like us, become us if they can, not least because it's a better way to feed, and to hide. Always they're at mimicry. We'd better find Jacob. He can deal with this. There's never just a fight, Jean: There is always an after, and a mess to clean up. I'm sorry that your childhood has ended. It was a long one, in its way, but you have work to do now."

The Summer Gate bell started ringing. It could be heard clear across the town, so there was no chance of mistaking it for anything else. Those visitors had come.

"That makes it easy to find Jacob," Nan said.

The bell rang again. It wasn't the insistent pealing of an alarm—no fire, flood, or incursion—but it was demanding enough.

The only thing that kept our town alive was the flow of newcomers. There was always someone new. That may have caused some trouble, but it had its benefits, too. People came to Casement Rise to escape the madness of the world, or to flee the direct gaze of the Masters to the north, who ruled with a cruel hand. Even Furnace hadn't completely stopped the flow.

We left Mrs. Card's house, and went down Coopers Lane to Main Street. The horrors lessened a little with each step, though I would see her face buried in that creature's throat in my nightmares for many nights after. Main Street was busy. Nan hunched forward, leant heavier on her stick, and I wondered what such a battle cost her.

She squeezed my hand. "Don't worry, child. I'm fast to get my breath back. Not so old yet."

"Nancy," Gail, our butcher called. Nan turned to her. "Nancy, I have need of you."

"I've got to get to the gate," Nan said.

"I know, I know, but my Ashton . . . I swear, he is troubled in the earth."

Nan nodded. "I'll talk to him for you."

"Tell him I love him."

"Gail, I always do."

"Thank you," she said, and we kept on.

"All the dead are troubled," Nan said once Gail was out of earshot. "All they do is moan and grumble. If I told each one they were still loved, I'd have time for nothing else, and they wouldn't believe me anyway. The dead are high in their entitlement; no one could ever love them enough. Remember this: We're not here to comfort the living, we're here to protect them."

There were two gates into our town. The Summer Gate was the common gate, the one everyone used. The other gate was on the southern side of the levee. People called it the Winter Gate. It was much smaller, and only Nan had a key to it. There were two other gates named for the lesser seasons, but neither opened.

The Autumn Gate to the west was the most decorative, its iron red and so densely curlicued you'd never see the same pattern in it twice. It was built into the western end of the levee, but went nowhere. The Spring Gate to the east was a slab of stone with a bird painted on it, some sort of pigeon. We didn't have many of those, so I'd go there sometimes, and run my fingers over it.

Most of the council was waiting at the Summer Gate, waiting for Nan, waiting for Jacob to open it. Five women and five men sat on the council. Nan didn't run it, but they followed her lead. The only one who was ever any trouble was Myles Preston, who still blamed her for his brother's stupidity. He scowled at Nan. She ignored him.

Myles hated my family. I'd heard once from Jacob that Myles had said something improper to my mum when she was in her cups, and she'd punched him so hard she'd broken his nose.

Dr. Millison was there with his bag. He dabbed at his face with a handkerchief. He wasn't the only one doing it; the day was hot. I still had a chill in me, though. Poor Mrs. Card, dead because of my bloody mindlessness and ignorance. She'd have been so much better off if I had been rude, if I hadn't carried her bags. Thinking of that, I felt a sob coming. I stopped it before it became more than the slightest shudder. Nan squeezed my hand.

Jacob came up to us.

"I'm sorry to tell you this," Nan said to him, quietly, "but you're going to have to go around to Sally-Anne's. There was a visitation."

Jacob's hands clenched, and his face whitened. "Poor woman."

Myles was watching us. I could see him trying to read our lips.

Nan moved so that her back was to Myles. "Take the sheets and what's on them, and burn it all. If you can do that before dark, it would be better."

"I will," Jacob said.

Myles came over. "Nancy," he said, smiling the widest, fakest smile I had ever seen.

"Myles," Nancy said. "There was a death."

Myles' smile snapped shut like a gate. "What happened?"

I was ready to sob again, but not in front of Myles.

"Something made it through."

"One or many?"

"One."

"We'll discuss this later. Perhaps we should send these folks on. There's enough of us here."

Nan shook her head. "That's not what we do, Myles."

"So you say, when you can scarcely keep all of us safe, it seems. And all the while, that Furnace burns. Perhaps we should petition the Red City, get an auditor to stay down here."

Nan's face grew hard—not rageful, but cold. "Auditor? Have you no other topic of conversation? You know nothing if you think that a fine route. They're trigger-happy. Oh, I'd love the holiday, but half this town would fear an auditor more than what's beyond the walls."

"Only those with something to fear would. I think if you—"

Nan seemed to grow, and Myles shrink, and I saw the anger of the day rise in her. She was leaning over him now, and every word she said was quieter and somehow more forceful for it. "Do you think people come here because they love the Red City? Do you think the Red City loves us? What kind of second-rate man or woman would they spare? Those city folk don't understand us. They don't want to, least of all when it comes to our troubles."

Myles wasn't satisfied, but he nodded. "We'll discuss this later. I need you to walk my farm."

"Yes, we will. And yes, I will, because that's my job."

He left us, then.

Jacob shook his head. "I don't like him, sometimes."

"I try not to be so judgemental," said Nan, sounding the very description of judgemental. "This town doesn't always bring out the best in us. I'm not immune to it, either."

Jacob shrugged.

Nan glanced at the gate. "Let's get this done," she said.

Jacob walked to the gate, looked at the other councillors, and they nodded. He undid the great bolts that held the doors shut, and the doors rolled back.

There they were. Half a dozen souls. Two men, scarcely out of boyhood, standing by a woman and three children, one of them a girl around my age, maybe older. They huddled there, waiting.

Nan let go of my hand. "Stay here."

She walked by Jacob's side. "You're all welcome here, if your intent is good."

"You'll have no trouble with us," said the woman. "Shelter's all we want."

"We've plenty of that, if you'll work for it. We only ask what we ask of ourselves. Labour in the fields, two days a week, skills if you have them."

"That's fair," the woman said. "You the Walker?"

"Amongst other things. And you?"

"Baker," said the woman. "I'm Catherine Merrikson. These are my children. They know the work, too."

"We've a bakery already, but I'm sure that Rachael would appreciate some help. Where are you from?"

"Somerton," the woman said flatly. "When there was a Somerton. It's all gone now. Something swept through. A madness, a nothingness. People changed, slow at first, then in a rush, two nights of screams and blood." I thought of Mrs. Card. What would that thing have become? Would it have wanted me to carry its bags? Would it have baked me pie?

"What of your Walker?"

"He was a clever fellow. Too clever. He was the first to run."

Nan shook her head. "Won't happen here."

"I believe you," Catherine said. "That road is hard. I lost my Gareth, to cold children, I think. Called him out into the dark. He was a good man. I lost my daughter when the creek flooded. She was the eldest, and a strong child."

The children started sobbing. Catherine hushed them.

Nan nodded, though her face had taken on that hard look again. Nan never played at stern; it was in her blood. "I'll want to know of the troubles there, when you are settled."

"It was more than troubles," Catherine said. "They say you're the best. I'm here because so many say it, and looking at you, I see the truth in it. Please don't let my children die."

Nan winced. "We've a new place opened up on Coopers Lane. Jacob will need to get it ready for you. It is fully furnished, though you will need a new bed in the master bedroom."

Jacob nodded. "I have frames and mattresses," he said. "I'll need a couple of hours."

"Honestly, I could sleep on the floor."

"You won't need to."

You could see something leave them. A tension, a fear.

"Thank you," Catherine said, and she gripped Nan's hands, hard. Nan let her, for a long while. At last, she pulled her hands free.

"Our town is strong," Nan said, "because we are all strong for each other. Dr. Millison will tend to you. You can stay in his surgery until Jacob's ready to take you home."

"Thank you," Catherine said.

Dr. Millison introduced himself; Myles, too. Nan had a quick conversation with Jacob.

As the family left, the girl my age stuck her tongue out at me. I was so surprised by such a childish thing, I stuck mine out at her in turn. Both of us were ignored by the adults doing adult things around us.

"What's your name?" I asked, as she walked past me.

"Alice," she said.

"Jean."

"You've a weirdness about you, I can feel it. You and your nan. We're not going to be friends," she said. I blinked at her like I had been struck.

Nan grabbed my hand, hard. Distracted me completely from Alice's goings-on. "Somerton, destroyed," she said. "Now, that's the sort of thing that can drive a deep despair into you. You'd have liked Somerton. It had a fountain. It was quite beautiful, and the water was sweet, would you believe! I was often envious of it. Now it is gone." She shook her head. "This day has had too much grief in it. I'll have to get word north. The Red City must know of this."

"You said they don't care about us," I said.

"No, but they care about dissent. We owe them some courtesies. Somerton will need to be avoided—places like that can become a trap; look welcoming enough, but they eat travellers whole."

I watched after Alice, and she turned her head, and stuck out her tongue again. This time, I shook my head, gave her a glare filled with the old me that lay always in wait. It must have been grim! She pulled her tongue in quick.

No, we weren't going to be friends, but what did I know of friends?

Nan squeezed my hand. "Are you listening?"

"I was—"

"Then you'd know I've told you to go with Jacob. There's a mess to be cleaned up."

Jacob spared me the worst of it.

He handed me a shovel, and we started digging a ditch. For the fire, he explained. I worked till my hands were blistered. Didn't take much, as my calluses were shaped by gentler chores. I didn't complain. We hardly talked, and Jacob did the lion's share. But my back was aching by the end.

Then I had to help carry things to the fire that he had built up in the ditch. The bed, once he had broken it with an axe; the table in the kitchen, likewise cut; the bodies. We carried those together, once Jacob had wrapped them in sheets.

I started crying as we carried the first one. I couldn't tell which it was, woman or monster.

"I'm sorry, Jean," Jacob said. "If your nan wants you here, then you must help. You need to know what costs failure holds."

"I didn't mean to," I said.

Jacob nodded. "You're a good child, raised to kindness. But this has happened." He spoke to me then as sternly as he ever did, but not without gentleness. "I don't suppose you will ever forget this. But don't let it break your heart entirely, Jean. You are this town, and we will hold you. Even this can be got through."

We placed the first body on the fire, then carried the other. Jacob was gentle and reverent of both.

They went up fast, and we stood before the crackling flame, the smoke stinging our eyes and our lungs. Jacob whispering beneath his breath. I could see him crying, and he didn't try to hide it from me.

"Thank you for your help," he said. "You can go now. Your nan will send you to me when you need your lessons."

"What lessons?"

"That knife at your belt, for one. It's a hard world, Jean. Many troubles, not just one. You're going to need to know how to use it."

When I reached the end of the street, smoke behind me, my hands blistered and sore, I dropped to the ground, and cried. Sobbed up smoke and snot, sobbed so hard I thought my chest might break. But it didn't, and after a while, I stopped crying, and walked the rest of the way home.

The whole town stank of that sickly-sweet smoke for a day, then rains came in from the south, and washed it away, and the only smoke that could be smelled was Furnace. That fire burned endlessly, no matter which way the wind blew, no matter how hard the rains fell.

That night I was playing with the knife when Mum found me with it. A look passed across her face that I could not read.

"You're not holding it right," she said.

"How should I hold it?"

Mum shook her head. "You don't want me to tell you, believe me."

A little later, hiding in my usual spot, I overhead Mum and Nan talking.

"You're giving her that knife?"

"You'll never use it again," Nan said.

Mum made a low noise in her throat. "No, I won't. But you trust her with it?"

"Yes," Nan said.

"Don't make the same mistake with her."

"I won't," Nan said. "She isn't you."

Mum laughed, and there was a cruelty to it that made me flinch. "I've seen her use it. She'll never be my match with a blade."

"Good," Nan said, and Mum said nothing.

Mrs. Card's ashes were buried in a lull in the storm. Everyone was there, and if they blamed me, I didn't see it. But I blamed myself.

There was no Threnodist to sing her gone—they didn't come this way that often—so we sang instead, and told funny stories, even about the time that grey bird ate her dog on my birthday. I didn't laugh at that.

Afterwards, at home, I put a toe down onto the earth.

"Miss Jean, Miss Jean," my dead boy said. "Where have you been?"

He giggled at the rhyme. I did, too, and the laughter made my grief a little easier to bear.

"I've been getting an education," I said.

"Was it you I felt cross the levee? Was it you I felt in the Huskling hall?"

"Yes," I said.

"You've found a bit of bravery, then."

"Yes, but I was scared."

"Everyone's scared, Miss Jean. I'm down here, where its cold and noisy, and I'm always scared."

"Why are you down there?" I asked. "Why don't you go?"

"I'm lost, I think. There's a way somewhere, but it's too bright here. There's a light so bright, it's like a wall. All of us are blind. The only thing I can see is you."

"Would you like a story?" I asked, somewhat selfishly. I didn't want to think of that place. To be honest, I couldn't really imagine myself there, and I'd had enough of such thoughts.

"Yes. I like the pirate one." I liked that one, too, so I read him a bit of it, doing different voices for the different characters. He laughed at the bits I thought were funny, and made sounds at other bits, too. The world unshed some shadows, and my spirit lightened.

Then he said. "Miss Jean, there's an angry woman here. She wants to talk to you."

I lifted my foot up quick. I knew whom he meant, and I didn't want to talk to her.

It didn't matter because Mrs. Card came to my dreams, scurrying onto my bed. Lying there next to me, all those insect limbs quivering, her breath a rattling wheeze.

"I don't need the earth to find you," she said. "Not when your sleeping calls me."

Lolly was standing outside my window looking in, his mouth a big, horrified O.

"You stole my life," she said. "You stole it from me. Now I'm burnt up, and hungry. Give me a bit of yours. You're young; you've years in abundance."

Her mouth opened, and her tongue lashed out, only it was long and hollow, and sharp at the end.

Lolly watched, his mouth wider and wider. His fear made me angry. I swung out at the thing, but it cut my hands, slipped on the blood, and shot towards my chest.

"Jean, you are a silly girl," the graceful man said, only he was Lolly now, and then Lolly kissed me on the lips.

I woke, my hands clutching the coin. I slipped it away. It was raining again, the roof singing. I went back to sleep, but that's how I dreamed all night long, lurching from horror to fresh horror until Nan shook me.

"Time to get up," she said. "No rest. No rest."

For once, I was pleased to rise.

Coffee, breakfast, then out into the rain. I had an umbrella with me. Nan walked beside me, seemingly happy enough without one.

I told her about my nightmares.

Nan nodded. "This work will find its way into dreams. Usually not so clearly, but we're partway there when we do what we do. Don't let them scare you. Interrogate them. A dream is a lie stretched until its true." We reached the eastern edge of the levee and the stone. It beat out a steady rhythm.

"Yes, that's better." We stood, and waited for a glimmer of sun through the rain.

"I'm serious about your education," Nan said. "But I can't do it all by myself. The Huskling King has agreed to teach you a few things, but there is also something else that you need."

"What?" I asked.

"I've enrolled you in school, Jean. I've kept you apart from the town for too long."

A new horror filled me. I wanted an education, but school had never factored into that desire. School. All those children. All those rules and mysteries.

Nan bent over a stone, and turned it three times to the right. "It won't be that bad," she said.

She didn't sound at all convincing.

When the school bell rang, I was already at the gates. I had dressed in my neatest clothes. Mum had combed my hair so that it wasn't its usual mess.

Mrs. Paige was there to greet me with a big smile on her face. Mrs. Paige had lost her boys and Mr. Paige to Furnace. She always looked sad to me, despite how she might grin.

"Hello, Jean," she said.

"I'm here to get an education, Mrs. Paige," I said.

"I know, and I'll do my best to provide you one, but you'll need to work at it," Mrs. Paige said.

"I will, Mrs. Paige."

She nodded at that. "Good. Your grandmother says you can read and write. Truthfully, at your age, I'd be horrified if you couldn't."

"I can read better than I can write," I said. "My hand's messy, but my spelling's good."

"We'll fix that." She led me to the classroom. "Are you nervous?"

"I am," I said, truthfully. "Kids are weird."

Mrs. Paige smiled at that. "Jean, some days I don't think I understand them either."

It wasn't too bad. I'd got it in my head that I was slow or stupid, even with my memory, but I could read better than anyone in my class, and better than most of the older kids, too. My maths wasn't that great, nor my grammar. I wasn't any genius. I had so much more to remember, and school was only part of my education.

Mrs. Paige was a kind woman, though. Not one of those awful teachers I'd read about in stories, the sort that would lock you up if you spoke a word out of place, or you didn't blot your paper.

Best of all, the school library had lots of books—old stories, too. Some written (but never printed) before the Years of Heat and Sadness, most after.

The hours in school ran the slowest. Mrs. Paige might have been a great teacher, but I had Nan, and where once she had closed me off from the world, now she was opening it. I knew my words and my histories, but I knew deeper things, like the way clever birds scratched their memories on trees, or the way monsters burrowed and crept and wheedled their way into towns.

But I did learn things, even if I was counting down to when the afternoon was done, when I'd run errands for Nan, or see Lolly.

And that's how my weeks passed for a while.

Every morning, I would walk the circuit with Nan, then see Jacob for fighting instruction, then go to school.

The circuit of the levee was the best. Nan and I would follow it east to west, then east again. Nan would show me how this or that symbol worked, or how to make a guarding from fox fur and warpweed. We'd head west along the levee, working our way around, touching the signal stones at each point of the compass.

Every day the circuit beat with its formidable strength.

One morning, we stopped at the western stone, and I pointed down along the road that ran towards the Slouches, the road that ran to Furnace. The smoke was thick in the sky over there, but it wasn't the smoke I was pointing at. "Isn't that Dr. Millison?"

Nan squinted. "Yes," she said.

Furnace had him.

"And who's that with him?"

"I don't see anyone," Nan said.

I knew who it was. I'd held his coin the night before, and it had been as hot in my hands as if I'd left it in the sun.

"Whom do you see?"

I wanted to tell her, but I didn't. "Just a trick of the light," I said, but kept watching.

The graceful man was holding Dr. Millison's hand, chatting away, and the doctor was nodding. He even laughed.

"He does look like he's talking to someone, doesn't he?"

"It's just a madness, isn't it?" I asked.

"Of a sort," Nan said.

We could have walked down there, and taken Dr. Millison home—it would have been a struggle, but he'd have come with us. It had been done before. But then the wildness would build up in him. He'd start hurting himself, and others, if they got too close. He'd start screaming to be let free, that he had to go to Furnace, that there was a place there for him, pulling at his bones. He'd tear out his hair, scratch his cheeks.

When Furnace hooked you, there was no point in fighting it.

I'd never heard that they were taken by the hand by my graceful man, though, and that he'd chat to them like you would about the weather or tell them jokes. Dr. Millison was walking like he was going for a stroll, or a visit, hand in hand with an old friend. It scared me. I should have told Nan, but that gold coin burned in my head.

The graceful man looked up. He waved at me, once, and got back to talking. Nan and I watched Dr. Millison walk to the hills until he was lost in the trees growing there.

"What's out there?" I asked. "What's beyond those hills where Furnace burns?"

"I wish I knew," Nan said. "But I fear that place more than anything. When it started burning, the dead were blinded, the Stone Road closed. That's a work of awful power."

"Has Tree ever sent a bird that way? Or the king a Huskling?"

"No, birds won't fly there. They refuse. And the Husklings say that the air grows hard against them in the west."

"We're going to need a new doctor, aren't we?"

"I'll write to the college in the Red City," Nan said.

"You ever been there?"

"I have travelled, but I've steered clear of the city. It's a long way. The roads are poor."

"And the troubles many," I said, mimicking her husky voice.

Nan grinned despite the worry writ on her face. "And that's the damn truth."

We walked the rest of the circuit, and Nan didn't say much, except to point out a line of force, or a weakening. She certainly didn't talk about Dr. Millison, or Furnace.

"How is your training with Jacob going?"

"Terribly," I said. "I can hardly hold a knife."

"Not all of us are fighters, but you'll learn. Today after class," she said, "I want you to carefully cross over the levee, and make your way to the king."

"Really?"

Nan coughed. "Do you take me for a joker?" She pressed the bone needle into my hand. "Keep this hidden," she said. "In case you need it."

"Will I?"

"Of course not," Nan said. "But, just in case."

I nodded. It was getting late, I ran down the levee and off to the schoolyard, thinking of Dr. Millison, and how happy he'd looked with the graceful man.

A school day's slow enough as it is. Conjugating verbs, shouting out times tables, and watching the other kids play at lunchtime because none of them will play with you, and you're not even sure you'd know how to if they did. When you know you'll be seeing the Huskling King, everything else is five times boring, and touched with trouble.

You feel like that last bell will never ring. And you want it to, and don't want it too all at once.

But it did, at last, and I was off like a shot. Over the levee, and down, careful this time not to disturb a thing.

Bird found me. "Miss Jean," they said.

"Bird." They settled on my shoulder, and I stroked their head.

"Your nan asked that I guide you to the king."

"Please do," I said.

We were much faster that afternoon. There was no Lolly to disturb us, no attempt on Bird's part to run us in circles. We climbed the hill, and went down it, then to the rings of sculptures. There was a new one there: a woman of Nan's age I didn't recognise. Someone from out of town.

I paused to look at her. "Who's that?"

"I don't know," Bird said. "Could be a Threnodist. See the chain and the symbol attached to it?"

"Yes," I said.

"Threnodists wear those sometimes."

"I've never met one," I said. I'd heard of them, though, and their sad and wonderful singing.

"Oh, they come down here, but rarely. I suppose Casement Rise is too practiced in its mourning."

I looked at the statue for a moment longer, then walked out of the grove and to the hall.

The Husklings were waking, unfurling like flags that had at last found a breath of wind. Amongst them, larger, fiercer, his eyes bright and knowing, without a thread of sleep to them, was the king. He grinned at me.

"There you are! I have been waiting for you."

"Nan said you are going to teach me."

The king nodded. "Yes, but it won't be with chalk and blackboards and books. I'm going to teach you about the land, as much as I can." The king sighed. "My kingdom is a tiny one. No matter that we carved the Defiant with our own raw hands, or made the watchers and the weepers on the Stone Road. The old Masters won't let us forget that we were made, grown into being, on steel benches by whitecoats. So we are banished to this edge of nowhere, which suits your nan well, for we help keep worse things out."

He leant in close. "Are you willing to learn?"

I was willing, but I'd had so much education lately that my head felt fit to burst. "Yes," I said.

"It won't always be like this. Your skull will grow bigger to accommodate it all."

How did he know what I was thinking? The king made a face like he was blowing up a balloon: a look part comical, part horrendous. Then he stopped, regained his dignity. "We'd best begin then."

Around him, his entourage roiled, the Husklings biting and spitting at each other. He was much larger than any of them, but they were scarier. No, that wasn't quite true: What wildness he possessed, he held within. The danger was no less great, just buried deep.

He led me back through the grove. Back to those statues.

"Each of these I made myself," he said, lifting a hand towards mine. His nails were long and sharp, almost claws. "We've no need of tools. Our flesh is hard enough to shape stone."

I looked long and hard at his carving of me. It didn't offend me so much, now that I'd gotten over the shock of it.

"How did you know what I looked like?"

"My eyes are not constrained by distance. You'll need that sight, too."

"Why?"

"Looking in other places, other ways, will make the world a little less surprising to you. You've a challenge ahead, and it may aid you. But it has its dangers. I can't pretend that it doesn't. There are others that see that way, too, and there are others that hunt there."

"Is the man from Furnace one of them? Will I see him?"

"He's a scary fellow, that's for sure. But I have never seen him there, hence, no sculpture."

"Who is he?"

The king shook his head. "You'll need to find that out. That's your challenge. I can't look at another's shadow. The west beyond the Slouches is sealed up to me, as though it's the land's end."

"Nan said that the monsters want to be like us. Do you want to be like us?"

The king's lip curled; he showed a bit of teeth. "Be careful whom you call a monster. We were you, but now we are not.

The whys and wherefores I cannot answer. Those Years of Heat and Sadness were days of transformation. The thing is, only some of us came back. Everything you see that is monstrous was a human once, or of human provenance, even if it was little more than a fragment of nightmare or a sliver of hope. It's no wonder that they yearn to be that way again. Most of what you see that is wondrous was a bird or a tree, or an animal, but is now something else. Like your clever bird."

"I've always been a bird," Bird said.

"Of course. Now, close your eyes, Jean," the king said. I did. "You need to find this place with your eyes shut. It's out there, and you can search for it, call it to you."

My eyes snapped open. "What am I searching for?"

"Nothing you'll find with your eyes open!" I squeezed them shut. "It's a kind of coldness, a twitch inside your heartbeat."

I tried to make sense of that.

"Listen." I listened. "You can hear it. There's a space in the silence that isn't quite noise."

There it was. I felt it. My heart twisted, my skin prickled with goose bumps, and I felt like I was falling and growing all at once. I stumbled, then my feet found their balance.

"Yes," the king said. "You are here. Open your eyes."

I opened them, but it was as if they were still closed. Everything was darkness. Bird was gone from my shoulder; I hadn't even felt them leave.

"This is the Long Between. It's the truth behind the real. Secrets fall away here. You will need to be careful," the king whispered in my ear. I jumped at his hot breath against my face. He took a step back. "You see without seeing, you feel without feeling, and you travel here by walking, and not walking."

"I don't like it," I said. The darkness closed in tight and hot, a dry heat, a brittle one.

"I'm not surprised. Some truths aren't likeable at all," the king said. "But you must use it. Think of home, think of your nan. Keep your eyes forward."

All at once I could feel her. She was a distant thinness in the dark.

"First lesson," the king said. "It is the worst, perhaps the most dangerous. All you have to do is find your way home."

Then he was gone, and I was alone in that dark. Not sure how I had gotten there, not sure how to get home. Far away, I felt something notice me. A great stirring presence, a storm with a mind.

"Jean," it whispered, and it sounded hungry, like I was all it wanted, the only meal that would suffice. And it was drawing closer. Soft footfalls, steady breaths, a little scrape, as of clawed feet.

I started to walk, away from that sound. I told myself it was just a wind blowing, some distant tree scraping, but the air was still in the Long Between. Everything was still, and yet something moved, and not just me. There was a sort of presence, a predatory consciousness, and it was drawing in on me.

How could I find my way home when I couldn't see? When all I could do was walk and feel?

"Jean," the voice that wasn't a voice said, again. I wanted to run, but I was certain that if I did, I would be lost. I looked around me, but there was nothing but darkness. I thought of Jacob's lessons—if only I wasn't such a bad student. But still I took out the silver knife, and it gleamed slick and poisonous in the weird light of the Long Between.

I heard laughter, caught a flash of a fire burning, and birds screaming, but a long way off. Someone called my name, closer now.

Somewhere ahead of me there was a subtle shift: a slight thinning in the dark.

How could I find my way home when I couldn't see in anything but bursts? When all I could do was walk, feeling out each step, as uncertain as a toddler?

I closed my eyes, and it came to me more clearly: a thinning in the murk. I walked towards it. Kept my steps steady. The dark flowed around me. I caught impressions, saw without seeing, deeper darknesses and moments of white—the memory of a colour. And then they took shape. The statues, the hill. Here, though, they were more like drawings, things I might scratch out on clay.

When I moved slowly, they became more vivid, easier to see. Not quite the real thing, but close enough. When I hurried, they fell apart, the world slipping from me, and I felt like I was moving anywhere but home.

So I took my time with each step, and the going quickened. I kept my gaze on where I felt Casement Rise must be, and the shadow space, that sketched space, moved around me.

Past the Robsons' farm I went. Quick sketches of cows, a flick of tail, a spray of dung. I thought I saw Lolly running through the scrub, chased by his brothers, but I was already at the levee.

The levee was drawn all mazed and prickly. I could feel its intense outward gaze, its power driven to keep the world from the town, keep everything at bay. It was like walking against the drag of a current in a weed-slicked creek. More than that! It was like having an argument with my nan, and I'd had plenty of those.

I grinned. I knew my way through this.

Up and over, and the going gentled. I moved effortlessly and swiftly through the town.

I knew these places. I passed through them, and they passed through me. I was almost home.

I turned back to see where I had come from.

And there it was: a shadow, terrible and smothering.

"Jean," it said, and snatched at me.

Five times my size, at least, the shadow was, and as it closed fingers around my wrist, I nearly dropped the knife. I reached for Nan's needle with my free hand. I had wits enough for that. The bone flared with a pale fire in the dark, and the shadow let me go, shielding its face. I moaned in fear, and so did it. I stumbled back, fell on my arse and . . .

I sat in the middle of Main Street. I cackled. Home! I was home!

"What are you doing?"

I rolled around. Standing over me was Alice, the girl I had met what felt like forever ago at the Summer Gate. She hadn't liked me then, and it was obvious she still didn't.

She was blurry, not quite there, but I could still see there was a glower to her. One of her hands was clenched into a fist. "Where did you come from? Where?"

"I don't know," I said.

Alice slipped into focus. She was glowing like a thousand candles, and everything was beautiful. Everything, all at once. I hadn't expected that. My mouth hurt from grinning like a mad old cat. "So gorgeous. And your hair looks nice."

Alice frowned at me. I was grinning up at her like a loon from there on my bum.

"Don't do it again," Alice said, and walked off.

"Oh, I won't," I called after her. "Maybe."

She didn't look back, just hurried on her way.

I sat there a while. The air felt good in my lungs. The first stars were out. They burned so bright and warm. I wanted to eat them.

It felt like a dream, and for a moment, I wasn't sure whether I was awake or not. Except that, where the shadow had touched me was a welt the size of my palm.

I got up, brushed myself down, and walked home. The whole town glowed, not a reflection of the sun's light, like the moon, but luminous with its own nature. This was the real world, and having seen its shadow, it shone even brighter.

I walked past a couple taking a stroll, greeted them so effusively that they looked at me like I was crazy. Maybe they thought I was drunk like my mum. I certainly was drunk on something, only I wasn't a bitter drunk.

A white shape found me out. "Where have you been? You were there, and then you weren't."

"I was somewhere, all right," I said. "You fly so beautifully, Bird."

"Yes, but I shouldn't be about. There's owls."

"Then wing away home."

"Are you sure you are well?"

"Yes, I'm as healthy as the stars," I said.

"Hmph."

Bird stayed with me until I was almost home. Then there was a nearby hooting, and they were gone like a shot.

Our house was brightest of all, though by the time I got to the door, the silliness had left me a little.

Nan had already started on dinner. Chopping greens. All the potatoes had been peeled. I went to help her, and she shook her head. "I'm almost done. Don't want to break my rhythm."

"But I'm particularly good at chopping!" I declared.

"Just sit!"

But I wasn't one for sitting, certainly not then. "Maybe I could help you knot that cord," I said.

Nan shook her head. "That's a gift. I have to make it, and me alone. That's the nature of the giving."

"But I can tie the tightest knots!"

Nan held my cheeks, and looked into my eyes. "Oh, but you are giddy. Where did he take you?"

"The Long Between," I said.

"Of course he did," Nan growled. "What reckless abandon! I tell him you require an education, and he throws you in with the sharks."

"There weren't sharks," I said.

"Oh, there were sharks. There are always sharks."

We ate dinner, just the two of us. Mum was already gone for the night. The house felt so bright, but it was already becoming as it always was. Out there, in the deepening night, something may have been calling my name, but I couldn't hear it.

By the time I started on the dishes, the glamour was mostly gone. I washed, and Nan dried. Our tea was steeping in the pot.

"Nan," I said. "The king said I had trouble coming. I don't understand what he meant, except maybe it's that graceful man."

Nan hung her tea towel on the rack, poured two cups of tea, and sat down. "You're right at that, Jean. It *is* Furnace, and that fellow with the golden eyes. Everyone has troubles, except in our family it's more . . . pronounced. We've, all of us, been challenged, since we started to walk the levee bank. That goes back past my grandmother, past her mother, too. It's something that we bear, a price we pay to keep the whole town safe. A great trouble finds us. Not that there aren't the usual things that push and pull at everyone, but this is bigger; this is singular, defining. And the troubles have been getting worse."

That didn't seem fair to me. Nan was tough as bones; I was just a kid. "What was your trouble?"

Nan sipped at her tea. "It wasn't any Furnace. Nothing raised when I was born; I wasn't so unlucky. It came upon me later, and I was waiting.

"There was a cold winter. The coldest I had ever known. My mother, your great-grandmother, had walked the Stone Road by then, so it was just me. I was thirty, and I had protected the town for thirteen years, and this was back when the town was much bigger. I thought I knew everything.

"Maybe that was my challenge, my pride. Maybe that's been my challenge all these years. That winter, the snows came all the way to town, swept in, and smothered everything. The dead were grumbling, and I was waking to a bitter chill every morning.

"Your grandfather woke with me. Les didn't walk the levee—I preferred to do that alone—but he would make me tea, and we would talk, and that winter you could see our breath, even inside.

"It got so everything was freezing. Even the creek had frozen over. One morning, I woke earlier than usual. There'd been an almighty crack, loud enough to wake the dead, except Les was still sleeping, and the air was warm.

"I got up, hoping it was nothing, but certain it wasn't. Grabbed my walking stick, which was more a weapon then than something I really needed to get around. I walked outside.

"There was a strange light in the north, and my hope faded. Each of us feels our challenge, knows where it is coming from, and I'd always known mine would be from the north.

"That crack had come from the west, but I knew what it was. The creek. It was so warm that the ice had shattered, and the water had started flowing again. I kept my ears on that, but my eyes were on the north.

"I went to the Summer Gate. The gate was shivering. I reached out to touch it, but the metal was too hot. Buckling, almost molten—go look at it next time, and you will see that it still bears that damage. I couldn't go that way, so I walked around and up the levee, no matter that the bank is steep that way. I was young, and I had my walking stick.

"Let me tell you, I almost turned around, and started walking away from what I saw from the top of that levee. I was shivering in my bones."

"What was it?"

"It had wings; it was big as two oxen, head to tail, in the body; and it walked low and flat to the ground.

"This was the thing. This was what I was born to face. It must have been coming for me from far in the north. I had gotten a sense of it—you will, too, if you are close enough to your challenge.

"I felt how it had been in waters deep and dark when it had awakened, and then how it had risen slowly. I felt the death on it, the lives that it had taken. The lives it wished to take, and chief of those was mine. It hungered for me, and it was terrifying.

"It lifted its head, and stared at me with fierce, bright eyes. I could feel the heat of it. Its raw stink.

"I closed my eyes. I took one step, and another, and I walked down to face it.

"I was terrified, yes, but when I reached the bottom of the levee, I realised that it was terrified, too. That its conception of death, of its own death, was bound up in me."

"Woman," it said, and it had the voice of an old man, hard and strong and confident because it had never been challenged. "I have come to kill you."

I didn't bother with speaking. I swung my stick, and struck it on the nose, and it howled, and lurched back from me, lashing out with its great claws.

"We fought. I was stronger back then, of course, but we didn't fight with our flesh alone. I was its bane, and it was mine, and in that we shared a weakness and a strength.

"You'd think that it would have been greater than me. But no, we were equals. And, when it realised this, do you know what it did?"

I shook my head.

"Why, it turned tail and ran. I stood there, panting, bloody, my stick held in one bruised hand, and I watched it start on its ruinous way north. I didn't give chase straight away; that would have been folly. I went home, cleaned myself up, packed a few things, and kissed my husband goodbye. I'd always wanted to go north, to see the world a bit, and now I had to.

"This time I went through the gates, not over them, and I followed that beast. It was a long hunt. I walked north for days, then weeks, then months. I passed no township nor outpost, though I did cross the railway, well after the Night Train had rattled west—I heard its whistle twice, one south of the line, the other north, and though I never saw it, it still haunts my dreams.

"One day, my trouble veered to the east, to a shore unfamiliar to me that I soon realised was the place where it had first entered the land. And we fought.

"Now it was ready for me, here where it felt strong, but I was ready for it, too. It was all swagger as it rambled, laughed, and cursed me with a thousand dooms, a hundred cutting insights. But I ignored them for the weapons they were, and I struck it even as it gripped me in its claws, claws strong enough to tear a person into strips of meat and bone.

"It beat its great wings and flew up, high and fast, and I was terrified. I struck it hard between the eyes, and it fell into death, and then I realised in the killing of it, I would fall into my own, and I laughed a bitter sort of laugh as I fell.

"But its landing softened mine, and while I was broken, I breathed. Slowly, moment by moment, I felt its strength seep into me. When I could walk again, I started walking home, and every day the walking came easier.

"I was gone nearly a year in all. When I came home, Casement Rise was still there, the townspeople were getting on, and your grandfather was waiting. He asked me if I would like a cup of tea, and I laughed at him, and he laughed at me, and we kissed like it was our first kiss, and the awkwardness of all that time apart fell away like the old cloak it was, and some nine months later, believe it or not, your mother was born. That's how I met my challenge, and I thank the god in the Sun that it was so easy when it could have been so hard."

"Didn't sound so easy to me," I said.

"At the time, it didn't feel that easy, but it was a simple challenge. I think, at the heart of me, I'm a simple person. You, my love, are not. Neither is your mother, and that's what terrifies me the most. Your challenge won't be crude and wild, nor rushing like the tide. It will be a web spun around you, and it's been that way since the moment you were born."

"How do I survive that?"

Nan held my hand. "We do the best we can, then do better, and hope that is enough."

I looked up at her. "What happened to Mum?"

Nan's face hardened. "That is a story I can't tell you. That's for your mother alone."

"You're forbidden to tell it?"

Nan shook her head. "No, my love, it hurts me far too much. I can't. And I won't. To bed with you now, Jean. This story's made me tired."

The next sunrise was the sweetest I had ever seen. I almost laughed with delight at it. Nan held my hand as we stood staring west.

"You seem too cheerful," she said.

"I'm all right. It's just, the sun is so beautiful," I said.

She dropped to her knee, looked me in the eye, and frowned. "Maybe I'm pushing you too hard."

I did my best to be quiet and normal as we walked the circuit. Furnace smoked—there was no one walking that way, thank goodness—and even it was beautiful, a grey feather that brushed at the sky.

When we were on the southern length of the levee, above the Winter Gate, we stopped, and looked at the road that led that way, and I asked about the mountains known as the Whispers. They were high and often snow-streaked, but this was a hot summer, so they glimmered dark and sharp.

"What's beyond them?" I asked.

"Why, the Stone Road, of course. The road of the dead," Nan said. "The road you must walk when you are ready."

"Is it a long way?"

"Yes, it can be."

"Is it beautiful, the road?" The mountains certainly were. I don't think I'd ever seen them so.

"Jean, you've grown peculiar," Nan said, squinting down at me. I couldn't tell if she was concerned or irritated. Probably both.

"I'm all right," I said again.

Nan nodded. "I *am* pushing you too hard. No matter what you say! It's Saturday. Once you are done with your chores, go and visit Lolly, and get him to show you where the best warp-weed grows. I'll need this filled for tomorrow." She handed me a hessian bag. "Now the levee is secure, and strong. Get to work."

I laboured all morning, and most of the afternoon, doing this and that. If that was me being pushed less hard, then I had no desire to be stretched. It worked, though; the world's high gloss was rubbed from my vision. Which was a relief, I realised, once it was gone. Such intense beauty was intolerable; it burnt at the senses rather than soothed. You saw everything and, in the end, saw nothing.

Still, it was later than I expected when I crossed over the levee, and walked to the Robsons' farmhouse.

Maggie Robson, Lolly's mother, was in the yard.

"Young Jean," she said.

"Mrs. Robson," I said, "I'm looking for Lolly."

She was amused at that. Who else would I be looking for?

Maggie called him out. He had a shiner, the biggest bruise I had seen so openly displayed. I must have made a face at it because Maggie frowned. "The boys get a bit rough, but I've punished them. They're all working the farthest fences today. Won't be getting any lunch, either."

Lolly's face flushed with embarrassment. I changed the subject. "Nan said you know where the best warpweed is. She needs some for tomorrow's work."

Maggie nodded. "Nancy's right. It's at the other end of the farm. If you hurry, you can get there and back before it starts to get dark."

"I know another place where there's plenty of warpweed," I said, remembering that horrible clearing I'd come across before I first met the Huskling King. "It's just west of here."

"No," Maggie said, all at once. "No, you'll not go there."

"Why? What happened there?"

"Lolly, you take her where I want you to. Be a good friend."

Lolly frowned. "By the hanging tree?"

"Yes," Maggie said. "Nothing hanging there now, but I've seen great bunches of what Jean's nan needs." She went inside, and came back with two apples and some water. "You two better hurry."

Lolly led me through the farm. "What's a hanging tree?" I asked.

"Place where they hang bad folk. Or they used to." He grinned. "They'd slip a rope around their necks, and hoist them up, and they would be twitching and thrashing until all the breath was gone out of them. Never seen it—there's not been a hanging since before your nan was a girl. At least, that's what Mum says."

"Seems an awful cruel thing to do."

"They were bad folks that they hung. Murderers, and worse. But they'd dance a jolly dance at the end."

"And that's where we're going?"

"Yep."

We walked a while in silence, Lolly looking at his shoes, me staring at my boots so I wouldn't look at that bruised face.

"Your brothers are cruel," I said to him.

I heard him sniffle. "I deserve it," he said.

"No one I know has ever deserved a thrashing." I thought of my mum, and the violence she'd visit on me when she got wild drunk, and Nan wasn't around.

Bird arrived then, which shows that such creatures have exceptional timing on occasion. They flapped around my head once—that brought back a flash of memory, of a hundred birds circling furiously. I gave them my arm. They landed on it neatly, and made their way along it to my shoulder.

"Bird!" Lolly said.

"Boy and Jean," Bird said.

"My name's Lolly."

Bird hopped up and down on my shoulder. "That's not a name, it's a sweet."

"My mam always said I was a sweetie."

"Where are you two going?"

"To the hanging tree," Lolly said.

"We're getting warpweed for Nan."

"Yes, that's where the best of it grows. That's the way, with warpweed. It needs a place all twisted about, all ruined with tragedy, to get a good bit of growing."

"It's just a weed," I said.

"If there's a clump of it, then you can be certain that there was a bad death there. Been a lot of bad deaths in this country, so it's all over the place. But that's a good spot."

We walked a while. I thought I heard the Summer Gate's bell ringing, but when I mentioned it, it stopped, and Lolly looked at me like I had made it up. He pointed out his family's farm, the dam, the cattle trails, and the new shearing shed—they had some sheep, too. There was a big flat space where they played cricket, though not as often as they used to. There were fewer Robsons now. Furnace didn't just take people from town.

It was a leisurely stroll. But we got to the hanging tree at last, and I couldn't help but groan. The warpweed was old, brittle, and thorny.

"This will not do," I said.

Lolly shook his head. "S'pose nothing bad's happened here in a while." Lolly pointed to a stout branch, its thickness marred with scars. "That's where they did the hanging."

"You know a lot about hanging," I said.

Lolly reddened, but it wasn't with anger. "Mitcham tells me. Says he might take me out here one day if I'm too much trouble."

It was then I thought that having siblings might be more trouble than it's worth. What a horror.

"Well," I said, trying to change the subject quick. "I know a place where the warpweed's good."

Bird flew into the air, fluttered before my face. "I don't think that's a good idea."

I puffed myself up. There was still a touch of the Long Between in me, an echo of that jubilance. I felt braver than I ought. "There's three of us." I looked over at Lolly. "You know where I'm talking?"

Lolly picked up a good length of stick, swung it in the air. "It's on the Prestons' land."

"Do you think we could make it in and out?"

"Yes."

"No," said Bird.

"We'd better hurry, then."

We ran. The day was getting on, but the grove wasn't far away. Over a creek and under the fence that tracked its bank, its posts half-eaten with termites, then it was a swift dash through a field. We even saw a few of the Prestons' sheep. They watched us, suspiciously.

Lolly paused, then. "You hurry home," he shouted at them.

"They look happy enough," I said, glad to catch my breath.

"This close to the Husklings, they'll get eaten."

I shrugged. "We need to get that warpweed."

Truth was, I didn't want to stay in that clearing after dark, and it was getting late. The memory of that place was growing heavy in my mind.

Finally, we reached the grove. It felt just as bad as last time. I paused, looking across the clearing at the tree. Ten circles, cut as with a knife.

"There it is. See?" Bird whispered in my ear. I was ready to turn around, take a tongue lashing later from Nan. But there it was: warpweed, soft and thick. She would be pleased.

"Oh, I see it," I said.

"We shouldn't linger," Bird said. "It's getting late."

"Won't take long," I said.

The shadows had a length to them. But my eyes were mostly on the warpweed. It was thick and green, and not particularly thorny, as though it could afford to lose some of itself to my needs. I took the blade from my belt and started cutting.

Which was why I didn't see it, until Lolly whispered low and painful. "Jean. There's—"

I swung my head up, and there it was. A thin shadow, taller than both Lolly and I, if I were to stand on his shoulders. And it towered over him now.

"Jean." Bird said.

The shadow gripped Lolly's head in its hands—if they could be called hands, for surely they had no substance to them. It bent low, from the waist, and whispered into his ear.

"Be strong for the boy," Bird said. "It's not too late."

"Go away," I shouted at the shadow. It turned at me, and took one step in my direction. I did not move, no matter that I wanted to. It took another step.

"Be strong," Bird said.

"Gone," I said. "Get." My voice cracked, but I didn't turn from it. In fact, I took a step towards it. The shadow fell into fragments upon the ground.

Lolly looked at me, and his eyes were wide as plates.

"You all right?" I asked. "Still with us?"

Lolly nodded, then fell backwards into the shadow of the tree. It swarmed over him. I rushed to him, dragged him free of the dark. He clutched at my wrist. "That was," he said, blinking and blinking, "that was unexpected."

"What?"

He laughed. "Sorry," he said, touching his brow. "Sorry. I wasn't expecting that to hurt."

Somewhere nearby, a creature called out, and I realised how dark it was getting.

"Time for us to go," I said. I didn't want to be there a second more.

"Yes," Bird said.

I tugged at Lolly's hand.

"Yes, we must go now," he said, and he let me help him to his feet. That he could stand made me grateful, grateful enough that I didn't question him more than to ask: "Can you run?"

He nodded.

Then I heard the click of a rifle.

"What in hell are you doing here?" Myles Preston demanded. He looked at us from behind that gun. He had it pointed right at me, or at Bird—I couldn't tell. I could feel Bird tensing, perhaps for flight. Myles was glaring at them, perhaps even worse than at me. I tapped my bag gently with my knife. "Just getting warpweed for my nan."

"On my land? In this place, of all places? This is trespass."

"I didn't realise."

"Oh, don't lie to me," he said.

I had my knife, but he had his gun.

"There's a few sheep in the east field," Lolly said.

"I was looking for them," Myles said. He lowered his rifle.

Lolly nodded, calmer than I could imagine. I guess it was the gun. Lolly lived with bullies, and knew how to placate them, though it wasn't always enough.

"We lost three cattle last summer. Dogs. Remember?"

"Yeah," Myles said. "East field, near the Husklings?"

Lolly nodded again.

Myles was already thinking about things more important than trespass. The Husklings love mutton. "You two, get out of here. But if those sheep aren't there, I'll be talking to your parents."

"They will be," Lolly said.

He glared at me. "Might just talk to your nan anyway."

I could see him tallying something up: Maybe this would be the thing to push the rest of the council into getting an auditor. But those sheep were more important.

"Get, then," Myles said.

We got, all right, quick as we dared. As soon as we were clear of the trees, we ran. I raced Lolly to his farm, carrying the warp-weed over my shoulder, and Lolly laughed all the way.

Maggie was waiting at the gate. I tried to look like we'd just had the most fun and uncomplicated adventure. "Brought him back safe and sound."

We said our goodbyes. I still had a ways to go, and it was dark now.

"Keep an eye on Lolly," Bird said as we walked.

"He's all right," I said.

"I don't know boys, but he seemed a bit peculiar."

"He's all right."

"Something's wrong with him."

"How many kids do you know?"

"Well, there's you."

"Exactly," I said. "I'm perfect. Every other kid seems wrong compared to me."

Bird considered this, then nodded. "Perhaps you're right. I know nothing of children. We birds are different as babies. The shell and the sky are sense-bringers, the roots of our tree are wise. You two are a constant confusion to me."

That's Bird, always trying to show how their kind are better. I rolled my eyes.

They flew away home once I reached the levee. Lolly hadn't been that different. Not really. I knew enough to see that, didn't I? I thought about going back, just to be sure, but changed my mind. It was getting late, and I had to go home.

When you're twelve, you don't always make the wisest decisions.

But this wasn't Mrs. Card. Lolly was walking and talking. His hand had been solid and hot.

I carried the bag of warpweed home. I would have said something to Nan, but Jim was there. That had been the Summer Gate's bell I heard ringing.

"Jean," he said. I threw myself around him, and he hugged me back.

"Well, that was a welcome!"

"Will you make us some tea, Jean?" Nan said. "And some for yourself."

The pot took forever to boil.

Jim was here, which meant the traders were here, which meant festival and food and fun. I came back with cups of tea: black with two heaps of sugar for Jim, straight old black for me and Nan.

Jim studied me. "You just keep growing, don't you?"

I nodded. I was tall for a child.

"Going to be as tall as Les, isn't she?"

"He was a tall one, all right."

I'd never known my grandfather; he'd died four years before I was born. If I had anyone close to a grandfather, it was Jim, but we only saw him twice a year, sometimes three, back when the roads were better.

He was a friend of Nan's, nearly as old as she was. He travelled and traded all the way north to the Red City, and west to Shipton, where the sea was. He brought coffee and cigarettes and chocolates, and news. There was always news, bits of politicking and plagues and storms. The world was bigger when Jim was here.

"Nancy was telling me that you're getting an education."

I nodded. "A proper one, from dawn to sunset."

"Finally! Something to fill that head of yours."

"What's the news, then?"

"Same old things. Masters jostling, Red City politics. There was some trouble in Midtown that had mouths flapping, but nothing to concern Casement Rise. There hasn't been a breath of flu or plague in months. We came here with your new doctor—Sue Williams is her name." He took a sip of tea.

"Did you get her measure?" Nan asked.

"She's capable, for sure. Stitched up a few of my boys when they got into a bit of bother at Knotbridge."

"That's a brawling town," Nan said.

"I don't encourage it, but we pass through some wild places."

"Don't *you* get into trouble?"

Jim chuckled. "Nancy, I'm an old man. I keep my fight for when I need it."

"You hear about Somerton?"

"Yes, that was a shock."

"The communities are shrinking."

"There's always room up north."

"Folk stay in Casement Rise for a reason: that it isn't the north."

"I'm not here to fight."

"Good," Nan said, and stroked his arm. "I'm in a mood to smoke. Want to join me?"

I was left to clean up while they talked on the verandah, low and close. Mum came in, and joined me in the kitchen.

She sat down carefully. "Those old lovebirds," she said, fondly. "They'll get to kissing soon."

She looked at the verandah, and there was a bit of a sadness to her. I made her a cup of black tea.

We sat in silence a while. "I miss your dad," she said. "I miss those lips."

I nodded, but I didn't know what she meant. I'd never been kissed by anyone that wasn't family, except in a dream, and I couldn't even picture my father. He must have held me, wrapped me up, rocked me to sleep, but that was so long ago that it was beyond my dreaming.

Casement Rise never seemed more alive than when the traders came. The town filled up with goods and laughter. And above all, there was Jim, who made Nan so happy, I'd catch her whistling.

The traders would set up their tents out on Weary's Park, and it was like Casement Rise had a second, brighter heart.

Everyone came: to trade, buy (there were folks who still used the Red City's money), gossip, and paw over the fashions and peculiarities of the north. You could get a paper that was only a month out of date, and you could get a fella to read it to you if you couldn't. There was a Threnodist there, too. Not a real one—those followed a call, travelled alone from town to town to sing the sadness from a place. This one sang the familiar songs, the sorrowful ones, mainly, and his voice was beautiful. There weren't that many men in town—Furnace swept them up more than women, for whatever reason—so there were romances, and there was a dance.

Dr. Williams pitched a tent with the fair, said she'd set up her practice later. Dr. Millison had left all his equipment, and she could move into his surgery after the fair.

The nights were still short and hot; the days long and slow as syrup. It was a happy time. The men would tip their hats to you, the women, too, for there were a few of them, worldly and clever, and quick to fight.

It was a week or two of fineness, and a sense that we were part of a bigger world. It let me forget a few things, or at least ignore them.

Still, it ended, and it ended the way it always had. Jim asking Nan to leave with him, virtually proposing, and Nan saying no, and her happiness sliding into bitterness.

This was the first time I had really noticed that. It had been a year of noticing things, of being noticed.

Nan and Jim argued, and there may have been a few harder words said than usual. He still came around one last time for dinner, and at the end of it, he gave me a present.

I unwrapped it. It was a small wooden box, and inside, a watch.

"Made in the Red City," he said. "My father gave me one when I was your age, and his father before him."

He lifted his arm so I could see his watch. It was battered and scratched, but it still worked.

"If yours breaks, I can take it north, and get it fixed for you, but if you keep it out of water, and don't smash it against a wall, it should last you a lifetime. That's Masters' work."

Nan sniffed at it. "Damn machines, with their ticking and tocking, and all those little gears turning. Always on at you with their demands."

"What nonsense!" Mum said. "I think it's a fine thing."

I did, too. I put it around my wrist, and hugged Jim. "It'll keep you safe," he said. "Not from those haunts your nan faces, but it'll turn smaller things away, and perhaps some big things, too. All my crew has them. I wouldn't travel this far south without it. Those ticks and tocks will drive some creatures mad to get away from you, and not just your nan."

Nan sniffed again.

I took off the watch, and looked at the inscription on the back of it. Three circles interwound, with Jim's name written in the middle.

"Should you ever need me, if your nan and your mother are in trouble, call my name. I will feel it through this watch. Well, that's what they say, and I have known stranger things than that on the road. It won't be fast, but I will come. Even if it takes me a month, I won't ignore the call."

I strapped it to my wrist. "I'll call, if it comes to that," I said.

"You better," he said.

Nan humphed. "Sun help us all, if it ever comes to that!"

I looked up to see a gaze pass between her and Jim that I did not understand, but knew I would not like if I did.

The next day, after Nan had taken me around the levee, and I'd finished my other chores—of which school was one—she sent me to Jim, who had a job for me.

The fair was packing up. Most of Jim's stalls were already packed away on wagons, the horses being fed and watered. When I arrived, Jim was pleased to see I was wearing my watch. "You like it?"

I nodded. "Yes," I said. "Nan doesn't, though."

"Good that you're not your nan. She doesn't hate me too much, though, not if she's sent you here. I'm off tomorrow, but today I'd like you to take me to the Huskling King. If that's okay with you."

Of course it was.

We crossed over the levee, me chattering away, telling Jim of my adventures (at least the ones I could tell), and he told me a bit about his travels, and how he had his own tricks for dealing with the creatures that stalked the south. There was a coin nailed in the rear of each wagon, a bit of blood painted on their corners, and curved symbols carved into the horse's hooves. There was a Walker like Nan who stayed with the caravan, only his circuit was looser, different every day.

"Your nan might have told you this, but Walkers don't just fight. Mostly, they try not to. Some of them, maybe the best, make their charges hard for monsters and the like to detect. It's better to avoid conflict when you can. Violence is a poison, and one that ruins everyone."

As we walked, Jim picked what warpweed he could find, and other supplies as well. He had a shoulder bag, and he'd slip things in it, not just weed or leaf. He found a lump of fox fur— nipped out by a hungry mate, he said—and he was very happy with that.

As we neared the hall, not far from the statues, he slowed.

"The Huskling King knows more than most," he said to me. "You'll learn plenty from him, but he isn't always to be trusted. Not like your nan."

"I know," I said, feeling a trifle affronted that he should think me so credulous, and a bit confused because, in most cases, I really did trust the king.

We reached the Huskling hall late in the afternoon.

"Jean," the king asked, "why are you here with old Jim?"

"Jim asked me to bring him here."

The king looked at Jim. "Do you expect my answer to be any different with the child here?"

Jim shook his head. "I just wanted her company. To see what you've been teaching her."

"Nothing too dangerous. Nothing too safe. That's all you need to know. She's still young."

"Good," Jim said. "You have always been a wonderful teacher."

I looked at them both, then, never thinking that Jim might have been taught here, too. I was shocked and delighted.

"I'm without peer, beloved of my students, eloquent in my wisdoms," The Huskling King said, puffing up his chest. "Were I not banished so far from the north, this hall would be crowded with pupils, all getting their education in the mysteries and histories. But I have her, and she's in possession of a supple mind."

I did my best to keep the pleasure at that flattery from my face.

"I'm not surprised. She's Nancy's grandchild."

"Yes," the king said. "And better late than never."

Jim looked around the hall. The Husklings were watching him. Some were wrestling, and some had flung themselves up into the nearby trees, but most stared at him. I couldn't tell if they made him uncomfortable.

He reached into his bag, and pulled out a small stone.

"What's that?"

"Something I thought might interest you. It's an ancient carving."

The Huskling King leant in close. "It is familiar to me, now that I look at it."

"It's a chess piece," Jim said.

"Yes, it is a king."

"A king like you."

"Don't try and flatter me," the king said.

"I could give it to you."

"That would be a fine gift, but such a gift isn't really a gift."

"I'm a trader," Jim conceded.

"Not only a trader, are you, Jim?"

"Show me a man who says he's just one thing, and I'll show you a liar," Jim said.

"What if I took it from you?"

"That's not how this works."

"Tell me, how did you find it?"

The Husklings had drawn in close.

"There was an old Master in the Red City who collected such gewgaws."

The king snorted at that.

"An old Master who was dying."

"Masters don't die like that."

"This one was very old. Sometimes they die from weariness, you know that. He wanted passage to the east, and the Soft Sea, and he wanted his Day Boy taken care of. I gave him both of those things. It's a long journey. I let him drink from me only; I couldn't ask that of my crew. That made it a longer road for me, but he was a good companion. At night, we would talk—he wasn't always hungry.

"Once something came amongst us in the shape of a man, despite the workings of my Walker. It tried to take what it thought was one of my crew, but what it found was a monster far worse than it was. I doubt I will ever forget its screams, when it at last succumbed. I gave more blood than usual that evening, enough that I was faint for days, but some bargains must be kept.

"By the time we reached the Soft Sea, I was weak and weary, but I had grown to like the old Master, and the journey had reduced his weariness somewhat—it can go either way, on the road.

"Still, he walked to the seashore, and waited for the sun. When it rose, I was with him. I held his hand." Jim raised his right hand up. "See that burn mark? That was from his last moments. I held him, till I couldn't anymore. No one likes to die alone, not even Masters.

"And that's how I got this carving. He gave it to me, there on that final shore. Said he had found it, when he was still a man, and that he had kept it for all the long years that he wasn't. He gave it to me near his death, and in that giving, it was a powerful thing. A kingly thing. And I offer it to you as trade."

The Huskling King nodded. "At last, you do me the honour of a trade I can endure." He shuffled behind his throne, pulled free a little statue, and held it out to Jim.

Jim reached for it, his grin fixed, but he didn't take it. "There must be some mistake. This is the wrong one," he said.

The Huskling King laughed. "So it is."

He found another statue, and gave it to Jim. Jim nodded, and passed the chess piece to the king.

"We will be going now," Jim said, putting his trade into his bag.

The king nodded. "Yes, it is best that you do. We are feasting tonight; it might offend you."

There was a box, twice as tall as me, to the left of the throne. It shook.

Jim's face turned a little grey. "Yes. We should." He squeezed my hand. "Hurry, Jean. I'd better take you back to your nan."

The king gave the chess piece a kiss. "Goodbye, Jean," he said.

I bowed, a shallow, swift bow, and we got out of there.

"Don't look back," Jim said.

When we were near the levee, I stopped. "What did the king trade you?" I asked.

Jim took the tiny statue from his bag. "Something very important, indeed," he said. "A piece of me."

It was a perfect little sculpture of Jim—much younger than he was now, but I recognised him.

I went to touch it, and he pulled it away. "This isn't leaving me ever again. You aren't his first student, but I guess you know that. He took this from me a long time ago, back when I thought such an agreement would give me more power. It didn't, not really, or it was the sort of power you discover you don't need. I lost something; but now here it is, returned. Be careful what you offer, Jean; what trades you make. The wrong gift given or received can take nearly a lifetime to correct."

I thought about that coin, but I didn't say anything. I couldn't.

The next day, they were gone. It was like they had never been there at all, except for a few patches of yellowed grass, and tracks in the mud. Casement Rise felt like half a town for a few days. There were broken hearts, the pub was less raucous, the streets so much quieter. But it did what all towns do: got on. The gardens needed watering, bread needed baking, cattle taken to slaughter, and so on.

Nan was angry at first, particularly when she saw that watch on my wrist—though she never asked that I take it off—and then sad. But my education continued. What else was there to my life?

Nan was trying to fit what should have been years of learning into a few months. She'd teach me, speak to the dead, and, afterwards, get back to knotting that cord. Used to be that Nan would read at night, but she didn't anymore. She knotted, one twist after the other.

I didn't understand the urgency.

Until the graceful man came back.

It was a weekend, so we did our circuit of the levee at a more leisurely pace. Then Aunty Liz had caught us on the way back, wanted Nan to speak with her long-dead husband.

Nan gave me a long look. "There's things you don't need to hear," she said to me. I didn't know the twists of some of my family then, so I didn't put up much resistance. I wasn't that interested in talking to anyone in the earth, except my little dead boy.

I walked home.

There was no dog to greet me, which was rare, but Elic sometimes liked to sleep under the house on warm days. I ducked my head under the verandah. There was a dark shape there, but it only shifted a little when I called it, and I wasn't going to crawl under there unless I had to: the floor was too close to the ground, and the spiderwebs were too thick.

I stood up. It was quiet. Mum would normally be working in her shed by now, but I couldn't see her over there.

I went inside, treading softly as I could. There was a soft weeping; a whispering coming from the kitchen.

That had me wondering, and cautious. I pulled out my knife, my hand shaking. I took a moment to quiet it.

I crept towards the kitchen. I was dead silent, but a few steps from the door, a new loose board found my foot, and creaked. The graceful man swung his head towards me. He was stroking my mum's hair. His eyes narrowed for a moment, then he grinned his toothy grin. The cape of leaves he wore rustled like the grove by the Winter Gate after the first frost. He was the colour of autumn. The kitchen felt cold with his presence.

"Oh, there you are," he said. "I've been talking to your mother, telling her about your lovely father. He's having such a wonderful time in Furnace, hardly thinks of her at all.

107

Everyone's busy and happy there; we have no troubles but one, and I'm growing more certain I must end it."

"Leave my mother alone," I said.

"Why are you so angry? After all, you called me here."

"Leave." I lifted the knife.

He left Mum by the sink, and came over to me. He gripped a blade, against which mine suffered mightily in comparison. It was long and sharp, curved like a tooth, blood dripping from its edge.

His golden eyes twinkled. "Now, this is a proper cutter. In Furnace, we don't need them: meat falls off the bone, the bread slices itself. But here, everything is cut, cut, cut, and one must be furnished with an edge. Your big dog didn't like me," he said, "so I had to teach him a lesson. How are *your* lessons going?"

"Go," Mum said thickly.

The graceful man turned, danced a step towards her, and pinched her lips closed. "Oh, you can't tell me to go. I'm not yours."

"Why are you here?" I asked.

"I wanted to see how you were enjoying your gift."

That coin. That stupid coin! Maybe that's what had called him.

"I don't want it anymore," I said.

"Once you take such a thing, you cannot untake it."

We'd see about that.

I raised the silver knife up.

"Shall we clash blades, then? Hee hee. It won't end as well as your stories do." He came a little closer, raised his knife, then stopped, and looked at my wrist. A tiny shiver of pain slipped across his face.

"Oh, whatever is that?" He crouched down, sniffed, jerked back. "What ever, ever is that ticking? I smell Masters."

"It tells the time." I said it forcefully, like it was a spell, and a cruel one.

The graceful man shook his head. "Time's not for telling. You can't bind time so. That is an abomination!"

"Look at it," I said. He did, and his face grew sour and pale. "Take it away!"

"A second, and another second, and another, and—"

"Take it away!"

"It's eleven fifteen," I said.

"My head aches!"

"All those wheels grinding, catching time and grinding. Look, look," I said.

"Take it away!" He brought a hand to his head, his thin lips quivering. "Why would you do this?"

"Tick."

I brought the watch close to the neat little curl of his ear. He tried to snap at me with his teeth, but he stopped short, grabbing at his head.

"Oh, sweet agony!" He rushed to the far end of the kitchen, and grimaced at me. I wanted to stay where I was, but I followed. I had to press this advantage, keep on pushing. It felt not only right, but necessary. His face displayed all sorts of pain, and he raised one hand weakly. "This is merely a reprieve. I will inoculate myself against all clocks. I will heal the little cuts of those little hands. You'll see." He turned to my mum. "At least we had a chat. I liked our chat."

"Go," my mum said, but I couldn't tell if she was talking to him or me. I kept up my walk towards him, even if it filled me with terror. My heart stuttered. My legs were weak.

"Back," the graceful man yelped, a final burst of exasperation. Then he bubbled and shrank and fell into himself, until there was nothing there but a pile of leaves and a knife rattling on the floor.

Mum and I held each other tight for a bit.

"Are you all right?" we both asked, and then, "Yes."

But neither of us were.

"You were lucky," Mum said. It sounded colder than I think she meant it to.

"Did I hold my knife right?"

Mum softened her face a bit. "A little better," she said. "Maybe Jacob's lessons are having an influence."

I walked over to the pile of leaves, kicked them apart, poked at them with the silver knife. Nothing, just leaves. Then I remembered Elic. I ran down under the house, and got him out of there.

He was sore, whining, and bloody, but he would recover. The graceful man had cut him clumsily; hurt him until he had run under the house. Mum said he'd done his best to protect her until then.

Once Elic was wrapped up and comforted, I got under my bed, found that gold coin, took it to the edge of town, and threw it over the levee.

When I got back home, the coin was resting on my pillow. I didn't want it, but part of me—a tiny part I could hardly admit was me—was relieved.

I put a toe down upon the earth.

"Jean," came that familiar voice. "Is that you?"

"Yes," I said.

Nan and Mum were talking in the kitchen. Nan had checked me over carefully, but whatever she had been looking for, she couldn't find.

"What do I do with this coin?" I asked my dead boy.

"The one the graceful man gave you?"

"It's the only coin I have, except that Roman one with the old queen's head on it."

"That's not a Roman coin," the boy said.

"Doesn't matter. I can't get rid of it."

I'd considered asking Nan, but every time I thought to ask, I'd forget immediately, and I forgot nothing. It was a vexing thing, and I wondered if it was part of the magic of the coin. I'd have thought Mum would have asked me about the graceful man's gift, but she hadn't, either. There was something odd about it, all right.

"He gave it to you, and you took it. They say gifts like that are permanent."

"But I don't want it."

"Jean, you wanted it when it wasn't trouble. You must keep it when it is."

"You're not much help."

"I'm in the ground," the dead boy said. "I'm cold and cannot see. How much help can I be?"

"I'm sorry," I said. "I didn't mean it."

I picked up a story, and started reading it. The coin I couldn't do much about, but loneliness was another thing.

I didn't see much of Nan until the next morning. Mum and Nan had talked, but they must have seen my shadow when I tried to listen in because Nan stalked out, and sent me to bed.

I was a bit sore about that the next morning, until Nan poured me a coffee. There was plenty of it after Jim's visit—we wouldn't start doling it out for another month—and a few hard ginger cookies that Jim had brought down (a whole tin of them that had lasted nearly a week, but was running low now).

We drank and ate in silence, then out into the dark we went.

"I can't be with you every moment," Nan said. "I've tried to protect you, but my vigilance has its limits. It vexes me that he can cross our boundaries so easily. I don't understand it. Did he tell you anything?"

"No. He was scared of my watch, though. Said he'd inoculate himself against it."

"Inoculate, eh?" Nan stopped for a moment, and leant on her walking stick. "I think he'll find that harder than he expects."

"Why did my watch scare him?"

"That fella is a creature of time. It moves differently for him. There's nothing else that binds you to him, is there?"

"Not that I know of," I said, thinking of my gold coin, but unable to speak of it. I told myself it was just me putting off telling her, and that nothing else was involved in my silence. Not that I believed that.

"Good," Nan said. "Good."

And then we went to greet the sun.

Afterwards, Jacob ran me through his training drills, hitting things, or failing to.

Swinging that knife and tripping over myself.

"You're trying too hard!"

"But I want to get as good as Mum," I said.

Jacob shook his head. "You'll never be like that," he said, almost to himself. He frowned. "Jean, you don't fight to win. You fight to protect. You're striking out, but sometimes the best way is to give in, to fall back, to let your opponent make the mistake. Sometimes the best defence is to run away."

"I can run pretty fast," I said.

He laughed. "That you can."

When we were done, I asked Jacob if he ever got lonely.

"Yes," he said. "All the time. Used to be that I lived for company, and I had the best of it. Used to be."

"What happened?"

"She died. You'd have liked her, my Agatha. She was pregnant, and there were . . . troubles. I thought she'd have a girl, she said it was a boy. I never had the heart to ask your nan which of us was right. What would be the point of it? It was before you were born," he said. "And, since then, it's been better to be alone." He wiped at his face. "You're going to be late for school."

When I got to school, Alice was there, talking to her friends. I watched them, close, but at a distance, and wondered how it all worked. Why wouldn't they talk to me? Alice saw me, and waved me away furiously. The other children laughed. I left them to it, my face burning.

That afternoon, Alice found me out in the school yard.

I grinned at her, but she wasn't smiling. "I'm going to hit you. Spying on me like that . . . time you had a lesson," Alice said, her hands clenched tight. She took a few steps towards me, then a few back. All I could think of were the dancing bantams in our pen, uselessly and furiously brave, even in the face of a fox or a snake, though they'd start screaming soon enough.

I laughed at her, spat at the dry ground. "You don't normally announce such a thing. You ever fought anyone?"

Alice shook her head. "No, but I'm gonna hit you."

"You know if you hit me, I'll hit back? I get fighting lessons from Jacob."

Alice considered this. "Why are we fighting, anyway?" Asking even though she had started it.

"Because you're an idiot," I said.

Alice laughed. "No, because I don't like the feel of you. There's a nastiness there. No one likes you, you or your drunk mum. Not just me."

My eyes watered like I'd been struck. I thought I'd been fitting in.

"You want nasty, you should listen to what *I* have to listen to. The dead don't hold their tongues." To be honest, I didn't know—I still wore my boots. But I'd heard enough from Nan.

"They don't have to. If I was dead, I'd be the same, having to talk to you."

"Just hit me then. And we'll see wh—"

Alice hit me, with a force I'd not reckoned with. I fell on the earth, and felt the quick touches of the dead and their shrill voices.

Kill her, girl.

Kill her.

She does not honour you.

I lay there a moment, and their whispers crowded me. I touched my lip, saw blood upon my fingers.

Kill her.

The dead's blind rage washed over me, pushed at me, pulled me, and I let it.

I do not remember getting up, but I remember Alice's look of horror. Alice wasn't scared of me, but of what she'd done.

I took a swing at her, missed, and she hit me to the ground. I got up, and took another swing.

"Stop it," Alice said. "You'll hurt yourself."

I swung again, and she knocked me down. This time I leapt up at her, scratching and howling like an animal.

After that, I don't remember much at all. Maybe Mrs. Paige pulling me off Alice, and me swinging at my teacher, and that swing connecting. But I was addled, my ears ringing, my knuckles stinging.

Nan came and took me home. The dead had called to her; they were such tattletales. She was so angry, it frightened me. I couldn't tell if it was at the school, at Alice, or at me—I suspected it was all of us, but I was the only one close enough to take her fury. I told her of the rage of the dead. She'd frowned at that, and bent down, and studied my face.

"I'm still in here," I said, though my voice sounded so tiny.

Her arms enclosed me. "I know," she said, after a while, "but we're going to have to do something about those voices. You should not find them persuasive."

"They're just the dead," I said, my voice strengthening again.

"Exactly," Nan said. "But there are other forces that you will contend with. Greater things than the dead. It's the living powers that will challenge and beguile you, and to which you can't succumb."

"Monsters?"

Nan shook her head. "No, the strength within you. For it can be bent against you. That's where every battle ends. That's the one you will fight all your life."

"I lost today," I said.

Nan rested her face on mine.

"Yes," she said. "Yes, you did. But you'll have to prove to me you know what losing truly means."

I touched my foot to the earth.

"Miss Jean?"

"It's me," I said.

"I heard about your fight."

"It was a thrashing, and I didn't win."

"Not everyone is good at fighting," my dead boy said.

"But I have to be."

"Do you? Maybe you're better at other things. Maybe you don't need your fists. I don't know much, but the world isn't a battle . . . not unless you're a pirate."

I took the hint, and found his favourite story.

When I was weary of reading, I cleared my throat. "Am I terrible?" I asked.

He laughed. "Never, Miss Jean. Never! You're always reading me stories. You're the very opposite! That Alice, she sounds awful."

I sniffed.

She was awful.

That night I lay in bed holding the gold coin. I squeezed it tight, my jaw clenched so I wouldn't start crying. I wanted Alice gone. I wanted her out of my town. She had made me so mad.

But then, I thought, why not make her really suffer?

I wished, and I wished, and the coin glowed hot in my hands.

The next afternoon, after a day in bed reading, hardly thinking about what had happened, Nan told me that Alice's mother had walked to Furnace. Mrs. Paige, too. I hoped she'd found her husband and her sons. It wasn't common for women to walk west, and two in a day was unheard of.

"Don't blame yourself," Nan said. I must have looked so horrified. "It isn't your fault."

But I knew otherwise.

There were plenty of good folk in town, and Rachael the baker chose to adopt Alice and her siblings. It didn't change that she had lost her mum, though, and I knew I was to blame, no matter what Nan said.

Word got around, too. That all this had happened after that fight with Alice.

Myles came over. He had hardly knocked at the door before Nan was up and jabbing a finger in his chest.

"Not here. Don't you come to me here."

Nan took him outside, out of my hearing, and they shouted at each other. I knew it was about me, but Nan never talked to me about it.

The school was closed for a few weeks, and by the time they had a new teacher, Nan had decided I had had enough of that sort of education.

What had happened disturbed her more than I'd thought. One late morning, not an hour after our circuit of the levee, she called me to the verandah.

"I need you to walk in my shoes," Nan said, "and for that you need to walk without them. Time you got used to the incessant chatter of those below. Take off your boots."

Bird sat on the deck railing, hopping from foot to foot. I took off one boot, and Bird shat onto the earth. One thing birds do even more than eat is shit. Bird was no exception, despite their cleverness.

"Why are there so many dead, anyway?" I asked.

"There's always been dead in the ground, and our town may have more than most. But after Furnace came, something happened. They lost their way. Where once there had been a beacon to the Stone Road, that light became a blinding thing. They can't see past it to the road, so most of them end up here instead."

"Where should they be?"

Nan tapped her stick impatiently. "That isn't the lesson. You'll find that out soon enough. But the dead aren't there, they're here. And you're here, too."

I took off the other boot, stripped the sock from my foot.

"Would you like me to hold your hand?"

"No," I said, and I dropped lightly to the earth.

I had my dead boy, had chatted to him from my toe touch with the earth, but this was different.

This time they were ready.

All words and hands, they grabbed at me, for the dead can grab those naked and sensitive to them. I was a rope to clamber up, a delicacy to nibble, an ear to listen. They spoke and snatched and bit all at once.

Jean! they howled.

Jean! they cawed and heckled.

"Jean," Nan said. "Keep going."

I took an unsteady step, then another. It was like walking on a current of stones, loose and grabbing, uncertain.

I looked at my feet. The earth was broken, faces pressed against it, hard, bony fingers reaching through it. Eyes stared at me, and they were enraged and hopeful and scared.

Listen.

Listen.

"Listen, girl," Nan said. "You have to focus, let it slide off you. You'll face this every day. I don't wear boots, and nor will you. You can't, when this work is yours."

"It hurts," I said.

Hurt? What do you know of hurt? We are dead. We are dead, and no one listens.

"I listen," said Nan, affronted.

Do you?

Nan huffed. "Keep walking, girl. To the levee and back."

Will you be good and listen, Jean?

My knees near buckled, my head pounded, and my feet were raw with scratches, but I kept walking.

We went through the town, and the dead grew in number, their voices swelled until they were a chorus. There was a woman that just laughed, a sobbing, mad laughter. There was a man that chattered, but made no sense. These ones felt as though they had lost hold of themselves, yet they came through so strongly.

Above all were the serial moaners: circular talkers that groaned over and over again, like branches scraping a house in the wind.

"Last of my line. My children have wandered to Furnace. They are lost to me. Forgotten and dead. No one remembers my face—they are all gone from here—but *you* can see it."

A mouth snapped against my instep. I moaned and stumbled, then turned my fall into forward movement.

"Keep walking," Nan said. She reached out, and I clutched her hand. "I'm here. Their talk is poisonous, insidious. It will seep into you, and fill you with despair if you let it. The dead are liars and gossips, but you must walk through it. Listen, listen to them, but do not believe them."

Their cries, their mouths and fingers grabbing at me, were so loud. We walked through the town, and the town was quiet, people going about their lives as though none of this was happening. Of course, it wasn't happening for them, but I couldn't believe they had no inkling of it, that they could be so unfeeling. And yet they were.

I fell to my knees. There was a great and terrible cry of joy and disappointment—the dead wanted both, both my strength and my weakness. How else could I do what they desired, be their advocate, help them find a way home, if I wasn't strong? How else could I bend to their will if I wasn't weak? They hungered and hated, blind in the earth, but for me and Nan.

"Up, girl," Nan said.

They pinched and grabbed at my flesh, at my wrists, at my legs. I lifted my head. Bird sat on a fence post in front of the butcher's. They slanted their head and blinked at me. I raised my hand towards them, and they leant forward, as if to fly to me. I shook my head; I knew Nan would not like that.

"Up, girl," Nan said.

I tore my hands free of the dead's grip. Pushed up, rising to unsteady feet. I took a step, and another, and another.

There is no other way to walk.

I reached the levee at last, and climbed it. They surged around me, hands grabbing for my ankles, pulling, and dragging. I kicked at them.

"Good work, girl. They can trip you up, they can drag you down, but they can never pull you into the earth," Nan said. "You are alive, and they are not. They do not have that power. Once you know that, once you understand that in your flesh and in your bones, their noise will recede, and their touch will weaken. Now, back." She pointed towards our house.

My feet hurt and my spine, for I had bent it low as I walked, as though the dead's efforts had come from above, pushing me down.

"Hurry," Nan said. "We don't have all day."

I walked back through that grasping chorus. When I made it to the deck, and sat down, I was sweating and shaking, and my feet were torn. Nan passed me a cup of water, and then another.

"Every day you will do that. It gets easier, but it is never easy. Nor should it be, no matter how effortless you make it appear."

Nan's feet were bare and dark and hard as horn—hard as the rest of her.

"Is it still like that for you?"

"Always."

I looked at the levee in the distance. "Why do we live so far from the levee?"

"Because it is safer for us to be deep in the town, as much as we are apart from it. Because every day that I walk to the levee, it helps me remember why I go. We are not alone; we are of the town. Anything selfish in me falls away as I wait for the sun, because I understand that what I protect is precious. There's only one other thing that makes me feel this way."

I curled my lip at her. "What's that?"

She touched my face. "You, my darling child."

For the first time, I saw the tears in her eyes. I'd not been the only one weeping. Effortless was only an appearance. Effort was all we had.

Nan walked back with a bucket and cloth. She gently washed the blood from my feet.

She did that every day until my feet were near as tough as hers, and it was no longer needed.

It got easier, that clawing, chattering, walk across the town, but it was never easy.

It was around then that the clocks started disappearing. First one, then another, until the town could talk of nothing else. Time was not cheap this far from the Red City. Some people blamed birds; some blamed my Bird. No one except Nan, Mum, and I knew the truth, and we weren't saying.

One afternoon, a few days after Nan had started to teach me how to walk with the dead, Lolly's older brother, Mitcham, came to see me. "Jean, I have need of you." It was the first time that anyone had ever uttered that phrase to me. Oh, but it wouldn't be the last.

I raised an eyebrow. "What do you have need of, exactly?"

I didn't like Mitcham; I didn't like how he treated Lolly. Too many of those bruises on my friend's face were a consequence of his fists.

Mitcham looked at his feet. "Lolly. He's different."

"How?"

"Better if I show you."

I felt all kinds of dread as we walked over the levee. Mitcham wasn't forthcoming, but I had my suspicions. I'd not seen Lolly since we'd gotten that warpweed for Nan. Why, I'd hardly thought of him, things had been so busy.

I came to his house, and his brothers were crying, all of them.

"What's happening here?" I asked.

"It's Lolly," said the oldest. "He's gone mad. Just this very day, after Mum's left for the Northturn Markets. He beat each of us, as though he weren't the weakest. He said he'd grown intolerant of our cruelties. And that wasn't the worst of it." He wiped at his weepy face.

"Out with it, boy," I said.

"When he did it, he laughed. Ah, that sound would put ice in your guts. I have never heard such a thing. And the words he'd whisper: cruel words, dreadful ones."

I thought of all the terrors these boys had put Lolly through. "Maybe he's sick of you, and rightly so."

The eldest shook his head. "I swear, it wasn't Lolly. But who else could it be? He's changed. You've given him a madness."

"I did no such thing," I said, but there was a chill in my belly, and I knew that I had. Bird would be so smug.

Poor Lolly! What should have been a liberation for him was a prison. He wasn't really there to enjoy it.

Lolly sat in his room, holding a knife. He was cutting his thigh with it.

"Lolly Robson, put that down."

His head snapped up. "Lolly would, I'm quite sure, but he's a long dark way from this hand."

"Quit your madness!"

The shadow said nothing, just looked back at Lolly's thigh.

"Where is he?"

Its grin was an awful thing to see, cruel and menacing. It lifted the bloody knife. "Bits of him are here, Miss Jean."

"Put that down," I said, all the while wondering how to unpick such a shadow thing.

"Oh, you shouldn't fear a knife. You're well acquainted with them—ask your mother." What would she know? I didn't fear the knife, I feared what it might do to Lolly.

"Put it down."

"It has a sharp edge. I'll admit. Shame not to put it to proper use."

I should have brought my nan. I never should have left Lolly like that. But I was here now. I had to fix this.

"You'll do no such thing," I said.

"How are you going to stop me?" Its limbs lengthened, filled with shadow, and it rose like smoke, tendons cracking. "I'm boiling with spiders."

I wanted to run. I wanted to be anywhere but here. I didn't, though, I couldn't; I was all Lolly had. "You're just a boy," I said.

It grimaced. "No, I'm not. I have messages for you. Furnace will grind this town away. Your grandmother's road is the wrong one. She is being played a fool. All she does is fret that you will be hurt, and in the fretting, in the failure, she hurts you more than anyone."

I didn't like those words, but I knew distraction when I heard it. I squinted at it. "You don't know anything." Something moved within me, some force that was older than I was, an ancient thing. Old as Tree, maybe older. I felt it push against me.

I took a step forward. Well, whatever was in me did, and I was carried with it. The shadow held its ground, teeth flashing in a smile that Lolly never would have made. I slapped the knife from its hand—would have punched out that smile, too, except I suspected it'd be Lolly with the bruise.

That ancient thing within me approved, grew sharp against my mind. "Get out of him."

"That's no fun," the shadow said. "I like it here."

"This boy isn't yours."

"Whose is he, then?"

For a moment, I hovered there, its face close to mine. I could smell the shadow on its breath, the rotted-meat odour of it.

"Mine," I said, and I touched Lolly's chest.

The shadow shrieked. The force within me bent to my will, like when you ride a horse, and it seems to be calling the shots at first, and then *you* are, and then both of you become one. I felt it dance a little. It could find joy even in such terrors, and I realised that I could, too. It moved within me like smoke, or a shadow, a counterpart to that which moved within Lolly.

I reached those shadow limbs into Lolly's chest, and curled my fist around the dark within him, and then I pulled.

The shadow came out, though it wasn't dark when it took its true form, but pale as a maggot. It closed itself around my fist, biting and stinging. I ran, trying not to howl with the pain of it all, past the wide-eyed Robsons.

"Your hand," the boys shouted.

"I know! I know!"

By the Sun, it hurt! Oh, this had been *inside* Lolly!

"Your hand!" Mitcham said, following me a ways. "What's that horror?"

"Worry about your brother, not me!"

I hurtled from the house and into the yard. There beneath the sun, bits of the creature sloughed off, tumbling to the earth and boiling away.

"Find me a spot," it said. "Find me a spot in the dark and the cold."

"And you promise to leave mine alone?"

"On my word. All I am is my word. Hurry, I'm boiling away. Please. That boy was a torment. Trapped, I was, in his soul; pushed at, by everything. I didn't like it, not really. It weakened me."

"And all your threats and torments, all your bully talk?"

"Nothing more than that. I'd never have used that knife. I was just showing off," it squeaked. "Mistress. Sweet Jean! Please. Please! Hurry, I'm tumbling to a bitter diminishment!"

I wasn't cruel enough to kill it. Instead, I took it as far from the levee and the Robsons as I dared go, then let it slip from my fingers. It rushed like a snake into the dark of a tree's roots.

"Do not forget my kindness," I said. It blinked its little yellow eyes at me, and was gone.

I stood for a moment, watching the shadows to see if I could unpick it from them, but there was only darkness.

I didn't go back to the boys, or to Lolly. I was too ashamed. I'd left that thing inside him. I'd let it take him, through ignorance, and incompetence. I'd failed him terribly.

I'd not realised that what I was could be so painful.

I was coming home from the Robsons', still trying to understand what had happened to Lolly, when someone cried my name. One of Alice's brothers, Travis. He ran at me, and for a moment I thought he knew what I did to his mother, what I had wished for her, and let happen. I didn't want a fight, no matter how much I deserved one.

I stood there, slack and still, but Travis didn't notice anything amiss. Some people don't see much at all.

"Jean," he said, his face all red with tears. "Jean, Alice is in trouble."

"Why would she want my help?"

"She needs you, Jean."

I wasn't going to say no, after what I had done, and considering the desperation in Travis' face.

"Where is she?"

He grabbed my hand like little children do, and led me to the playground, then across it. I knew where we were going: to the part of town every child was forbidden to visit.

White Tree rose up—not as high as the gum that hosted Bird and their kindred, but a tall tree nonetheless. And there was Alice, near the top, clinging to a branch.

"Jean," Alice shouted.

"Why don't you climb down?"

"I want to, but I can't. Something's keeping me up here."

I looked around for Bird. When I couldn't see them, I whistled: three sharp peeps, like you might in a storybook to summon something useful.

"Why are you taking so long?"

"I'm waiting for some advice. Doesn't look like it's coming. What's keeping you up there?"

"The tree says she wants me dead."

"All she is, is a grumpy tree. Ignore her."

"Says she's going to let me go, and I'll crash to the ground. And I'll lay there, all broken, and she'll drink my blood."

Still no Bird.

"Okay," I said. "I'm going to climb up and get you."

"Hurry," Alice said.

I gave White Tree a speculative glance. I'd never thought about climbing her.

White Tree gave off a harsh anger that I feared. The dead seethed beneath her, and I don't know if they fed off her, or if she fed off them, but there was a brewing badness. I took off my boots so I could get a better grip on the tree.

The dead scratched at my feet. There were so many of them—children, mostly. Why were there children here?

Let her die. Let her die, they crooned.

I touched the trunk, and felt her anger at once. Soon my hands were covered with biting ants. Where the old Tree had clever birds, White Tree had angry insects. Wasps tangled in my hair. I did my best to ignore them, but they were everywhere, and in their presence, I felt the age of White Tree, the sheer harshness of her existence. She'd stayed alive through years of rage, and she'd done what she must to survive. I felt her arc from seed to seething fury, and the ages in between, when trees had been cut, when her children had died. Maybe for the first time, I felt sorry for her.

But those wasps didn't stop stinging. I climbed through pain so fierce it made me cry, but I didn't stop. It was easier to keep moving; that way I didn't have to think about what came next.

It took me a while to reach Alice, but when I did, she grabbed me tight.

"Loosen your grip," I said. "Or we'll fall to our deaths."

She did, but not by much.

I noticed that the wasps and ants ignored her, and then I noticed nothing, keeping my focus on getting down. When we reached the bottom, Alice looked at me, kissed me once on the cheek, and ran away. I was wounded and sore. One of my eyes was swollen shut. Travis hesitated. I could see how bad I looked written on his face.

"Go," I growled. "Go!"

Travis ran off after Alice, and I stood beneath the tree, with all those dead snapping sharply at my heels.

"Foolish child!" Nan said to me when I got home, feeling weary, guilty, and sorry for myself. She was tying more knots in the cord. "You should have made her climb down. Look at you! Who climbs White Tree, anyway? What madness!"

I couldn't argue with that, but I was glad that Alice was safe. I had never seen anyone look so frightened.

"You look exhausted," Nan said. "Which is a pity. You best have a bath, then come talk to me."

Afterwards, I told Nan all that had happened with Lolly, how it was my fault, and what I did to salvage it. I won't say that Nan was happy, but she listened to me tell my story. While her face grew greyer as the details unfolded, her ears pricked up when I mentioned that old voice that had risen inside me, and those ancient shadow limbs that had become mine.

"How did it feel?" Nan asked.

"It felt . . ." I paused. "It felt powerful."

Nan made a face. She pulled a knot tight on the cord, then put it down. "I wish you'd come straight to me, let me deal with Lolly. You're changing, my grandchild, and you're getting strong enough to face what will come. But you must let me help. I may get angry, but I respect honesty. Everyone makes mistakes, but a secret only compounds an error. You've been lucky. You faced a darkness, and drove it from the boy, but that darkness could have just as easily leapt into you, and that would be a powerful residence. It didn't today, but that doesn't mean the next thing won't, and there'll always be a next thing.

"You seem to have fixed the problem, but I'll visit the boy tomorrow, and make sure your assessment is correct. That there isn't a . . . residue. I suppose that's the word for it. Something left over."

"I'm sorry," I said, and I wondered what it was I was changing into. Nan and Mum had both gone through this. Whom would I turn out like?

"At least you came to me, even if it was too late. That's something else you'll learn with time. There's always another trial, and that's a reassuring thing, though a terrifying one, as well."

"Nan, Lolly's shadow said your road is the wrong one. What road? How's it wrong?"

Nan shook her head. "Don't listen to such things. Whatever wisdoms they possess are warped and broken. They hold truth up to them like a flickering candle, and make shadows from it."

A few nights later, I woke to the sound of thunder, only it wasn't thunder. I got out of bed, and walked out onto the verandah. Nan was standing out there, smoking.

"What's happening?" I asked.

She shrugged. "I'm not sure. Something's crossed over the levee. I felt it for a second, and now it's gone."

"Do we hunt it?"

"Not in the dark. Not if we don't want to be hunted ourselves. Besides, it wasn't predatory. All I could sense was fear. Try and get some sleep."

The next morning, we found a trail leading over the wall, just west of the Summer Gate. It was made of deep, dark, boot prints, far enough apart that you could tell that whoever had made them had been running.

We followed the trail straight across town, and it stopped at the Winter Gate.

Nan put her hand against the lock, and closed her eyes. "They used the gate last night."

"What does that mean?"

She stared at the last of the footprints. These were even heavier at the toe. "Nothing good. Whatever's chasing them will be here soon. You don't run that fast if you have a good lead.

That afternoon, auditors paid a visit to our town. They did what all travellers on business did in those days, be they Threnodists, traders, or auditors: They went directly to Nan, whether she wanted them to or not.

These two had all the glamour of the law, their guns gleaming on their belts, their hands tattooed with the symbol of the Masters: a circle with seven lines radiating from it. It wasn't until you looked at them directly that you saw it was little more than that: glamour. Their work had put a bend in their spines, and their eyes were hollowed by the miles that they had put behind them, and those that lay ahead.

I couldn't see the fatigue back then. I certainly didn't understand it, but something about them made me feel uncomfortable. I guess it was partly deliberate. No one was meant to feel at ease around them.

"Hail, Protector and Ear," the female auditor said.

"Hail, Old Mother," the man said.

Nan showed her teeth at that. "Old Mother! Young enough to bruise you, young man."

He got just as toothy. "Oh, I know it."

"Will you let us in?" The woman asked.

"All your northern civilities!" Nan said. "Why do you ask when you mean to come in regardless? You're raised in the way of Masters, beneath the circle and the seven, and that way takes what it wants."

"We are not Masters, though," the woman said.

"May as well be," Nan said, then looked at me. "Get to brewing tea, girl," she said. "And, yes, you are welcome in my home."

"That's a brittle sort of welcome, but we'll take it," the man said. I thought Nan would start up again, but she didn't.

The auditors dismounted, tended to their horses, then came inside, and sat down.

The woman, who was called Sarah, sipped her tea. The man, Rob, held his cup in his hands, and looked at it.

"What brings you this far south?" Nan asked. "Someone summon you as my replacement?" Rob blinked.

"Like we could replace you," Sarah said. Nan scowled at that.

"You know what brings us," Rob said.

Nan put her cup down. "You're hunting something. The same thing that came through our town last night."

"Yes. A man. Well, he was once a man. He's a murderer. He's got some power to him, and he's running."

"I don't like those who chase such things into my town."

"We didn't drive him here. He knew where he was running, and so do we. We've a mind to follow him onto the Stone Road, and we need a guide."

Nan sniffed. "Why should I help you? You can't bring your Masters' Imperatives to the dead. You've done nothing to help us here, and I have written many letters to ask. Furnace still burns. If some fool is trying to hide on the Road, he'll be dead soon enough. That way has its own laws, and they are severe."

"Not severe enough," Rob said.

Sarah looked at Rob reproachfully. I could see whose side she was on, even if Rob chose to ignore her. He raised his hands, all placation, perhaps not aware how annoying such a gesture was. Nan's face didn't soften; she just looked at him and his raised hands. He lowered them, and shrugged.

Nan was getting under Rob's skin like a tick, burrowing beneath the calm, even if he wouldn't admit it. He sipped his tea. When he was done, he lifted his head, and looked at her square, without a hint of artifice in his voice. "The Road's laws aren't ours," he said at last. "We're chasing a killer, and I mean to see him face proper justice."

"Justice!" Nan said. "What's justice, now? Nothing more than stories we tell ourselves to make the world seem fair."

"You know it's more than that," Rob said. "There's a weave to the world, and without it, there is only madness. This man needs to know that terror catches up to you."

"So says a man that kills to stop a killer. Who speaks of terror like it is justice. The Road is easy to find. You should know it; you've sent enough people down that way."

Rob nodded. "I can feel death all around here."

"Why don't you follow your feeling, instead of asking me?"

Rob turned to look at me. "We could always take another guide. She's old enough. She could lead us down that road."

"Jean isn't ready. If you're so intent upon death, why not train your pistols at your skulls right now? That's the direct route to the road."

Rob clenched his fists. "I've asked nicely, woman. Don't make me call upon our agreements."

"I know what binds me," said Nan, "and what I must do."

She looked at her empty cup. "Make us tea, girl. Hurry to it. I'll leave with these fine folk"—oh, what venom she said that with—"tonight. You'll walk the levee alone tomorrow."

I left them talking in the kitchen, and hung my foot off the verandah, big toe touching the earth.

"Who are those visitors, Jean?"

"Auditors," I said. "They say we have agreements. What agreements?"

"The Red City rules everything, if they want to."

I snorted. "Not in my memory. Now they're taking Nan away. I'll have to walk the levee by myself."

"Maybe you're ready," the boy said.

I didn't feel ready.

I kept my foot down. "You know White Tree?"

"I can feel her," my boy said. "She likes the children; she gathers them. There's babes and all, right up to your age."

"Why?"

"I don't know. She's a special kind of nasty, I guess. Doesn't like anyone. Maybe there was a child that cut her branches once. Or near snapped her trunk. Children do that."

That didn't sound right to me. Would something so simple create such rage? "Don't you go there."

My boy laughed. "I won't, Jean. I promise. I'm here with you forever."

I felt a bit of relief at that, but mostly I felt sadness.

They were gone the next day. Nan's work was left to me, as well as her walking stick and her bone needle. I was free! It was terrifying. I pulled myself from bed, now that there was no one to do the waking. Coffee slugged, a mouthful of oats, and off, striding through the dark town, the dead mumbling beneath my feet, but no singing, no Nan. I felt her absence more completely in those weeks than any other time in my life. But I wasn't completely alone: Bird would find me, sit upon my shoulder, and keep me company. They were my closest friend, along with the dead boy.

Each morning I would circle the levee, testing the stones one by one, after which I would attend to the tasks of the day. Every afternoon I would sit on the southern ledge, and stare down towards the low hills that broadened and rose into the mountains on the edge of sight. Hoping to see Nan and the auditors, dreading that the next day something might go wrong, something I couldn't cope with.

One morning, I stood on the levee looking down, and there he was: the graceful man, walking the plain between Casement Rise and the Slouches, those low hills beyond which Furnace lay. He stepped slowly, his eyes on the ground. All at once, I saw him drop, an arm plunging into the earth. He stood up, and a dark shape was wrapped around his hand. It squirmed and struggled in his grip, and I realized what it was.

One of the dead. He'd caught one of the dead.

He opened a bag that he'd hung from his shoulder, and dropped the dead thing inside. The bag bulged and squirmed—even from here I could see that. He laughed and danced, then suddenly looked up at me.

"Jean," he said. I heard it as close as if he had whispered into my ear. It made my skin crawl. There was something wrong in that intimacy, something horrifying. I spun around me, looking for him; tripped and stumbled backwards; and fell down the levee on the town side.

There was warpweed and sawtooth down there, and cat heads, too—those are the worst, with their sharp, pointed seeds. I was cut and raw, and I landed at Alice's feet.

"What are you doing?" Alice demanded. She'd gotten a tad peculiar since her mother had left. I'd not seen her with her friends. I felt that familiar burst of guilt that horrified me, and made me angry all at once.

I glared at her. "Why don't you tell me what *you're* doing?" There was nothing here except the orchard and the Autumn Gate, useless and rusted on the levee-side. Not another person around.

Alice went red. "I was—"

"Spying, that's what you were doing!"

She shook her head. She was embarrassed, and I was on my hands and knees, covered in scratches. "Just help me up, will you?"

She gripped my hand and pulled. I stood, and yanked out the burrs and the cat heads. Each one had a knot of points dipped with poison. I'd swell up that night.

"I'll leave you, then," she said.

I shook my head. "Please stay with me," I said. I didn't want to be alone. I could hear the graceful man, the echo of his voice inside my head.

We walked back into town together, but as soon as we were in sight of others, she took off, and I was alone.

Bird found me, then, and I had never been happier to see them.

The dead whispered constantly. They were hardly supportive, but I think they feared that I'd put my boots on, and silence them.

Talking to the dead or holding the levee doesn't excuse you from chores. There's always washing and cleaning and cooking. We never just cooked for ourselves. There were plenty in need of food, and company. We did our best to give it. Out of kindness and practicality. And my mother took it upon herself to drink less, stopping almost entirely. The verandah quickly filled with pots and cups, newly turned, and Mum was happier than I had ever known her.

It couldn't last. There came a day when the stones didn't beat their regular rhythm.

I dashed around the levee, finally coming not to a scratch or a wearing down, but a rift, a man-sized furrow, that ran from the outer levee lip to the inner one, as though some serpent had dragged itself through.

Bird tsked on my shoulder. "This isn't good," Bird said.

"What've I done wrong?"

"I don't know, but this isn't good."

I called Bird onto my wrist, and glared at them. "You are not very helpful."

They hissed at me, then demanded a head scratch. I obliged as I studied the damage.

I would have feared that what had entered was waiting for me if I couldn't see the path it had taken out nearby. I repaired the damage as well as I could with Lolly's help. We worked for hours, but at last it was done.

Lolly was talking to me again, though we hadn't spoken of the thing that had lived inside him. I'd tried to bring it up, but he had waved his hands furiously, and put his fingers in his ears. I left it at that.

Besides, I had more pressing concerns now.

Later, I heard that whatever it was had taken three sheep.

Perhaps that would be enough. Sometimes a little snack was all a creature wanted before moving on. Nan had told me that most of our visitants were like that.

This time, I wasn't so lucky.

The creature came back the night after, and the night after that. Each time, it chose a spot I had worked over carefully, as if to show it was immune to my trickery. I began to sink into despair.

Mum was no help—she refused to offer what she knew—so I was left responding to attacks long after the visitant had gone.

Jacob and Myles visited me one morning after I'd spent a day fixing the ruined levee yet again. I wasn't in a great mood, but I saw them in the living room, which I think was better treatment than Myles had gotten from Nan.

Jacob looked at Myles. "He wanted to see you, and I said I'd come along."

"We are worried at your proficiency," Myles said. "The council's considering sending for another Walker. Or an auditor."

I was horrified. I felt like a failure.

"There's no shame in it," Jacob said. "You're still a child."

How could I not feel shame at that!

"Nan will be back before another Walker makes it here, if you can even find one."

A Walker without a home was a rare thing, Nan had told me. If they'd lost their town, they'd most likely died with it.

Jacob nodded.

"*If* your Nan comes back," Myles said.

"She will!"

Myles raised his hands. "I don't mean to offend. Something needs to be done before it decides to stop with livestock, and take something else."

"Let me see what I can do tonight," I said. "Just one more night."

"All right," Jacob said. "One more night, then we send a rider north. Just remember your lessons. Keep your stance loose. Try not to trip over yourself."

Mum watched them leave. She'd listened in on the whole conversation. "Like they understand how hard it is," she said.

"Everyone expects it to be easy, seems shocked when it fails. Would you like my opinion?"

"Yes," I said. *All* I wanted was her opinion!

Not long after, I visited the Huskling King, and we made plans.

Each time the creature had made the crossing, it had entered the town a little farther to the west. I set myself up on a chair about a hundred yards down from the last entry point. Lugging that chair onto the levee had been a real effort, but damned if this thing was going to make me spend the whole night standing up.

I had a blanket, a thermos of tea, a few matches, and materials to start a fire. Bird came to me, a white shape through the rising dark.

I stroked their head, and they let me. Their eyes shone red with the last lingering light of the sun.

"Shouldn't you be sleeping?"

"Shouldn't *you* be sleeping?" Bird replied, then promptly fell asleep.

I faced out into the dark, hands around the thermos. Mist followed the river, began its slow, thickening dance, the roof of it rising, and the sky above so clear I could see through to forever. The moon came up, and there were the Husklings, sheets of flesh rising and falling with the air, circling the moon like a ring, then drifting apart. At night, they were different creatures, elegant and foreign. Light called them: the lights of evening, moonlight, starlight, fire. They might chase fireflies, if they saw them. There was a trick to summoning the Husklings that the king had taught me, but mostly it was safer to leave them to their dance.

They called and hooted, and gossiped and bragged, and followed the moon. I sat and waited.

The night passed in dozes and fragments, as fitful as I felt, though I kept a rein on my attention. It does not do to give into restlessness, nor lose the focus of waiting for a possible doom. The problem was—and this is the problem with all impatience—it is so dull to wait. It eats at you as much as anything dire and predatory.

I sat in my chair, and watched the world. I rose, and walked along the crest of the levee, Bird sleeping on my shoulder. The sky turned above me, and the trees creaked, and the earth shifted, and the owls hooted, and the dogs howled. Finally, there was silence and stillness, except for a breeze blowing up from the river that smelled of rot and mud and the ever-present smoke of Furnace.

Nothing happened, except those many things. Nothing happened until all of that nothing sunk into me, and I was yawning and falling into a slumber that felt as inevitable as death, and as chasm-deep.

The sound of footfalls woke me. Bird buried themselves in my hair. They were the only warm thing about the world; all else had grown cold. Steps, distant, then drawing close. Then I saw him. Down the slope of the levee below me stood a man, old and bent low. The last light of the moon and the first suggestion of the dawn described him. He was all shadows and squiggles, but I could feel his eyes, see the sharp curve of his smile.

"I'm coming to eat you, child," he said, his voice bright and courteous. His body flickered, became something else, became itself again. "If you would be so patient as to wait for me."

"Careful," Bird whispered. "Careful."

I said nothing, and the old monster sighed. I felt almost sorry for him.

"Wouldn't you like to talk to me?"

I kept my gaze steady, and my mouth shut.

"This is quite intolerable."

Still, I stayed silent. There are rules in these engagements. You can't just start flapping your mouth.

The old man moved a little closer, except sometimes he wasn't an old man, but rather the branch of a tree, or the limb of some great and reaching creature.

"Very well. I submit to you, and release any obligation. All rules but for the basic back and forth of conversation are undone. You may talk to me as one of the living. Surely I'm alive if I hunger."

I felt that release. A force shifted, and the rules did change. I felt a corresponding power within me, that old force that I'd ridden when I faced Lolly's possessor.

"You're a monster," I said. "I'm not here for small talk."

The old man laughed, and shrugged. "I have released us from everything but small talk. Big talk would grind your soul to dust."

That presence rose within me. "Do not belittle me."

He raised an eyebrow. "Oh, ho! Now this is interesting."

I wanted to know why, but I didn't trust him, nor did I wish to offer any hint that I may not know what I was doing. It was obvious enough.

He had reached the bottom of the levee, and stood there, staring up. The shift of forms was more frequent and dramatic now. Man, beast, tree, as though he couldn't quite hold on to any of them in this reality, and had become a flickering show instead.

"Why are you here?"

"I have wandered for years, always seeking a way into a town. They are usually better guarded than this."

I winced. "Do *not* disparage my attempts."

"My actions do more than disparage. I have found that the way in isn't closed to me. My presence will soon draw more of my kind, the things afraid of that Furnace in the west—this will encourage them. I have little time to indulge my hungers. I do not play well with others."

I laughed at that. The clouds were shifting in the sky, dawn was far enough away for me to die, and I wasn't sure who was stalling whom. "Neither do I."

The look he gave me was almost too tender. "Fortunately, it will be over soon."

The old man was halfway up the levee bank. His face broadened, that mouth opening wider and wider. I could see the sharp points of his hunger; I could see the desolation beyond; there was an urgency to his steps. Perhaps he had realised that he had lingered overlong. Time works against us all, in the end.

Just a few more steps. My heart had quickened, my fingers shook, and I worked a match from the box next to my chair as I pulled a paper tube from my pocket.

"Have you ever wondered what makes your kind different from us?"

The old man-monster's face wrinkled. "Hunger?"

"Planning," I said, and I lit the match. It flared, and I pressed it against the tube. The light was unexpectedly bright. The old man's face flickered in the wind.

"You cannot undo me with light," he said.

"No, I can't." I tossed the burning tube in his direction, and watched the Husklings that it called dive down upon him.

"It was nice talking to you, sir," I said.

The Husklings snapped and bit at his flesh, stripped away the illusion, and gnawed at the truth beneath, and the old man howled.

"It is coming, girl."

"What's coming?"

I stepped down the levee towards him, careful of the Husklings, though we had an understanding. Even in predation, their nighttime forms had a beauty that bordered on heartbreak.

"You'll suffer the most mournful of pains."

"Quiet," I said, and I tapped Nan's walking stick against his chest. Once, just once, and it passed right through him, like he was no more than a spiderweb.

Then the monster was gone, and the Husklings looked at me, and I remembered where I was. Their wide mouths flapped.

I scrambled back up the levee, a little dignity lost in the rush to save my skin.

I quickly re-marked the path I'd taken, sealing up the town again. Weakness draws things; it is a cry to the predators of the night. I knew that the old man wasn't lying about that. I built that section of the wall stronger than it had been before. It was hard work.

The sun rose into dawn, true dawn. The Husklings hovered a moment, battered by the light. Then they lifted into the blue sky, and were gone. I stood in that nascent morning, breath and blood thick in me, and stared into the valley, where the fog lingered, and the sun had yet to make its furrows and sow the day.

Bird shivered on my shoulder. I'd forgotten they were there.

"I said to be careful, and you were not," Bird said.

"What? I was! It worked!"

"You made yourself the bait, and you risked the whole town."

"You are a remarkable creature," I said. "Ready to pretend that there was a way without risk."

Bird turned their head so I might scratch it. I looked down into the town for the first time all night, and I saw my mum, asleep on a chair directly behind me. I held in a sob as I walked down to her, and kissed her cheek.

She woke, and kissed me back.

"It's gone," I said. "It's dead."

"What happened? I didn't want to leave you alone to face that thing," Mum said. She pressed her face against mine and stared into my eyes. "Are you still in there?"

"Yes," I said.

"Good. Come home as soon as you've walked the levee. I'll make us breakfast." And then she laughed and pointed.

There, twenty metres behind us, sat Jacob, a rifle in his lap, snoring gently. We walked over to him, slipped a blanket over his legs, and left him there.

A few nights later, we had our first storm of the season. These things were always fierce, but this was a bad one. Trees whipped at the earth, and our roof sang, and hissed, and finally roared. I thought we might lose it—a few lost theirs that night—but we were lucky. Elic begged to come into the house, and who was I to deny him? He slept on my bed, curled up against me. I was pleased to have the solid warmth of him there, even if he whined with every rumble of thunder.

At its worst, I knocked on Mum's door— from underneath it there was a light burning.

She looked up from the book she was reading. "Do you need to go out in this?" she said.

"Not for a while yet."

"Let the storm die," she said. "Nothing will be wandering through it."

Mum lifted the covers of her bed, and I crawled in with her, and she held me. She smelled of soap and clay, and I lay my head against her heartbeat.

"I dreamt about Nan last night," Mum said. "I don't think she is far away."

"Do you miss her?"

"I like missing her. It's easier to miss her." She stroked my head. "Now sleep," Mum commanded. "I'll wake you when the storm has ended."

She didn't, but I woke anyway, and walked out to greet the dawn.

The morning was a fury of work to match the fury of the storm, this time with a bedraggled Bird upon my shoulder—they had found me at the eastern stone. All along the levee, marks had washed away. Yet the world had spun a perfect sky, as beautiful as she was fierce, and I felt at one with it. I worked, and for the first time I did not miss Nan until all my work was done. Job done, sweat dripping from my brow to my fingertips, I walked home, where half the town was waiting for me.

"Jean, we've need of you." "Jean." "Jean." "Jean."

One by one I spoke to their dead; the storm had upset them so. The dead, upset, were a calamitous force. Everyone complaining and moaning, and me trying to unpick their knotted grievances.

I didn't get home until much later.

Nan was sitting at the table drinking tea. "What kept you?" she said.

I threw my arms around her. She hugged me back, and we laughed. Even Mum was smiling.

"The storm blew her in," Mum said.

"Where's Rob and Sarah?"

"They went another way. You know what they say: An auditor's business never ends," Nan said, and sipped her tea. "You look taller!"

Part Three

The Stone Road

After the storm, things went back to normal for a while, but Nan was restless. She'd work as she usually did—though harder, to make up for her absence—and then she'd get back to knotting that cord.

I could tell something was building in her, and finally, it broke.

That night, Mum had visited me in bed, giving me the longest hug and kiss, and her eyes were wet. She didn't explain herself, and I was so tired that it didn't stop me from sleeping.

Nan woke me by candlelight.

She handed me a duffel, rolled tight. I slid it under my arm, and curled around it. It was as comfortable as any pillow. I was wrapped in dreams, and it felt like a dream itself.

"Jean . . ." Nan shook me again, and I looked at her through a slit in my too-tired eyes. My lids were heavy and sore. Nan had her tobacco pouch and her papers and a small candle with her. I looked at my watch in that dim light, and it was scarcely past one. But there she was, scowling down at me with all the ferocity of the sun, as though it were morning already, and I wasn't in need of sleep.

"Tired," I said, and Nan's scowl deepened. She lowered her face close to mine, her eyes as hard as stones. I could smell the tobacco smoke on her, mingled with coffee.

I pulled a face.

"None of that. The road's calling," she said. "Time we did what I've been putting off."

I sat up straight. "What? Really?"

"You're of an age, and I'm nearly at the end of all my ages. We need do this while I have the strength to see that it is done properly. Believe me, I have held off as long as I could, and that's been to your detriment."

All I could see was strength. "You're not old!"

She put her hands over my eyes. They were rough and warm, but could I sense a slight shaking there?

"Ah, you can't see it," she said. "The sliver of weakness within me. But it is there, and I have work for you. Work for both of us.

I sat up, put the duffel aside, and dressed. Nan gave me a moment to wash my face, then handed me a cup of bitter coffee, which woke me up in a hurry.

Then Nan handed me a thermos of something else, a musty smelling broth. "Take a sip, quick."

I did, and winced. It was very bitter, much more so than the coffee.

"You'll get used to it," Nan said. "It's all we can consume on our journey."

"What is it?"

"It's made from mycota, dried. That's all you need to know. I have a supply of it, enough to sustain us. We'll know little hunger on the road, but we still must remember what it is to eat." She clapped her hands. "Now, we've got to run."

"What about Mum?" I hovered there. Despite the coffee, I was still stuck between sleep and dreaming.

"It's her job to wait for us. Now, hurry."

Out the door we went, duffels heavy on our backs. Nan had a big hunter's knife belted to her waist, and a stone for sharpening it in a tiny pouch tied to her waist. I could see her wince: The dead were challenging her, demanding that she tell them when she'd be back.

"Enough," she said. "Enough, you belligerents! I'll be back. That is all you need to know."

She rolled a smoke almost without thinking, an effortless twisting of fingers, of lips to paper, face stitched with a frown—not at the act, but the voices and their demands. She started puffing on the smoke, and at last, she gave a sigh of contentment. She pinched my bare arm with a strong hand, fingers cracked and yellow. "You are never to indulge in such bad habits!"

I didn't tell her that I'd smoked once with Lolly, two whole cigarettes, and been sick. There was enough smoke coming from the west; I didn't need more in my lungs.

Bird flew above us, then landed on my shoulder. Nan looked at them speculatively. After a while, she shook her head. "You are not to join us, creature," she said.

They said nothing. I scratched under their chin.

"Off with you. Some things, only blood can share." She clapped her hands, and Bird, giving me a quick study, as though they might forget me, flew back in the direction of Tree.

"I'm not fond of them," Nan said, under her breath.

"They're just a bird."

"They're no such thing, and they shouldn't follow you so. It is not the Tree's way. They have become something a little more and a little less than Tree. You must never grow dependent on one another."

"I do *not* depend on them." But I still wanted them with me.

Nan brought her face close to mine. "You must seek no comforts. They're a weakness."

"What about your coffee and your cigarettes?"

"I regret them every day," she said, as she rolled herself another smoke. I could just make out the tight, thin smile on her face. "Do as I say, not as I do, my child. It's how I was raised, and it should be how you're raised, too."

"Did you like growing up that way?"

Nan laughed. "What do you think?"

We came to the Winter Gate, and Nan pulled a thick iron key from her bag.

"This demands deliberate ceremony. We walk through doors to find other places; we open doors so that the other places may find us. Sometimes you open the wrong door, and it doesn't matter if it's the right road; it'll take you somewhere else."

She made a low noise—a word, maybe, or something a little more complicated than a sigh—and slid the key into the lock. The whole door clunked as she turned the key. The night held its breath, and I held mine with it. My heart was beating thick and hard in my chest, as though my blood had turned solid. Nan put her weight against the door, and it opened, but not without resistance. It moved on rarely used hinges, in opposition to the world.

"Close your eyes a moment," she said, and I did.

As we walked slowly but steadily through the opening, a light blazed. Even with my eyes shut, it was intolerable, and then it was gone.

The door slammed shut behind us.

"You can open your eyes," she said.

It was like Casement Rise had never existed at all.

The road that lay before us was wide and pale as the belly of the moon. You could have had fifty men walk it shoulder to shoulder. It was ageless, in the way Nan was ageless.

Nan didn't let go of my hand. She tapped the road with her stick, and the sound rang out hollowly. Somewhere, something dripped. We were outside—a few stars shone above us—but it was like we were inside, too, deep within a mountain or the earth. The sky had a weight to it, enough that my back bent beneath it.

"This is the Stone Road," Nan said. "This is where the dead walk, and have since the Years of Heat and Sadness. Those that don't cling to life find it easily—or they used to, before Furnace—but we have to work at it. I wouldn't take you here, except you need to know this way, you need to walk as the dead walk, or you will not understand their power. Should you meet anyone here—and there are some dead who linger—don't talk to them. Be polite, listen, nod, but be as though tongueless. Words are a nourishment to the dead, and a goad. Silence is your only shield here.

"It wasn't always this way," Nan continued. "These roads weren't always so quiet. Once, before the Years of Heat and Sadness, they shivered with the thunder of carriages and engines, and the only death upon them was what the vehicles themselves made. I've seen them in visions; they were cruel and wondrous machines. But then the world shrugged, and they were shrugged from it. Roads, however, have utility. All roads can be repurposed. The dead called out for service, something ancient listened, and this became their road."

The slap of our feet echoed ahead and behind us. Away from the road, grey lands stretched featureless; then they would take on a haunting shape—a fist of rock, a burning tower, a giant

Trent Jamieson

dog—only to fade when I tried to take a closer look. It was as if the sun didn't burn here. What was revealed to us was through the memory of light, and that memory shifted.

After a few days, our skins took on the pallor of the road. The way was flat, the walking easy, but interminable, and I yearned for the slopes and falls of home. I yearned for the dry and heat.

The road lightened with the day, and darkened with the evening, but it was never really one extreme or the other. The dead, those who had somehow missed Furnace's raging light, would pass us, singularly or in groups. This was their road, and they moved swiftly upon it: shadow shapes that hardly paid us any mind. They knew where they were going, and they were intent upon that path.

"Why do our dead stay in the ground?" I asked Nan.

"Not all of them do," Nan said. "It used to be a handful, but now most of them keep to the town. It got worse when Furnace started burning, that's for sure. The dead call the dead. Maybe they won't let them go; maybe that's why they settle and seethe beneath the earth in anger."

"Why didn't the dead follow us?"

"That gate is hard for them, since Furnace. It burns so bright there—you felt it when we crossed over. Whatever blinded them knew this would make it impassable to the dead. I tried, years ago, to take them through, but they wouldn't follow."

I thought about that. My birthday, my first moments of life, had closed this way to the dead. "And it's my fault."

"No, not your fault. We don't choose the troubles that find us," Nan said. "We'll find a way."

"What about you? Once it's fixed, I mean."

"I've made my peace with death. I have no intention of staying to curse at you. When my work is done, I'll leave, and walk this road properly."

"I'll miss you," I said.

Nan kissed my face. "Jean, you are a sweet child sometimes. You wouldn't like what remains of me."

Walking the Stone Road is to walk a dream. A familiar one, a shared dream: You recognize the landmarks without ever having seen them. Perhaps three days after we left home, statues began to appear, the watchers and the weepers carved beside the road out of a white rock. There was the Knotted King, the Shuttle Bus, the Memoriser, and the Moreman.

"When the Husklings were banished from the place of the Defiant, they set about making these," Nan said. "They talked to the dead and the angry and the monstrous, and they carved out a sort of human history, a record of misery in stone. We are walking through the past in all its glorious ridiculousness. The world was different, then."

The statues crowded around us at night, things we had seen hours ago come to us again. They shared our thin broth with us.

It felt right that they should. This was their land; we were only travellers passing through.

On the road, footsteps were dulled. All talk, no matter how loud, became muted. Everything was a whisper. Wariness was the greatest consideration, but weariness dominated. On that road was the intimation of all the great exhaustions of my life ahead. It settled in me with its terrible weight, until all I wanted to do was drop to the road, curl into a soft ball, and never move again.

Nan seemed less affected by it, but I suspect that's because she had already grown familiar with life's exhaustion. I was so young; I had no true idea.

For all our tiredness, sleep was hard coming. It slipped away like a fish from any attempt to catch it, leaving me breathless and weary, my eyes wide open.

Nan lay next to me, snoring or mumbling, swiping at dreams, and I envied her. At least she could sleep.

Each day became a waking dream, a cruel series of steps. That is how one walks the Stone Road. There is no choice in it; it is only to be endured.

One morning, not long after we had started that day's walking, an old man joined us. Nan gripped my hand like a vice, but she did not say anything, and neither did I.

"It is a long road, this," he said. "Don't you agree? I'm waiting, but I want to know that you are happy. Are you happy?"

Nan shook her head at me.

His face fell. "Cat got your tongue?"

I said nothing.

"Speak. Speak. Don't you know it is rude to ignore me?"

Nan's grip tightened.

"Speak!"

I turned my back on him. Nan's eyes were wide.

"Speak!"

A cold wind blew, a sudden lightness. Dust spun around us. I dared to turn.

The old man was already a hundred metres away. He did not look back.

Nan squeezed my shoulder. When the man was finally gone from sight, she kissed the top of my head. "Silence is your only shield here," she said again.

"Did you know that man?" I asked.

"Yes. He was my Les."

I felt such a horror. To have turned my back on my grandfather!

"He would have been proud of you. Don't confuse the harsh notes of the dead with those of the living," Nan said. "He understood the ways of this world, even when he was alive. And he understood me."

"You miss him?"

Nan shook her head, though her eyes said yes. "I cut him out of my heart. How else could I survive all this? The heart is a ruinous thing; love, a thread of rust that always threatens to flower into deeper decay. Don't feed it, child, no more than scraps. Even that may be too much. It always wants more."

She didn't sound convincing; I doubt she believed that herself.

The road ended at the Mumbling City. It was called a city, but it was scarcely a town. It was a scattering of shanties built onto a ridge overlooking a plain of yellow earth that rose into a miasmic dust, as though it couldn't quite decide if it was earth or air. Far to the southwest, through that ochre haze, were structures I first took to be towers. I felt a sense of longing—mine or the towers', I couldn't tell; it was so pervasive. Every day I had found it harder to separate myself from the landscape.

Maybe this was what those called to Furnace felt. I pointed the distant structures out to Nan. "Are we going there?"

"The Defiant?" Nan shook her head. "Those colossi were made by the Husklings at the command of the Masters. A grand gesture at the end of things so, even here, we're reminded of their rule."

So Lolly hadn't been making it up!

"Stop your gawking, girl. We've no business there. We're not touristing. You're here to come into your powers, nothing more. We stay here with the dead, and when it's time, we leave."

She stared back down the road, back the way we came. "It's not too late to go home. Here on the edge, you can still turn around, and the way back is swifter than you think. Once we enter the city, it's harder, slower; you'll have to trust me, and your boots. Are you willing?"

I nodded.

Nan gave my hand a squeeze. "Brave child."

I didn't feel all that brave, but I yearned for her to believe it. "Is this really the land of the dead?" I asked as we crossed into the city through a gateway, unguarded, crumbling, ancient.

"Yes. It is as far as we can go. I have heard there are tunnels that burrow down into the deepening dark. But who can give credence to the rumours of the dead? Those ways are closed to us while we breathe. Be careful here: Time is wrong in this place; it's forgotten the world we know. It moves however it wills. Look at your watch."

I did, and saw that it had stopped working. Three fifteen, it was, and would remain, until I left that place.

There were no more than fifty people in the Mumbling City, though they looked different every time I saw them. We were to stay a few days, no more than that, Nan promised.

The people there were polite. They spoke to Nan with gentleness, and Nan returned the courtesy, for in this city of mumbles, talk was allowed. But I did not talk, except to Nan.

We drank and ate with them, too. In the city, there was plenty of food, but it was not filling.

There was a room for us in a small hotel, the most substantial structure in the town. I learnt there was always a room here for anyone, if they had walked the proper way.

Some evenings, there was celebration. Once I saw a parade from my window: balloons and elephants and other creatures, and a troop of dancers, faces pale as the white levee mud back home. They moved silently. I ran to the door and onto the road, but they were gone.

Nan had followed me, and she held my hand, perhaps to stop me from running after them. "All we catch are glimpses, here," she said. "It's home to which you must put your mind, now."

That night we ate a lean dinner. Nan watched me, making sure I took every bite. "Please trust that I love you," she said. I looked up into her eyes, and they seemed so sad.

"I do," I said. "I do. But when can we go home?"

"Just finish your dinner," Nan said.

I hardly slept at all that night. Every time I closed my eyes, all I could see was Nan's sad gaze. I must have slept a little because the next morning, Nan wasn't in her bed beside mine. All her things were gone, except her walking stick. I scrambled out of bed, and rushed around the hotel, asking anyone if they had seen her. Each shook their head, and went on with the unknowable tasks of the dead.

I ran through the city, calling her name, but there was never an answer. My calls disturbed the dead, and they started to avoid me. I stopped at last, certain of what I already knew. Nan was gone.

I was in the Mumbling City alone.

I panicked, at first; went back to my room and cried. How could she have done this to me? The world lurched with those tears, then steadied. Finally, out of tears, I studied my possessions.

I had my duffel and my shoes, though I had taken to walking barefoot because everyone here did. On the duffel was a note I'd missed in my haste to find Nan.

I'm sorry, Jean. We can walk here together, but we must leave alone. I will be waiting for you, I promise.

That was little comfort.

I sat on my bed for a while, composed myself as best I could, and packed my things.

I left the hotel, and walked in the direction of the Stone Road, but when I reached the place where we had entered the city, I discovered something: The road wasn't there.

"Did you expect it to be so easy?" The graceful man leant against a nearby door, kicking up yellow dust with a boot. "If it was so easy, why would your nan bother leaving you here?"

"Go away," I said.

"Oh, I'm not really here. I'm working a busyness in the north. I'm the merest breath of a sending."

I had my little silver knife, and I pulled it out.

The graceful man laughed. "How do you hope to cut air? Your stupidity is more painful than that blade."

I looked at my watch. Three fifteen.

"Yes, and that little ticker won't save you. It's broken: Time is as dead as everything else here. Everything except for you, and my tiny breath."

"Go away," I said.

"I'm here to help you. Am I not the giver of keys?" the graceful man said. "I'm not the one that deserted you here."

"I don't want your help," I lied.

"Do you think you can leave the city on your own? People who stay here too long are driven mad. Some become monsters. Is that what you want for yourself?"

"I'll find a way."

"Who's here, and who isn't? Who can return home with a click of their fingers?"

"Click them, then," I said, and then he did. I stood, alone, staring across the flat lands where the Stone Road should be, but wasn't.

I walked around the edges of the city, an hour's walk, if that. It wasn't much bigger than Casement Rise. I went back to the hotel and my room, which had remained empty, and I sat on my bed, and thought. What I needed must be in this room. It had to be.

I dumped the contents of my bag onto the bed. No answers there.

I picked up my boots. Something rattled in the toe of one of them. I reached in, and found a key. I recognised it as a copy of the one Nan had used to open the Winter Gate. Nan must have put that there. Why hadn't she just given it to me?

I slipped on my boots, held that key like a talisman in my hands, and clomped back outside. Another parade approached, but this one was not silent. I could see it before I could see it. It grew firm in the spaces of my mind. Formed there steadily. All those instruments playing, animals dancing, and calling, people clapping. It got louder as I walked deeper into the city.

All at once, they were around me. A wave of people and music and creatures, unfamiliar to me outside of the darker sort of dreams. They pushed and pulled at me, and I could hardly move unless I went with them, but I knew that was the wrong way. I kept walking, and that parade kept coming, I couldn't even imagine how the Mumbling City might fit such a procession. I knew that if I gave up, and let it pull me along, I would never go home.

It was tempting. I'd eaten very little for days; I was weary, delirious. Indeed, behind me, I could smell food. Every meal I had ever loved, every trader's market, every feast. Spit fell from my lips, and my limbs shivered with hunger, as though they had lost the strength to keep still.

But I didn't give in. I was used to the grasping nature of the dead; Nan had taught me well. I kept walking because I had to.

The music stopped. No delights remained, only brute force. The nearest dead scratched at me. The smell of food became a stench. I walked harder now, and when they pushed at me, I didn't cry. I'd walked against the dead for months; my feet were hard. I knew this force. I laughed, and met it with my own. That ancient ageless thing within me awoke, and I swung at the dead with Nan's walking stick. Where it touched them, they crumbled to dust. They roared with a wild anger, then backed away. I grinned at them as they opened a path before me, but my grin faltered once I realised that they weren't parting for me, but something else.

A beast, larger than any animal I had ever seen, all teeth and claws, came running at me. I wanted to turn, and run screaming the other way, but what was the point? It could easily run me down. I would not look away. I knew what I was fighting for. I grabbed my little silver blade.

It charged, faster and faster, but halted just in front of me, dropping and sitting like a dog. I reached out, and touched its face. Its great dark eyes studied me.

"Good," it said. "You'll do."

"I'm leaving now," I said.

"You can stay. You are safe here."

I shook my head.

And, just like that, I was alone, and the streets were empty.

When I reached the edge of town, I noticed for the first time a tiny gatehouse, not much taller than me. Perhaps it hadn't been there before.

I walked inside it, and there was a door, painted red. That first splash of colour in so long was shocking. The door was warm to the touch, a blood heat. I turned the handle: locked.

My hands shook as I tried the key. It took three goes to fit it in the lock. I breathed deep, then turned the key. The door juddered, it jolted, and I pushed against it. I thought of home; I thought of Nan and my mum. There was an ache in my chest, a quiet place, and I let myself fall into it. The door opened, and I walked through.

Not home, but somewhere I recognised. The Long Between. Shade and flame. I'd not been here since that first time the Huskling King had showed it to me, but it scared me less than it ought to have. At least it was familiar. In the distance, I could see a tiny sliver of grey light. The memory of light, the softest, oldest breath of it.

Somewhere distant, something was calling my name. I rushed towards it, felt the world expand, and contract around me, though I was not sure that it was leading me where I wanted.

I can't say how long I walked before I reached a shimmering, crackling fire, a blinding brightness that grew until I had to shut my eyes; that seeped through my closed lids; that I had to crawl against.

But as I did, I knew I'd reached my limits. This close, and I couldn't make it any further.

Too much. It was all too much!

Someone called my name, and fingers closed around my hand.

"Got you, Jean," said my dead boy. "Hurry. Not far to go."

Hand in his, I kept moving. Then my free hand found a door, and I pushed. I felt his fingers slide away.

The light was gone. I opened my eyes. The door was open, and beyond it, a sky lit with the modest brilliance of stars.

I stepped through.

The air was warm and murky.

"Jean." Something rose, and smothered me. "Jean! My Jean. I was so frightened for you." Nan wrapped me in her arms.

I sobbed into her shoulder. "Why'd you leave me?" I asked.

"Because I had to. I didn't lie; you can't leave the city with another. But look, look where you are!"

I lifted my head from her shoulder.

We were in Casement Rise, just by the Winter Gate. It was late, but I could still make out the familiar shapes of home.

"How?"

"Sometimes it works, and other times it doesn't. A door can lead anywhere, and that door in particular leads where your heart wills it. I was beginning to worry. I've been waiting a long time."

"How long?"

"Five months," Nan said. "It's almost your birthday."

My watch started tick, tick, ticking. The frozen hands were moving again, but time hadn't waited for them. I wondered if they would ever catch up.

I started sobbing again. Nan let me cry until we were home, and I was in Mum's arms. I wondered, briefly, if she'd found it easier to love me while I wasn't there.

"You're home," she said. "You're home."

Her breath smelled of liquor, but I didn't care. Here were Mum and Nan. Here was everything that was important to me.

"Yes," I said, and Mum let me go.

Nan stroked my face. "Get some sleep," she said. "You'll be meeting the dawn with me, tomorrow."

I realised then that nothing had changed. I could go to the land of the dead, and still not be ready for what was coming.

Mum ran off to the verandah, and was sick. Nan carried my things to the bedroom, and left me there.

The next day, we walked the levee together, and it was almost as though I had never been gone. But the seasons had shifted, and I'd been cheated of part of my life. Afterwards, with Nan out on business and Mum suffering in her sleep, I walked back up the levee, and stared west at the smoke of Furnace, then north.

I could step into the Long Between. I could walk north, keep on walking, and never look back. What did I owe anyone? I hesitated there a moment, then turned, and looked back into town. This was my home.

I saw Gail walking out of the butcher's. I waved down at her, and she waved back.

Who'd do that anywhere else? Who'd know me? While there was an attraction in anonymity, there was a fear in it, too, worse than that of Furnace and monsters because it was unknown.

A white shape crashed onto my shoulder. A white head pushed against my cheek. "You're home!"

I scratched Bird's head. Kissed the top of it.

"Home," I said, and my heart swelled with the word.

My anger softened to sadness, and I walked back down the levee. There are always chores to be done, if you're not set on running away.

Maybe that's the way it is when you walk the Road. You lose something of yourself. Isn't that what life is, too? Each day a gaining and a loss.

But I did find that the dead held less power over me now. Their touches had lost their sting, and I knew that it wasn't just that my feet had toughened up.

Nan's cord had grown so many more knots. Almost all my hair had been used up, so she cut it again. This time, it was locks that had been to the land of the dead, and back.

"I missed you," the king said. We were walking along the edge of his kingdom. Three days since I'd come back, and I was anxious to resume my education. The day before, Jacob and I had sparred with knives over and over again. I was sick of it, and just as terrible. And his patience with me only made it worse.

I wanted someone who wouldn't be so patient. I wanted something with a bit of magic to it.

"I missed you, too," I said.

The king sniffed. "Oh, my dear, I do not doubt it, but you have your family. All I have are my Husklings, and they are from me, but they are not quite like me. They don't understand." He huffed. "What do children know?"

"Some things," Bird said.

"What do birds know?"

"More than you think."

"Why do you underestimate my regard for your kind?" the king said to Bird. "Jean, let me show you."

The king took me to Tree, travelling via the Long Between. I heard laughter, caught that flash of a fire burning, someone calling my name. The king could sense my discomfort.

"You must get used to this."

"Something hunts me here," I said.

"Child, something hunts you out in the world as well."

"The graceful man," I said.

"If only it was that easy," the king said. "Your graceful man is part of it, but only part. The world is the hunter, the challenge, the trouble, and so much more."

We walked through that scribbled world, passed Lolly's place and the hill, then down into the valley, out of the Long Between, and into the light.

Tree and her birds watched as we approached them.

The king bowed. "They are very powerful," he said. "And yet they are also incredibly fragile. That is the nature of power. Power's a story that we tell ourselves, and the most persuasive story wins; not necessarily the right one, nor the strongest."

"That's not fair."

"Equity is just another story we tell, isn't it? Tree has her birds, and they could strike at us—we are hardly allies, Tree and I—but she holds them back. We're all invested in your education, Jean."

He gestured at the red scars on the tree trunk. "I suppose you are cognizant of these markings?"

"Stories," I said.

"Yes, the same as my sculptures are stories, as the lessons you learn are stories. It's how we web the world, how we make sense of it. This is part of what makes the clever birds so clever. These stories are their thoughts made concrete. What a wonder that is, don't you think? Perhaps it's time you experienced a different sort of story, Jean. An old one."

We walked a little further, came to a thicket of lantana. A small tunnel had been cut through it.

"Do you trust me?" he said.

"I trust you."

He smiled with a warmth that surprised me. "Good, Jean. I'll do my best to earn it. We need to go through here, where time is slippery."

"Why's it slippery, exactly?" I looked at the tunnel uncertainly. I'd had enough trouble with time of late. "Is this like the Long Between?"

"Yes, I suppose it is, but not as giddying. This place is aware of the truth. Well, one truth: Lantana wasn't part of this land, until it was. It's rooted here, when once it wasn't. It's the simple stuff that sometimes has the most force. There is no here and now, or then, or what will be. There is only the Instant. Time is simply a matter of perception, but it is a persuasive one. One that we all believe. One that you need to stop believing."

"Uh . . ." I hesitated.

"What?" He cleared his throat. "Look, experience is the best sort of understanding." With a quick movement, he wrapped his wing around my back, pulled me down, and pushed me into the tunnel. "You said you trust me. Let's go."

I started crawling. It was a tight squeeze, and the lantana scratched me as I went. All around me there was a low sound, like a kind of moaning, or laughter, or the stuttering of an engine. I scowled. Why had I told the king I trusted him?

I wanted it to stop. I thought of crawling backwards, but the lantana had pressed in so tight that I could only move forwards, so I kept going, that noise rising up and up, and washing over me. And then I was standing. In a city. People walked around me, so many people. They wore such bright clothes. Everything was busy, machines snarled and rumbled, and the air smelled of smoke and oil. I was barefoot, but I couldn't hear the dead. The ground was all concrete and stone.

"There you are, Jean," someone said. "You've made it."

I turned towards the voice. It came from a man in a white coat.

"Bartlett?" I asked, but I already knew the answer.

"Who else?" he said. "Before I became a king, I was a man."

I could see the king in him, but here his face was gentle, his teeth the blunt pegs that all of us are born with.

He reached out, and grasped my hand. "Would you like to see my workplace?"

I nodded. "You're a whitecoat," I said.

"I was. I mean, I am. See how confusing this time thing is?"

I looked around me at the motion of the city.

"When is this?"

"It's long ago, at the beginning of the Years of Heat and Sadness. I'm glad that you could make it. Now, time waits for no one. After you."

We walked through the crowd. It was almost as horrible as that lantana. People pushed around us, too close a reminder of that dead carnival, with all these oblivious people, going this way and that. How many lives there were in just this little patch of city. More people than I had known in all my life, crowding, and rushing like the ants and wasps on White Tree's trunk.

Bartlett caught me staring. "I know," he said. "And this is a small city."

Great steel towers crowded out the sky, carriages fumed and filled the roads, and there was hardly a hint of green or blue. A few birds pecked at crumbs, others dug around in rubbish. For all its noise, it was a dead place. Its rhythms had no life to them. I looked up and up, trying to find the sky.

"Yes, so much is going on. We built towers then, as though we wished to smother the sky."

Bartlett led me into a tall grey building. Here, everything was quieter, though there were still so many people. The building was also full of statues.

"This is it, these first carvings," he said, pointing at the stone figures. "Every time I come here, there are more of them. Here, things are fluid."

We walked through a set of metal doors that opened onto a tiny room, then shut behind us.

"It's a lift. It takes us where we need to go, up or down."

"I know what a lift is. My education extends that far, at least," I said, but I still gripped the handrail when we started to fall.

Bartlett patted my hand. "It's all right," he said.

A few moments later, the doors opened, and we walked down a long corridor. We passed rooms filled with cages. I could see clever birds, though these ones didn't look so clever. I could see rooms filled with potted plants and trees and other things.

When we got to the last room, everything was dark. We stopped at the door.

"I don't like it in there," Bartlett said. "I was an artist even then, but my artistry was changing the fundamental nature of things. We were trying to save the world, trying to adjust it. The Years of Heat and Sadness were coming—in fact, they had already begun. We all knew it, but still thought we could avoid catastrophe.

"There were places like this all over the world. Grand, hot-house-in-the-end-of-days endeavours. All of them were follies.

"Problem was, we didn't do enough. All of us were scrambling, which only made things worse. And then there were the

Masters, and the sicknesses that lingered. They changed us, they made us fight in those final wars, but we were too much like the enemy, and too little like our makers. In the end, all it did was hurry the fall."

Bartlett shook his head, and his shoulders began to hunch, his fingers lengthen. He took a step back from me, stumbling.

"It wasn't this quick," he said, his voice thickening, skin falling from his face, teeth falling from his mouth, gums bristling with new edges. "But, time. You know about time now. You had better run."

I knew I had to leave, but I didn't want to. "Hurry, girl," the king said. "The world is onto you. This time is ready to catch you."

Something rattled in the dark room. I felt the scrutiny of a dozen eyes burning red, and one pair that shone golden.

There was nowhere else to go but forward. Behind me, the building lurched. Somewhere, an alarm was blaring.

I ran into the dark, and for once it was a welcome thing. The noise grew muted, the motion of the world lurched to stillness, and the darkness turned from comfort to terror. I thought myself alone, until a sharp finger scratched the base of my neck.

I jumped, hissed at the stinging touch. The dark had fled. I was in the shadow of the lantana tunnel, branches against my neck.

The lantana scratched at me, and I scratched back. By the time I had forced my way through the tunnel, I was bleeding, and the king was standing there: not human, but rather, the inhuman thing he had become.

"Was that real?" I asked.

"What magic isn't a little false? The end of days wasn't so quick, and I don't remember working at a lab in the heart of the city. But it was something like that. We made mistakes, not least of all a furious greed. And those mistakes compounded, and the heat and the storms came, and the world grew ragged and wild."

I thought about the great press of people in the city. "I couldn't live that way."

"It's unfamiliar, that's all. The world was faster then, denser somehow, and more crowded. There's not a day goes by when I don't miss it. Not a single day."

The next night, my dead boy was waiting. I could feel him before I even put my foot to the earth.

"I saved you," he said proudly.

"I'd be lost but for you. How'd you find me?"

"I could feel you there. I hardly even had to look. And there was the Stone Road behind you. It was hard to turn my back on it."

"You mean, you could have walked down it then?"

"Yes, but not if I wanted to save you. Can't see it anymore, but I still have you."

Selfish as it was, I was glad.

It took me a while to adjust back to life among the living. Five months gone. Though it had passed in what felt like no time at all, I had aged. I could see it. I'd had a bit of a growth spurt—my limbs were longer—and my hair, before Nan cut it, had crept down my back. There's not a child that doesn't want to grow up, become an adult all at once. There isn't an adult that doesn't regret it in some way. I was between both, anxious at what I was gaining; fearing what I had lost.

The town was a little wary of me at first. I'd been missing, and now here I was again. But as I settled back into the routine of Casement Rise, the town settled back into me.

I visited Lolly to see if he was all right, and he was the same old Lolly, though he treated me a little differently now. I don't know how much of that time with the shadow thing he remembered. He still refused to talk about it. I sensed a sort of resentment had built up while I was gone, and I knew that I deserved it.

"Where have you been?" Lolly asked me, straight up.

"Went away down the Stone Road," I said.

"Saw Bird a few times. They seemed as lost as I've ever known them." He bent down, picked up a rock, and hurled it at a fencepost. "Did you suffer?"

I shrugged. We'd known perhaps a little too much suffering for our age.

"People thought you were dead."

"Close enough," I said. "Nan said it was something I had to do, to become what she is."

Lolly digested that, nodded. "Like me. I'm to be cut soon, so I can become a man."

I laughed. "You're a boy."

He nodded sombrely. "That's because I'm not yet a man. But I will be."

I knew about the Robsons and their secret ceremonies. I thought it was all pretty silly, and I know Nan did, too. But then, what was it I had gone through, if not something similar, just with more miles involved?

"I'd like to see that," I said.

Lolly shook his head. "Well, you can't. It's for men only."

So we went, and got warpweed and fox fur and a few other things that Nan wanted, and the Robsons' farm had in abundance, and I tried not to think about sneaking over the levee to see my friend come of age.

It was Mum who was the strangest to me when I got back. She'd become distant and sad.

I hardly noticed it at first, but every day it got worse. I'd walk into a room, and she'd walk out of it. We'd be working in the kitchen, and she'd just stop singing, and turn her back to me. It started to hurt.

I was used to her anger and her fierce love, not this chilly sadness.

"Mum," I asked her finally. "What's wrong?"

"Nothing," she said. "It's just been a long year."

"That's not true," I said. Why, even though I'd lost five months of it, I knew that wasn't what she meant. "There's something else. I can see it."

Mum sighed. "Please, don't tell your nan." She sat down at the table, gestured for me to sit next to her. "When you and your nan were away, he came. Your father. He knocked on the door. I was so happy to see him.

"We drank together, and did all the things we used to do. It was a good few nights. Then something changed. He'd say strange things. He never told me why he had come back, and sometimes I would find a golden leaf on the bed or tangled in my hair, and I would get suspicious. Then he would tell a joke, or he would kiss me, and I'd forget my doubts. Didn't stop them from coming back because I think I knew the truth, from the very beginning." She looked at her feet. "It wasn't your father, it was that graceful man. Finally, I confronted him. Terrified that I was wrong; even more terrified that I was right.

"He was sitting where you are now, and I demanded that he tell me the truth. He smiled, and it was my Jack's smile, but it was the graceful man's smile, too. 'Ella,' he said to me, 'I'm all of them. I'm your Jack, and Dr. Millison, and all the others. I give them a place in Furnace, and they take it, and they're all so happy.'"

Mum lowered her gaze. "I won't lie. I begged him to take me, too, but he shook his head. 'Not yet,' he said. 'I have plans for you, but there's a place waiting when the time is right. I've set it aside for you, and only you.' He said that, Jean. He said there's a place waiting, and he kissed me on the lips. It was a good kiss. Then he walked out of here, and I'd never felt so alone."

It made me shiver, the thought of that. The graceful man sleeping in my house.

"I'm sorry, Jean. I just want . . . I would have run away if he had let me. What kind of mother am I?"

I got out of that chair, walked around, and gave her a hug. After a while, she hugged me back.

And things were right between us for a while.

It was meant to be a secret, but the Robsons were a little too proud to be secretive. We all knew where the ceremony was held—you don't have drama without a stage to play it on. There was a hollow in the thicket out past the levee, east of the Robsons' farm. You could find it easily enough if you were small and curious and had time on your hands. I lacked for none of those things, even at my busiest.

I'd snuck into that mannish place several times when it was unattended. I'd never needed nor desired to see what happened there in the past, but Lolly made that different.

A day came when all the Robson men from the towns north and east of Casement Rise gathered.

I waited until the evening. I had work to attend to, no matter my curiosity. When the dark fell, I crept out to the levee, then crossed over it and down into the deepening shadow. The air was cooler than I expected. There was no moon, and the stars spanned the arch of the sky.

There I was, furtive in the dark. The landscape turned unfamiliar, though I had walked it a thousand times.

I approached from the west. That way held more cover, a dense thicket of lantana. It meant I had to travel farther, but I knew no one would see me. I wore my thickest boots to spare me the chatter of the dead, and hoped that no one had noticed me leave the house. My movements were familiar to the dead; they were creatures of routine, tied to the rhythms of the world. I guess we all are, whether we admit it or not.

I worked my way through the brush and bush and burrs. Silent, biting back curses at the stinging touch of nettles. My hands would be swollen the next day, but at the time, nervous and excited, I hardly noticed.

Slowly, I reached the edge of the scrub, and the low sound of men's voices carried through the air.

I had a clear line of sight from my hiding spot. They'd spread out in a circle, Lolly standing fearful and defiant in the centre. Michael, the eldest, raised a knife. As it swung down, a hand, cold enough to sting, clamped over my mouth, and another grasped my shoulder so tight that I would have yelped if I could.

That touch had a wild energy. My hair stood up on end all over my body, and the flesh beneath those fingers rippled.

"If that watch ticked any louder, I'd be deaf." The voice was honey and fire. I tried to pull free, and the hand tightened. It was no human hand, though it had been, once.

"Quiet, girl. Quiet, or I will devour you now."

So I was quiet. There was no defying that voice, no matter how far south of the Red City we were.

The ceremony itself was brief and brutal. I remember little of it. When a Master is behind you, his clear, cold presence absolute, the world beyond falls away as though there is nothing real but him.

Afterwards, the Master took me from that place, the scrub parting in front of him, and closing behind us. That makes it sound precise, but it wasn't. The world moved to accommodate him, the earth shifted, and the air around him shivered, dense with energy, fury and silence bound up together. In the dark, he studied me. I took a fighting stance, but he laughed at that softly: not mocking, but, rather, melancholy.

"So you're the Walker of this town?" he asked.

"Yes, one of them. I'm Jean March. My nan's teaching me," I said, proud that it didn't come out as a squeak. "I know enough not to be frightened of you . . . sir."

He laughed again. I could hear the human in him, faint beneath the beast. "That suggests you know very little, then. Settle your racing heart; I have no harm in me tonight, not for the likes of you."

"Then tell me your name, if you will?"

"You want a little power over me, is that it?"

I shrugged. I just wanted to know his name. I didn't know much of Masters, but I'd read about some of them. Old Dain the exile, Egan the cruel. I wanted to see if he was one of the famous ones.

"That is not how it works for us. The dark that hollows our flesh is far older than words. My name's Dav."

He seemed surprised that he'd told me that. I knew at once that he wasn't an old Master, but a young one. Raised as a Day Boy, then kept in cages beneath the Red City, and made into a monster. That's how they do it, turn flesh to something else, something hungry and strong. His eyes were lit with a hard radiance, almost in the way the graceful man's eyes burned gold. I wanted to tell him that the dark hadn't emptied his flesh entirely, but I knew he would deny it.

"Why are you here?"

"The blood," he said. "The blood draws us. We don't belong here, but we know when these ceremonies come, and, quietly, we officiate."

"Do they know you're here?"

"Some of them, perhaps. This land isn't big enough to hide such things from us, nor are we quiet enough to be completely hidden." He smiled. "This is so far from home."

"You miss the Red City?"

"Yes. More than I expected."

"It's your home," I said.

"Wasn't always my home," Dav said. "I lived in a place not unlike this before that. But, yes." He stared down at me, his eyes shining, then he nodded, and turned his bright gaze back to Casement Rise. There were still some lights burning.

"Your town is well protected. I don't think I could enter it if I wished. It pushes at me, even here."

"Nan . . ."

"I know of her. Perhaps I should say my hellos."

I shook my head furiously; I had no desire for this Master to meet Nan.

Dav laughed. "You think it unwise?"

"What do I know?" I replied.

"You know enough to keep this town safe, even as that monstrosity burns to the west. One day you may even learn to sneak quietly." His face shifted. He became more of the dark, and less of a man. He nodded to the west again. "Be careful, Jean. That Furnace is building. I can feel it. There are challenges ahead. It may be best to run."

There was a crack of branches in the distance. I looked up, and caught a flash of gold, smelled that choking smoke.

Dav spun towards the sound, then moved towards it, putting himself between me and the visitor. "He won't approach. He knows not to challenge me." He didn't sound so confident, though.

"Why don't you approach him?"

Dav laughed. "I'm not that foolish, either, child. You're a brave one, aren't you? I'd have liked you, growing up. I've fought monsters before, but this is a different thing entirely. It is yours, and you are its."

I looked past him. The graceful man was gone.

He seemed to sense it, too, and something else. He sniffed at the air, then glanced to the sky. "You've kept me long enough. I have many miles to travel before dawn, and little time. Good luck, Miss March. You're going to need it," Dav said. And then he was gone, at a lope I knew would not slacken, heading north towards some safe place that he might hide in from the sun. How precarious life was, even for monsters.

Nan was waiting up for me when I got home. "You were lucky," she said.

I tried at innocence. "What?"

"That you weren't found out by the Robsons, and that whatever found you there wasn't hungry. Once I thought you too timid, now I'm worried that you're too damn reckless. You're grounded for a week."

My dead boy loved the story of the Master, and Lolly's ceremony. I swore him to secrecy.

"Who am I going to tell down here?"

The next time I saw Lolly, he was pale, his wrist bandaged.

"Did you see it?" he asked.

"Not gonna say." Now that he was initiated in all the secrets of manhood, he seemed different. Even if he looked like the same old Lolly, I knew how secrets could change a person—I had my share of them. He held himself more assuredly, and looked at me a bit more steadily.

"Good," he said.

"Good that I didn't, or good that I did?"

"Just, good."

I handed Lolly the book I'd brought him. He looked at it as though it were a childish thing. "Thanks. I'll read it when I have time," he said. He looked so discomfited by my presence that I decided it was better to get out of there.

The funny thing was that, after that, he seemed to grow a foot in about a week. His voice deepened, and his face took on the shadow of a beard. Maybe ceremonies can shape you. Maybe the words he'd heard reminded him that he had to grow up. I didn't appreciate it. With Lolly's manhood, a silence grew between us, and our friendship waned.

A few days later, I walked up the levee wall. Something was itching in me, a sense that I had to get up there, and quick, and I found myself facing west.

The dirt road that led to Furnace stretched that way, visible until it reached the low hills and the scrub. I stared along it, and I realized that someone was walking the path. I squinted. It looked like Jacob.

I was horrified. I thought of his pony May, and how sad she would be. Who'd look after her? Who'd teach me how to hit things? We could replace a doctor, but Jacob was indispensable.

I was determined to do something to stop it, if I could.

I could be there in an instant if I took the Long Between. It was like falling into a cave so dark that I was I drowning in shadow. If I turned east, there was light and fire, but the west engulfed me. I fled that space at once.

I had no option but to use my feet on real earth.

I looked behind me to see who might be watching. No one, though people had the habit of suddenly appearing and paying me no mind, only for whatever they witnessed to get back to Nan in great detail. I'd endured so many punishments for things I'd done when I thought no one was watching. I gave the town another glance. I could see all the way to White Tree—now, that was something that watched. But White Tree was resolute in her silence. I couldn't imagine her ever slipping secrets to Nan.

I stepped down the levee bank, careful not to fall. When I reached the bottom, with the road to Furnace laid out ahead, I hesitated. Jacob was farther away than I'd thought.

I could catch him, though, if I ran.

I sprinted along that road, which I had been told never to set foot on. It wasn't so bad.

Except I started to vomit.

I stopped. I'd made quite a mess.

"Peculiar," I said.

"And how is that peculiar?" came a voice.

I looked up. The graceful man bowed. There was something calmer about him, almost gentle.

"This road's not for you, Miss Jean. How is it peculiar?"

"I can't remember ever vomiting so."

"Oh, Miss Jean, you were a vomiting child, and that's a fact."

"And how do you know that?"

"Look at me, Miss Jean," the graceful man said. "Am I not made of leaves, and earth, and assorted critters? It's not only the dead that can wander. I'm a little bit past, a little bit future. I've eyes all over the place. You, who chats with Masters like they're old friends, ought to know that! Why, once there was a chair I liked to sit in, in a tidy little kitchen."

"You!" I said.

"Who else? I was there until your nan talked me away. That woman is a conundrum, always getting between us. She made me a promise, though."

"What sort of promise?"

"That she wouldn't always stop me. Gave me a few things, too."

What things? I shook my head. This wasn't what I needed now. "I have to catch up with Jacob. He needs to come back," I said. "But I can't, if I'm sick."

"That's the problem right there. If you keep on this road, you'll keep getting sicker. This way is closed to you, Miss Jean, and not just because I say it is. Look at how you're feeling: Isn't it an unpleasant way to feel? You should be home."

I put my hands on my hips. "But Jacob can walk the road."

"The road is made for him. It's made for most everybody, but not for you. Not yet."

"And if I were to take another step?"

"I wouldn't recommend it, not one little bit."

So I took a step, and one after that. I vomited again.

"Oh, you really are a silly child, Miss Jean." The graceful man rubbed at my face with a handkerchief.

"I wouldn't touch her." I turned my head to see the Huskling King, then back to the graceful man, who grimaced at him.

"Too late for that," the graceful man said. "It's been too late, since the day she was born." The graceful man laid a hand on my shoulder, then grunted. Bird had flown through his chest. Leaves burst this way and that.

"Oh, this is a curious bunch of allies," the graceful man said.

"I'll tear you from limb to limb," the king said.

The graceful man stepped away from me. He moved with all the precision of music and water.

"I believe you would all find that hard."

Bird had settled on my shoulder. They gave a loud hiss.

The graceful man smiled. "What could you tear apart that would scare me, when I can tear myself apart so much better?"

There was an awful ripping noise. The graceful man jolted, reduced himself to a pile of leaves and bugs blown on the wind.

The Huskling King frowned. "Now, that is a clever trick."

"I'm feeling terribly poorly," I said.

"Of course you are," the king said. He nodded west, towards Furnace. "That place will sicken you. Surely your nan has told you that?"

"She told me," I said. "Many times."

"Oh, you were never one for listening, were you?"

I shook my head. "I listen all right, but that doesn't mean I obey."

"Some instructions are for your own good, you know."

The king gripped my arm. His fingers were rough and warm. "You concern me, Jean."

"I needed to talk to him," I said, and nodded at Jacob, walking towards the horizon.

"What would he tell you? That Furnace calls and promises? That it is all the sweet things in the earth, and none of the sour? That it's an itch that you can't scratch except by walking that way, walking until you go over the hills, and arrive?"

"Yes," I said. "Yes! But what *is* it?"

"The sort of thing that none of us can know. Except that whatever the graceful man offers is a lie. Promises like that are emptier than the mouth that offers them."

I threw up again.

"You must turn around, now. Turn around for your nan, and your cruel mother, and for me."

I wiped my mouth. It tasted sour. I looked to the west, and the figure receding in that direction. I'd never catch him. I could hardly stand. It made me angry as sin, but I turned towards the levee. I walked back up it, Bird on my shoulder, the king watching after me.

When I reached the top, Alice was standing there. "Who were you talking to?"

"What?"

"I saw you shouting, but no one else was there."

"I was talking to the graceful man, and the Huskling King," I said.

Alice shook her head. "No, you were talking to no one."

"How would you know?" I retorted.

I looked at Bird for support, but they were gone. I leant over the levee, and vomited again.

"You are disgusting," Alice said.

I couldn't help but laugh. "Yes, I am," I said.

Alice shook her head. I watched the west a while, then realised that Alice was still there, standing beside me.

"What do you feel?" I asked.

"What do you mean?"

"The west. Furnace. It makes you feel something, doesn't it?"

Alice rubbed her chin. I noticed she had a smudge of flour across her cheek, and one of her knuckles was bleeding. I could suddenly smell her sweat, and it wasn't a bad thing. She held a dry crust of bread in her other hand.

"It makes me feel sad," she said. "I can't explain it otherwise. I think of home—not this place, but Somerton, when we had the bakery, and Da was still alive, and Mum hadn't . . . What does it make *you* feel?"

"Nothing," I said. "It feels like nothing."

I wanted to tell her how I had a mother I didn't understand, and that I didn't remember her being any other way. But I couldn't, same as I couldn't walk that dirt trail west, or speak of the gold coin to anyone but my dead boy. The words stopped in my throat. How could I say anything about mothers when I had wished Alice's mother away?

I must have stared at Furnace for a while because when I looked up, Alice was gone. I wondered if she'd ever been there at all, until I saw the bread crust at my feet, already covered in ants.

Nan was waiting for me when I got home. She had never looked so furious.

"Where were you?"

We both knew that she knew where I'd been. I could have burnt away beneath that gaze.

"What foolishness infected you? What madness?"

"I saw Jacob," I said.

"No," Nan said. "No."

"I'm certain it was."

She clenched her hands. I could see her anger, and her sadness, the way it made her body shake. "Furnace calls all in the end," she said, taking a moment to breathe deep and slow, and then she stroked my cheek. "Please understand that I do not make up these rules. I say no for a reason. I do my best to keep you safe, and you walk into a nest of storms and knives as though it were a garden, plucking at this and that, all the while skirting the edges of a terrible death."

"I felt sick," I said.

"Yes, it will make you sick. I walked that way once, and it nearly killed me."

"Did you see the graceful man, when you went?"

"I saw nothing but the hard yellow earth of the road, and the dark streaks of my vomit. I crawled back here. I nearly died. You were a babe, and I feared I'd be leaving you to the mad cruelty of the world. But I didn't die. I survived, and oh, how the dead crowed; they had never seen me brought so damn low. And I swore I would never let you walk that way."

"But I did, and I'm all right," I said, just as I fell on the floor. Even my body was anxious to prove me wrong.

When I next woke, I was in bed. Bird was sitting by the window, watching first with one red eye, then the other.

"I've thought about why Nan went that way," I said. "Thought about the timing of it."

"And?" Bird said.

"And maybe she must have gone after my Da, but she couldn't get him."

"Some people can't be saved," Bird said. "But some can. I saved you!"

"You and the king."

The clever bird coughed. "Let's not speak of it again," they said.

It was dark outside. I thought about the graceful man, and that chair that had horrified me so as a child. What had Nan said to him? What had she promised? Those burning rose bushes, those men who'd left for Furnace? Maybe I wasn't the only one who'd sent people that way.

"You want to come in?" I asked.

Bird didn't say no. They landed on the foot of my bed.

"Tell me a story," I said.

"A story. A story." They preened their feathers for a bit, and then they started on one about a mouse who was a tailor—don't ask me how—and a giant who was cruel, and their inevitable confrontation, and that was how I fell asleep.

Some days don't end so badly, no matter how they start. And the very next day, I was walking from the levee wall, and there was Jacob coming the other way. I ran to him, and hugged him. Nan wasn't far behind.

"Miss Jean, Nancy," he said, extricating himself. "What's all this about?"

"Never you mind, Jacob," I said. "Never you mind."

Not much later, a Threnodist named Sal arrived in town.

She stayed in our guest room, though there were plenty of others willing to lodge her. Everyone was keen to host such a visitor. News of world, and of the Red City in particular, was welcome. But just like the auditors Rob and Sarah, she came to us directly. She knew whom she needed to see.

"Jim sent me," she said. "Said there would be no better lodgings."

"Did he, now?" Nan said, looking Sal up and down. "You are young for a Threnodist."

"I'm seasoned enough," Sal said, though her face found a little colour.

"Yes. You've made it this far south; that says something. Are you here to sing away our grief?"

Sal shook her head. "I'm not here to sing a Threnody for anyone. No one called me. That takes a certain kind of grief. Even if they had, this town is too full of sadness; it has permeated everything. The grief's beyond my skill."

Nan looked towards the west. "As long as Furnace burns, it won't change."

"Oh, I can feel that! I was warned, but I'd not quite expected this. It's a desperate thing. If I could, I would resolve it for you, but I fear it would swallow me whole. No, I'm here to see the art."

"The Husklings'?"

"Yes, the Husklings'."

"They are quite dangerous. I don't know if I can be a party to such a request."

Sal laughed. "I've charmed my way past cold children and hunters. I've huddled in the mud and in the sharp scrub, hidden from predators, while the winds blew ice down from the mountains. You'd deny me a guide?"

"That's the risk of mere tourism. Besides, it sounds like you don't need one," Nan said. "You've song and trickery. What else do you require?"

Sal looked at Nan, and Nan looked back. They stayed that way, no word between them, until I could stand it no longer.

"I'll take you," I said.

Nan scowled at me, then shrugged. "Yes, Jean can take you. Why not?"

"You know the way?" Sal looked at me, and I could see surprise there. I suppose in other places they didn't let children walk with monsters.

Nan nodded. "She knows the Husklings well; you probably won't be eaten. But please don't fill my granddaughter's head with stories. She has enough as it is."

"That's what stories are for," Sal said. "Your head would be empty otherwise, and what would you think but a great, silent nothing? And then you'd hear nothing because your head would have sunk in on itself." She tapped my skull softly, and I laughed.

"It's no laughing matter," Sal said. "I've seen it. It is horrifying, all the terror that is silence."

"We enjoy our silence," snapped Nan—Nan, who sang almost as much as breathing.

Dinner was interesting.

I took Sal to the Huskling hall the following day.

"Who's that girl watching you?" Sal said.

I looked back, and groaned. "It's Alice. She beat me up once." "Why?"

"She called me a nastiness, and I hit her," I said.

"You are children! What do you know of nastiness?"

"Enough," I said, though I wondered what *she* knew of children.

I waved at Alice, she waved back.

"We don't hate each other anymore," I said. "I think she's even stranger than me now."

Bird chose that moment to fly onto my shoulder. Sal looked at me curiously. "She must be a very peculiar little girl."

"Hello, Threnodist," Bird said.

"Hello, bird," Sal said.

Bird looked at her. "How did you know my name?"

"What else is one to call a bird, particularly one as clever as you are?"

Bird preened their feathers, "I like this one," they said to me.

We reached the Huskling hall by midmorning. I'd taken her by a route that steered clear of the art because it didn't feel right to show her that without their blessing.

The Husklings were sleepy, which is how you want them to be when meeting someone new. But they woke up quick.

"Who's this? Who's this? Have you brought us dinner, child?"

"I've done nothing of the sort. This is a Threnodist. She came to see your art."

"Ah," the king said. "Then she must sing for it."

Sal gave that a moment's thought. "That is a fair price," she said. "But I have no song for here."

The king walked towards her, and with a hesitation I had never seen from him, he touched her arm gently. "What if we tell you our story? What if we tell you that, and you sing?" His dark eyes searched her face. "Do you think you could do that?"

"Yes. If you give me the song, I will sing it. I'll need to see the art first."

The king nodded. "Yes, it is part of us. You will need to see it to understand. Take her there, girl. She does not need our talk to muddy it. The art speaks for itself."

So I took her to the art. We walked around it for a while in silent contemplation, two living figures amongst all that stone.

"What do you think?" I asked.

Sal touched the nearest statue. "Look at this," she said. "It almost has a pulse." She circled the grove, and shouted at me excitedly when she came upon a sculpture of an old woman. Bird had once told me it was a Threnodist; now I had confirmation.

"This is Beth. Mistress Beth. She was my teacher." Sal's breath caught in her throat. "I don't think she even knew that they did this. She would have been delighted!"

The sculpture had the sternness of a grandmother about her.

Sal must have caught me frowning at it. "Yes, she always seemed so grim. But look at her eyes, at the lines around them. She watched the world with such generosity. Oh, I miss her. I'd forgotten her face, and here it is." I realized that she was crying. "The world is so cruel, Jean. It strips away memory, and you're lucky to be left with stone."

"I don't forget things," I said. "I close my eyes, and I'm there. I can walk through my memories."

It was only partly a boast.

"Oh, I think that may be even crueller," Sal said. "I'm not sure whether to envy or pity you."

"It is what it is," I said.

In the distance, there was a rising hooting call.

"We better go see the king," I said.

I sat on a stool in the airy Huskling hall as they talked to Sal, one by one. It took all day, and some of the night. They spoke to her, and led her to the stations of their art. Of course they wanted to talk of it—despite what the king had said about muddying the intent—and at great length. There were boasts and grumbles and sadnesses, things I'd never expected.

At last, long into the night, Sal nodded. "I think I have the measure of it," she said.

Nan came in as she was getting ready to sing.

"Where have you been, girl? What's going on?"

For once it was me waving her to silence. Nan nodded, and stood next to me.

Sal sang.

I had never heard anything like it in my life. It was now clear how she could charm monsters and cold children.

Her voice started small, but it grew, slow and steady. She sang in a tongue I didn't recognise, beautiful and sonorous. I looked at Nan.

"It's the Husklings' language. I know the barest smattering of it, but they keep it secret. How does she know it? How is that possible?" Nan marvelled.

The song lasted no more than a few minutes, but it seemed to echo on. I felt it every time I visited the Husklings thereafter.

They were silent for a long while after she had finished, and then they hooted, and cheered. I looked at Sal, and for the first time, I saw her as she was: small, frail, and old before her time. From that moment, I loved her, the first person I had ever loved who wasn't family.

"Hurry, girl," Nan said. "See to her, before she falls."

She didn't fall, though she leant heavily on my shoulder. But I'd fallen for her.

Such is the way of Threnodists.

We took Sal home, almost had to carry her. I had never seen anyone so weary.

"Don't worry about me," she said. "It's like this every time."

I made her tea, and she sipped it slowly.

"You didn't come to see the Husklings' art, did you?"

"Oh, I came for that."

"Not just that. You came to sing for them. As much as you might deny it, that's what you did."

"That's true." She smiled at me, a smile that seemed to shine through me. "I lied when I said I wasn't called here. The Husklings called me, even if they didn't realise it. So much grief, so much sadness."

"But they're monsters, mostly."

"Who made them, Jean? Who made all of this?"

"We did," I said repeating the first verse of the Years of Heat and Sadness. "This is our construction. This is the monument of our falling. These are our miseries. We let this happen."

Sal patted my hand. "Those are cruel lines, but we need to remember. We made all of this, in our ignorance and pride. We were capable of so much, and we tore it down. We can never forget that. These monsters are ours, and we gave them art and misery. They deserve a song, at the very least." The Threnodist studied me more closely. "You're a clever child. A little too clever. I don't holiday. I travel when I am called. Those who summon me may not even know that they are calling. Not every song I sing is meant for human ears. Not every call goes answered." She gestured west.

"You recognise Furnace's call?" Nan asked. I hadn't even heard her come into the room.

"I recognise its feeling. It is like the thing, the song, that calls me. Once I've submitted to my song's call, I cannot resist it. I'm somewhat inoculated to Furnace, but it is persuasive and pervasive, nonetheless."

Nan considered this. "Perhaps there are techniques we could glean from you."

Sal shook her head. "I'm bound by oaths. The things I know, the things I have opened myself up to, they cannot be shared. You cannot turn this town into a community of Threnodists. It would not be forgiven."

Nan's lips thinned. "How punitive can singers be?"

"My order is the most unforgiving. They would destroy Casement Rise."

"It's dying already."

"Yes, but you could always get up, and leave. Towns die all the time. Even before the Years of Heat and Sadness."

"You don't understand towns at all, then."

Sal laughed. "I understand them all too well, Nancy. I have travelled the length and breadth of this land. I have sung for Masters and children. I know towns."

Nan said nothing. She walked to the kitchen. I could hear her pouring tea, but she didn't come back.

Sal looked at me. "You, I could train," she said. "They allow me an apprentice. Your memory, that would be a boon in this work, believe me. And you'd be free of this place. Your nan's too accustomed to death, too tangled in its consequence. She has forgotten that there are other things. Death comes, but there's living beforehand, if you take it."

Nan was standing at the door, her tea in her hand, and I thought that she might throw it at Sal.

"Enough of your poison," she said. "Leave her be while your song's still loud in her head. Let the enchantment die a little before you garnish it."

Sal nodded. "I'm garnishing nothing. I'm a guest in your house; I'll respect your wishes. I have sung enough today."

A boy died somewhere far away, drowned in a distant sea. Sal woke calling his name. Nan and I were almost ready to leave for the levee, but I hesitated when I heard her cries.

"No," Nan said, "this is her burden. You can't make it any lighter. There is only one place that can, and it is calling her."

Still, I hesitated.

"She'll be gone by the time we come back. Leave her some tea in the pot, and set out her breakfast; that's something concrete we can do."

Nan was right: She was gone by the time we returned. She didn't even leave a note to me, just a bag of coffee, which Nan appreciated greatly.

Lolly saw her go. "She was almost running," he said, scratching at his stubble. "Never seen anything like it. She barely saw me."

"You've seen something like it," I said.

He seemed to think about it, then nodded. "Yes. My father, when he gave in to Furnace's call. He looked a bit like that. It was a terrible thing to see. Every day I feel that call, and the feeling grows a little stronger. Sometimes a little weaker, but it always comes back. I think I understand it."

"Don't you dare give in to it," I said.

Lolly laughed. "Never. You'd beat me up if I did."

I didn't beat him, then; I hugged him. And we talked of other things that were not Furnace.

Jim arrived not long after that. A couple of weeks before my birthday.

None of the other trading parties came with him. There was only his crew, and they kept to themselves.

Nan grumbled about it.

"Furnace scares folk," Jim said. "We feel it, all of us. The last time we came down here, Terry Barley lost three of his men a mile out of town. I lost one of my own. The roads are poor enough without that threat."

"What are we going to do?" Nan said. "We need you."

"I'm here," Jim said. "This time, but I can't promise that I'll be back. I have a responsibility to my crew."

"What about to me?" Nan demanded.

"Yes, well. I do have a suggestion for that."

"No," Nan said. "We can't go with you. I have responsibilities, too."

"For how long?" Jim asked. "This town's dying, Nancy. You tell me that every time I visit. Furnace is bleeding it dry. How long until everyone is gone, and it's just you and Jean walking the levee, guarding nothing?"

"It won't come to that."

"Really?"

Nan glared at him. "Enough. I won't leave with you."

"What about Jean? I thought that Threnodist might have talked some sense into you."

"So that was your idea? Trying to take away my grandchild?"

"Yes. Trying to keep her safe."

"You think the roads are safe?"

"Nowhere is safe, but she may have had a chance that way. You're the one who stole five months of her life."

Nan's face grew white. "Don't you throw my words back at me. Don't you dare."

Jim turned to me. "Jean, I'm sorry. You can come with me if you like."

I shook my head. Jim nodded. "I've tried. That's all I can do."

"Trying would be coming back, not giving up." Nan retorted.

"Ten years I've been coming," Jim said. "Ten years of this conversation. And I've kept having it because I love you. But these are my limits. I have my crew to think of. They're family as well, and I can't keep them safe anymore. The call is building. Surely you can feel it."

"It's all I feel," Nan said.

"Then—"

"No," Nan said. "I won't see you to the door. Jean, take him out."

I led Jim outside. On the verandah, he seemed to shrink, and I realised that he was crying. I stood there, not sure what to do.

"If you would be so kind as to give me a hug, Jean," he said.

He smelled of dust and coffee and cigarettes, and I wondered if I would ever hug him again. When he pulled away, he looked at me, wiping his eyes. He gestured at a package sitting on a chair, wrapped in red paper.

"That's for your birthday," he said. "How is your watch?"

"It's good," I said. "It's gotten me out of some scrapes. It stopped when we were in the Mumbling City, but it started again."

Jim gave that some serious thought. "Nothing works there. I'd tell you to be careful, but you're not a foolish child. Jean, if you ever need me, truly and deeply, you know to call my name.

I'll come to you and yours. I'd tell you to tell Nan that I love her, but she knows it. It'd only get you in trouble. Be careful, Jean. Please be careful."

He hugged me, one more time.

The next morning, he and his crew were gone.

After Jim left, Nan grew quieter and grimmer.

She visited the Huskling King alone for various items: a few raw stones, some weeds that grew only on Huskling land.

She walked to Bird's tree several times. She even started talking to White Tree again.

One day, I decided to visit the Huskling King because I'd hardly seen him since the Threnodist came. When I reached the grove, I heard an argument. I knew the voices: Nan and the king.

By the time I reached the hall, both were shouting so loudly I could hardly make out the words. Nan was holding her bone needle in her hand, and it was shaking.

I didn't announce my presence, but they turned, and stared at me.

"Jean," the king said. His eyes had such a sorrowful look about them.

"Go," Nan said. "Go home."

I nodded, but as I retreated to the grove, I heard him say to her, "You don't have to do this. There are other ways. Think of your daughter, and of Jean."

"My mind's on nothing else," Nan snapped. Then they were out of earshot, except as a background mumble of aggression.

Bird had been sitting on my shoulder the whole time.

"What's she doing?" I asked them.

"Protecting you," Bird said, as though it was obvious, as though it was unwise.

"She already does."

"Not in this way. This way is dangerous."

"We could leave."

"Jean, I think if you left, your graceful man would follow you. You can't leave until this is settled."

"What else can I do?"

"I don't know. But I think what your nan has planned is wrong."

I shook my head at that. Nan was never wrong, not when it mattered. Bird must have sensed my frustration because they took to the air, flew to a nearby tree, and watched me from it.

I considered throwing a stone at them, but I didn't. I wasn't cruel: The cruel one was west of here, plucking at the dead, calling the living, waiting to come and kill me.

Maybe I could have ended it, demanded that Nan stop, that this challenge was mine to face.

The truth was that I was twelve, and I was frightened, so I let it happen. It wasn't me that should have known better.

The week before my birthday, Nan showed me the levee in more detail than she ever had. She ran me through every seam and bound-together-edge of the town.

"Study this," she'd say. "Remember it."

Because it was me, because I didn't have any choice, I remembered it all.

The dead, too, were unsettled. They mumbled and moaned, and I couldn't find my dead boy at night. It was as if he had gone away.

Nan stopped going into town after each circuit, and ignored the requests of the townsfolk. She took me home, and kept tying knots, singing her low mumbling song beneath her breath, where you could chase the words, but never quite make them out. Her fingers twisting, looping the cord, knotting it tight.

I tried to help Nan, but other than my education, and a few curt words to stop this or that, she had very little to do with me. I wished that Jim was there. Several times I rubbed that watch, and thought of calling him, but I didn't do it with any fervour. I suspected that Nan would not appreciate the visit, and certainly not if I called him, rather than him travelling here on his own inclination.

I needed cheering up. Every book I owned, I had read at least ten times, and I knew the words before I even looked at them. There was usually some comfort in the act of reading, but none of my books were inviting.

I went to find Mum. She was working on a bunch of pots, and I could see that she had a sore head.

"What do you want?"

"I need something to do." I picked up a piece of clay.

"Not here, you don't," she said. "Go for a swim."

I went down to the creek, but it was soupy green in the still heat of the summer. The playground was thick with children, but none of them looked interesting. I thought of visiting Lolly, but the awkwardness between us was growing unpleasant. I needed someone to come with me.

Alice was working in the bakery, but she came over to me when I entered.

"Are you nearly finished?" I asked.

Alice looked over at Rachael.

"Go, and do something," Rachael said. "I've nothing for you here. Apply yourself to mischief. Just not too much, either of you!"

Apparently, I wasn't the only one getting on people's nerves.

"You must be bored," Alice said, "to find me."

I nodded. "I'm bored, and it's hot, and the creek is green."

"What are we going to do, then?"

Both of us were too old for toys.

"We could visit Lolly."

Alice scrunched up her face. "Lolly Robson?"

"He's all right."

She shook her head. "He comes in here all haughty, and stomping. All those Robson boys are trouble."

"He's a good one," I said. Even though I'd had a hand in making him a little less so.

Alice sniffed at me, but she still followed as I led her up the levee.

Bird flew in from the east, and found my shoulder. They peered at Alice.

"You've met Bird, haven't you?"

Alice shook her head.

"Bird, this is Alice."

"Yes," Bird said. "I know her."

Alice reddened. "Oh, you were the bird I threw that stone at?"

"I am a forgiving creature," Bird said. "Where are you two going?"

"Off to see Lolly."

"That's good. I'd thought you might be visiting the Huskling King."

201

"So it's true!" Alice exclaimed. "You know him."

"I'm not one for lies," I snapped. "He's a teacher, all right, as well as a tyrant and an artist. Now, we best go down the levee, don't you think? You've gotta be careful, Alice," I said. "One wrong step, and you could bring all manner of awfulness upon the town."

"And what do you mean by that?"

"You know," I said. "You fled your town, remember?"

I regretted the words the moment they left my mouth. Alice's eyes turned cold.

But she didn't say anything after that, and she stepped so carefully that we virtually crawled down the levee, Alice gasping if she so much as disturbed a clod of dirt. I wanted to be angry at her, but, if I'd been as careful as she was being, then Mrs. Card would still be alive. That didn't stop me from sighing dramatically at each slow step, though.

"Sorry," Alice said when we reached the foot of the levee and the unmarked land. "Sorry."

"Think nothing of it," I said, even if I didn't sound so casual.

We walked through to the Robsons' place. Lolly was sitting under a tree, reading a book that I'd lent him an age ago.

"Jean," he said. "Alice. Welcome to our farm."

"You still reading that book?" I asked.

Lolly nodded. "You know I'm a slow reader," he said. "Who'd have thought animals could talk and build boats and the like." He looked at Bird. "Apologies, Bird, for thinking you were so hopeless."

"You're forgiven." Bird really was in a forgiving mood.

Lolly nodded, and maybe remembered that he was now a man. "How may I help you?" he asked.

"You can bloody well help us by keeping us company," I said.

Alice snorted. "What she means is that we're bored, and we want someone to play with."

"Torment, more like," Lolly said, and Bird surprised us all by laughing.

We stood awkwardly around the tree. Lolly ran inside to put away the book. I supposed I wouldn't see it again.

When he came back, there was some more awkward standing, as though none of us knew how to have fun, which was probably true.

"We could go swimming," Lolly said.

"Creek's green," we both said. Lolly nodded as though that were the grimmest news.

"There's a fort, not much more than a shed, really, on the northern edge of the farm," he said. "We could walk there, and have a look at it."

"Sounds good," I said.

Lolly ran inside. Ten minutes later, he was back with a bag of food: a few apples, some sandwiches.

"Come on, then," he said, taking us north.

I looked back at their place.

"How do you keep your house safe, outside the levee?" I asked him.

"Mostly that's Mum's work, but she says your nan's reputation does most of the work. We've had some absolute horrors come through, but the house has never been so much as touched. Not until . . ." he looked at me, and I looked away.

"We've a hill to climb. It's the least scrubby way. Watch for shit when you're walking," he said. "Cows love this hill."

The hill was steep, keeping us silent and sweating for most of the climb. Bird flew straight up to the top of the hill, and waited for us. I think all of us wished for wings right then and there. My limbs were aching by the time we reached the summit, but the view was glorious, no matter which way you looked: back down towards the town, or the plains and hills to the north. The day was hot, but the air was clear. Everything looked so real that despite the distance, you might think you could reach down, and pluck a gum tree from the earth.

Lolly stood next to me, and we smiled at each other. For the first time in a long time, I felt that maybe we were friends again.

He frowned. "There's someone in the fort."

"I can't see anything," I said.

"There's a shape there, a shadow by the window, and it just moved."

"Maybe we should go home," Alice said.

Lolly shook his head. "I need to see who it is. I've responsi-bilities." He took a step, then stopped. "Jean, you don't suppose Bird could check for us?"

I looked at Bird. They ruffled their feathers, flexed their wings.

"I can look," they said, "though my eyes are better than any of yours, and I can't see any man. Just an old, empty fort."

"Please check for us," Lolly said.

Bird leapt from my shoulder, and dived down the hill. We followed at a distance. They circled the fort three times, getting a little closer with each circuit, then they darted in.

We waited.

Nothing.

"I don't like this." Lolly said.

I was already running.

I was nearly at the fort when the graceful man walked out of it, holding Bird by the legs like he was going to cook them for dinner.

"This your bird I've caught?" he asked.

At first I thought Bird was dead, then they struggled in his grip. He gave them a shake, so vicious that it took the breath from me.

"Be still, Bird," I shouted.

Bird stilled, whether from that brutal shaking or my demands, I couldn't tell.

"Come inside," the graceful man said.

All of us hesitated.

"You don't have to," I said to the others.

Alice shivered. "It's like he isn't there, and then he is," she said to me.

"Oh, I'm here all right," the graceful man said. "And I want you all inside, or I slit this bird's throat, and see what makes it talk."

I looked at the others, and they looked at me, and I led them into the fort.

Lolly gasped. The single room within had a table and chairs, and was laid out with food. So much of it! I'd never seen such a feast.

"I thought we all could eat," the graceful man said.

"I'm not hungry," I said.

He opened his toothy mouth wide, then closed it with a crack. "I am. So hungry. I could die." He picked up a chicken leg, started to gnaw at it.

"What do you want?" I asked.

"Just to talk," he said.

I glanced back at the door.

"Don't worry, there won't be any interruptions. I set a fire on the edge of Huskling territory. The king's busy with that, and your nan . . . well, the dead are shivering in their darkness. I went fishing today. A very nice catch. It will keep my Furnace burning."

I studied that table closely, and all at once—whether through my skill, or his indifference—I could see that the table was laid not with food, but the shadows of the dead.

Lolly reached for something on the table, and I slapped his hand.

"Don't," I whispered. "You don't want to eat any of this."

Lolly nodded. The graceful man looked terribly disappointed.

"Always see too much, don't you, Jean?" he said. "Fine. You don't have to eat anything."

"You said you wanted to talk. What if I don't want to?"

"Nothing much I can do about that, except exert force where I can." He gave Bird a little shake. "This bird, on the other hand . . . this I can kill."

"Talk, then."

"You and I have been separated too long," he said. "We need to be together. But I'm frightened."

That threw me. I couldn't imagine him frightened. "Frightened of what?"

"Victory. What if I kill you, and you cease to be? Where does that leave me?"

"Why would you kill me?"

"Because that is what I do. What I'm made for. I woke with your name on my lips, and your death as my inclination, and my terror. Just because I want something doesn't mean I'll like the outcome."

He reached out, and touched my face. "You feel it, don't you?"

Truth was, all I felt was dread.

"Ah, you're terrified."

"Am not." I reached into my pocket, and pulled out the silver knife.

"That old thing? Knives are the last resort of the fearful, hasn't your mother taught you that?"

I slashed out, and the graceful man split, became leaves. A man-sized pile of them. They started to quiver, then rose, and danced. They filled the room, spinning and rushing like a twister.

"Violence begets violence." The graceful man's voice entered my ear.

The whirling leaves snatched at me. Their edges cut. It took me back to the first time I had been smothered by spinning wings and claws.

I grabbed Bird from the ground, put them in my shirt, and reached for Alice and Lolly. The leaves kept spinning, scratching, and slicing, trying to force their way into my mouth. I tasted blood. They were going to suffocate us, or cut us to death.

"Hold my hand, now," I said, spitting out leaves.

They did, both of them. Lolly's grip was terribly tight, Alice's less certain, but they held me.

I closed my eyes, and found the quiet place, the Long Between, and I took them with me.

The fort fell away, becoming something else, something less concrete. Flame and shadow. I was standing with Lolly and Alice in a landscape that flexed around us like it didn't know what distance was. I took a step, then another, moving back towards the hill. To the west, something that wasn't the graceful man noticed me. I pretended that I didn't notice it.

It was hard work, with the others, but I dragged them through that space until I couldn't. Finally, I dropped to my knees, coughing out leaves.

We were back on the hill. The Huskling King would have been so proud. I smiled, and wiped at my face, smearing blood across my cheek.

In the valley below, the fort creaked, groaned, and fell into itself. A great gout of leaves spiralled and spouted into the air. It swung south towards us, then west, then tumbled into nothingness.

"Look at that," I said. I was filled with the giddiness of the Long Between, instead of its terror. Bird moved in my shirt. Alice was crying.

Lolly was on his back, eyes vacant.

Still as death.

"Lolly?"

Nothing.

I crawled next to him. His mouth was full of leaves, his nose stuffed with them. I yanked out what I could, fishing in his mouth with my fingers, until everything was clear, then put my ear next to his mouth.

"He's breathing," I said to Alice. "But he's not waking."

Lolly looked out at the world with blank eyes. I'd failed him again.

"I don't know what to do."

Alice frowned. "I do," she said.

I stepped away from him, and Alice crouched down, brushed Lolly's face with her hands, and kissed him square on the lips.

His eyes sprang open, and he sat up all at once. "My mouth tastes like leaves!" Lolly cried, though he touched his lips as though they tasted sweeter than that.

I watched with my arms folded.

Lolly looked at Alice. His face was red, and I felt a heat on my own.

"Where did you learn to do that?" I asked her.

"I suppose we don't read the same books. Kisses solve everything, don't they?"

I shook my head. I hadn't saved Lolly with a kiss; I'd pulled monsters from his chest. I looked to him to back me up, but he was staring at Alice, rubbing the fingers that had touched his lips.

Alice had saved him where I couldn't, and her solution had been so simple. He regarded her as if she had invented toast. No matter that I'd sent the graceful man running, sort of.

It was a victory that felt like a defeat, which was hardly a victory at all.

"We'd better get home," Lolly said, and we hurried back to the Robsons' house. Lolly asked Alice questions all the way, questions he had never asked me. I gave up listening to the answers.

I told Nan everything, except about that kiss. Nan listened closely, tying knots as she did. When I was finished, she smiled, a thin, terrifying smile.

"This is good," she said. "He's scared. He doesn't know what's coming."

"What's coming?" I asked Nan. She patted my arm, before getting back to tying her knots in the cord.

"An ending," she said.

My birthday was five days away.

On my thirteenth birthday, the graceful man came to visit, and he was invited. Summoned. By me, or my nan, or the golden coin, I couldn't be sure.

There was no party.

That morning we did the circuit, another close inspection, sipping coffee from a thermos as we went. The stones thrummed their steady beat, everything holding, not a single intruder. Nan squeezed my hand, studied me almost as closely as the levee.

The old part of me ached. I felt its memories, the hints of warning, but I couldn't make sense of them.

"Remember this," Nan said, as if I had a choice. "Look at every stone, every marking. Remember it; hold it in your mind."

I did. I didn't need to try. I closed my eyes, and all those markings were there. I closed my eyes, and I could be in the Mumbling City, terrified, or at the top of the levee, not sure if I was going to be eaten, or walking barefoot through the town while the dead clawed at my feet.

None of it came with effort. All of it just came.

I opened Jim's present: a leather belt. There were loops for things, including one for my small silver knife. I wore it, with that knife hanging from my hip. Nan had given it her approval, despite the hurt that anything that reminded her of Jim brought.

We sat on the verandah, drinking cool tea. None of my aunties had visited. Perhaps Nan had told them to stay away.

Nan sat working more knots into her cord between sips of tea. I was leaning on the railing, staring out.

Under the house, Elic started growling.

"We've a visitor. Don't look at him," Nan said, but she didn't have much force in her words, and it was an impossible thing not to.

He walked so elegantly, step after careful step, my graceful man. When he reached our yard, I could hear his boots, the heavy slap of them. He was smiling the widest of smiles.

"Jean, and Nancy," he said.

"Yes, young man," Nan said. "What do you want?"

"I guess we know what time it is?" He lifted his hand. He was wearing a watch: Jim's watch, or one very much like it. Nan hadn't been expecting that.

"Where did you get that?" Nan demanded. Her face twisted, then she brought it under control.

"The river gave it to me," he said. "For my birthday."

The door behind us opened. Mum walked out, and her face was dark with fury, but Nan gestured at her, and she kept quiet.

"What time?" I asked.

The graceful man looked at me inquisitively.

"What time is it?" I elaborated.

"Aren't you going to wish me a happy birthday?"

"Happy birthday," I said.

"It's not right to beg for it," Nan said.

"I don't get a thing, Nancy, unless I ask for it. Fortunately, I can be insistent. And you made a promise."

"Yes, I did," Nan said.

"What have you got there?" He looked at the cord dubiously.

"A present," Nan said.

"A present? I'm here for Jean. I didn't come for any present." He continued to study the cord, cautiously, and not a bit pleased.

"Trust me, you'll love this."

The graceful man took a step up and onto the verandah, moving like the world carried him along. I flinched, and felt that old power rise in me.

He took another step up, and Nan casually placed the knotted cord over his shoulders. Casual but swift, two graceful motions, his and hers colliding. There was a distant boom—not a thunderclap, exactly, but of a great gate slammed shut.

"Happy birthday," she said.

The graceful man moaned, and scraped at the cord. "Get it off me."

"I can't do that. It's yours. It's a gift taken."

"Get it off me. I'm not your challenge; I'm Jean's."

"That rope *is* Jean. Every knot contains her hair. Every knot is bound around my blood, and Jean is of my blood. And now it's bound around you."

His golden eyes locked with mine. "Jean, take it off me, please."

I shook my head.

"It hurts. I'm begging you."

I took a step towards him. Nan touched my shoulder. "No," she said. I stopped, and she did what she had told me not to: She stepped towards the graceful man, and he stepped backwards. Down they went to the earth, moving as one creature.

Nan stopped when she touched the ground.

I wondered what the dead were saying. I couldn't hear it, but I could see their force in her face. Their furious questioning.

The graceful man bent down, and plucked at the earth. A darkness came up, entangled in his hands. A death-like smoke.

"Oh, they're so loud and fearful." He popped the soul into his mouth. "But they've a sweetness to them, even now. They're going to love your company."

"Enough," Nan said. Then she took a match, lit it, and dropped it at the graceful man's feet. Where it touched the ground, a fire found its tail in a loop of flame, only there was no heat; at least, none that I could feel.

"I'm the one with influence here," she said. "I'm bending the rules. You'll not have my granddaughter."

The graceful man sighed. "You're not the only one with influence," he said, and nodded at my mother.

Mum dug her fingers in my shoulder. It hurt down to my wrist. Before I could even yelp, she had reached over, and snatched the knife from my belt.

"What're you doing, Mum?"

She looked right through me, her eyes empty, and I could tell she was in a trance. Those visits from the graceful man hadn't been for nothing. Who knew how long he had whispered to her? Who knew what knots he had tied in her mind? Regardless, she held the knife like she'd been born with it. I'd not seen anything as dangerous, and she wasn't even awake.

I tried to grab her wrist, but she punched me in the stomach. I bent over, the breath knocked out of me.

"Hurry on, Ella," the graceful man said.

A shadow passed across Mum's face. "What do you think you can do to me?" she asked. Her voice sounded young and frightened.

She took each step down lightly, the knife held loosely in her hands.

"You know what needs to be done. You've been here before," the graceful man said. He gestured at my nan.

"Don't listen to him," Nan said. I straightened. I could almost breathe again.

"I'm not listening to anyone," Mum said, and drove the blade deep into Nan's side. Nan didn't make a sound. Mum started to twist the blade. "There's nothing there. It's not the same."

I grabbed at Mum, and she struck me in the face. I hit her in the chest so hard that my fist ached. The breath came out of her. She blinked, saw without seeing, and closed her eyes. Her hand dropped away from the knife.

Nan looked at Mum. "I'm so sorry, my darling," Nan said. Then she turned to me. "It's okay, Jean."

It wasn't, no matter what she said.

"It's okay, Jean," the graceful man mocked.

Nan shuddered. I knew that she was dying, that something raw and awful and shocking, even to her, had been done. But dying or not, she steadied, and looked at me as though the graceful man was the mildest inconvenience. "Don't listen to him. Take your mother inside," she said to me. Her voice was low and small, but still so strong. "Quick. And then hurry back to me."

I led Mum up the steps. I glanced back at the graceful man. He was grinning like he'd performed the cleverest trick.

Mum came with me gently; all her violence was gone. I sat her down in the kitchen, and she stayed there, eyes sightless, bloodied hands resting on her lap. I ran back outside. Maybe I'd been mistaken—maybe it wasn't so bad.

Nan was swaying. The graceful man remained in the burning circle, the rope draped around his shoulders. He shuddered, and his teeth ground against each other in his mouth.

They'd been chatting, and it sounded like nothing more than inconsequential talk. Something of the weather, or a teatime visit. But it wasn't.

"I'm not yours," he said. "And you're dying, anyway."

"I've breath enough in me," Nan said. "And look at you, in your cage."

"I could step out of this any time I want to."

Nan laughed. "Try it."

I reached for her, but she pushed my hand gently aside. "It's all right, Jean. It's all right," she said, then turned her attention back to our guest. "Just take a step. It's such a simple thing to walk out of a circle, even a circle of flame, is it not?"

The graceful man smiled, but he didn't move.

Nan raised her hands, and blood ran down her side. She clapped her hands three times, and each time that distant door slammed. She turned, and looked at me.

"Sorry, child," she said. "I was hoping it wouldn't . . . This wasn't what I wanted."

"Don't," the graceful man begged, his voice so soft.

Nan wasn't smiling anymore. I looked at her. She shook her head, brought a finger to her lips.

"Quiet," she said. "He thinks I didn't know. Coming here, trying to take my daughter. Well, I knew."

The graceful man's eyes were wild. "You still don't know everything. Jean has a gift from me. She's had it since her twelfth birthday. This won't last."

Nan looked at me. "True?" she asked.

"I'm sorry," I said.

"Don't you be sorry, not for that. I should have taught you better earlier," I could see a bitter resignation cross her face. "Nothing's permanent, but some things will stick for a while," she said, turning to the graceful man. "A gift isn't always what you think it is."

She gripped the knife by its handle, and pulled it from her ribs.

The blood spilled from her in a rush. Her eyes fluttered, and she fell.

The moment she struck the ground, that distant door closed, this time so loudly that the windows in our house shook. I slapped my hands over my ears. A shadow passed above us, and when I looked up, the sky was dark with birds, or dust, or leaves, screaming in their passage. When the sky was no longer a chaos, when it fell away to quiet all at once, I knew that Furnace had stopped burning.

The graceful man was gone, no trace of leaves left behind. The circle was just a circle of fire in the earth. I dropped to the ground, and crawled to Nan.

"It's all right, darling," she said. She forced a smile.

"He's gone," I said.

"Yes." Her smile faltered. "He's gone, and he wasn't lying. He's banished for a little while. So that's something. When you're older—when you're closer to ready—you'll have to finish this."

"What do I tell Mum?"

"Don't tell her the truth. Tell her—"

I put my face against Nan's lips: no breath. I searched her eyes: no sight.

Nothing. She was gone.

I lay there weeping beside her for a long time.

I wasn't strong enough to carry Nan inside. Mum, sitting in the living room, was still and empty.

I washed the blood from Mum's hands, and then I went, and found Jacob, and we laid Nan in her bed. Dr. Williams came not long after.

She saw to Mum first—there was nothing she could do for Nan. She took Mum to her bed, gave her something to make her sleep. When Mum woke, I did what Nan told me to: I lied. I said the graceful man had killed her, which was true in its way, a hard and horrible truth. Too much for a child of my years, but I had no choice.

The choice was later.

Jacob, Dr. Williams and I stood on the verandah. Nan's blood—Nan, dead, stabbed by my mother! I felt so panicked I could hardly breathe—painted the stairs. Blood so dark with flies, you could almost pretend it was something else.

"How did this happen? Why?" Dr. Williams asked me. This was a world thick with monsters, but here, this house, should have been the safest place of all.

I couldn't speak; all I had were tears.

Jacob threw a bucket of water over the stairs. The flies scattered.

"It's Jean's birthday," Jacob said.

That night I took the gold coin, and buried it behind the house. Dug down six feet, and placed it under a stone.

It didn't reappear upon my pillow. But I dreamed of it, and a shining tree, and I dreamed of a dark wave behind me that rippled, and waited.

I slept until the dark before the dawn, and when I woke, I was neither happy nor sad. I just was. Half awake, thinking of a radiant tree. I got up, made my coffee, and checked on my mother, but she wasn't there. I half panicked, ran to the verandah.

Mum was sitting there, asleep, one arm curled around a rifle I hadn't even known that we had.

I walked to the levee, and waited for the sun.

"Jean," Nan said, as my feet touched the earth.

"Yes."

"Jean, the light burns. The gate is closed. I can't find the road. I can't find the road. But I can see you." Her hands grabbed at my feet.

"Death is filling me," she said, "with all its conundrums and bitterness. I never meant to fail you."

"It's all right, Nan," I said. "I'm here, and I'll listen to you."

"Good," she said, after a moment. "You still have so much to learn. He's gone, but he is coming back. Those knots are finite. Furnace sleeps, but it will wake. I did my best, and I have failed.

"I'll be ready," I said. "I'll be waiting."

I tried to visit Furnace, but the sickness still held, and it extended to everyone else in town now. Several times, people tried to make the journey, but they couldn't; the road pushed them back. There was no approaching that place, and we gave up trying.

I had plenty of work to attend to. It wasn't as if the world stopped its encroachment.

Myles petitioned and petitioned for an auditor, but none came. He may have wanted someone else, but he still let me walk his farm, still let me risk my life for him.

A few traders trickled in, now that Furnace slumbered. Jim and his crew hadn't reached the Red City. There'd been flash floods in the gully lands north of Casement Rise. Word was that the whole team had been washed away. I guess that's how the graceful man had ended up with his watch.

I cried when I heard that.

Nan laughed, a thin, mirthless sound coming up through the earth. "He's not down here; trust him to find his own way to the Stone Road," she said. "He said it'd be safe. We'd all have died if we had gone with him."

Monsters came and went. I didn't see the Huskling King as often, or attend to my education as closely as I should have, but I still read. I stopped celebrating my birthdays, and nobody reminded me about them. It was as though I had never been born, as if I had always been Jean, whole and powerful.

I grew. I fought, though mostly I found ways that didn't involve fighting. Jacob could never quite get those skills inside my limbs. And Nan remained: bitter as the dead are bitter.

I was the town's shield, if not its wit and wisdom in the way Nan had been. For all that, Casement Rise prospered; word got out that Furnace was gone. The town grew, and with it, my responsibilities.

The dead were always at my feet, blind except for what they could see of me. The moaning, raving dead, whose wisdoms came hard-won, even from those that loved you. The way was closed, the Stone Road gone. The dead were left to gather in the earth at my feet, and the earth became a surge of voices and of hands, but I walked it anyway.

Furnace didn't call me (though I felt it there, slumbering, not completely gone), but the people of the town still did.

"Jean, I have need of you."

"Jean, I have need of you."

"Jean, I have need of you."

Those needs were always the same. I protected the town, but the townsfolk yearned for their dead.

And there were so many of them.

Lolly and Alice married. My two closest friends became something else. I won't say I was unhappy for them, but they made a tight pair, and I couldn't be part of that.

Lolly's mother died, not long after the marriage. Snake bit her. It was a rough sort of ending: She was gone before Dr. Williams made it over the levee.

The Robson boys were bereft. They may have had their ceremonies, but they were lost without their matriarch.

I was made to suffer her bloody lamentations, all those secrets that the dead reveal. That she wished she'd had a daughter—just one, not all those rowdy sons—and that she'd loved Alice, a daughter at last, though once she'd feared it may have been me.

Well, that stung!

My mother's drinking didn't worsen, nor did it get much better. I never shared her love of the bottle.

That was the shape of my childhood and beyond. Up before dawn, circling the town, keeping it safe. I'd like to think I was good at it, though in truth, all I wanted was to be left alone.

No *Jean I have need of you*'s.

Just me and my books, perhaps a friend who didn't want anything of me but company.

Some nights, though not frequently, I would dream of a frantic, bloody-fingered creature working at the cord around his neck. Picking, picking, endlessly picking.

Every time, there were fewer knots.

Part Four

Furnace Take You

On my twentieth birthday, I walked the levee wall, and watched the mists bleed from the river and the valley where they had pooled. The signal stones beat with their regular rhythm, and Casement Rise was inching to wakefulness behind me. I'd be back there soon enough, to people coming for me with their *Jean, I have need of you's*.

Right then though, it was quiet, and almost cool, the sun yet to turn its harshest gaze upon the town. Bird sat on my shoulder, and we both took in the day like it was any other.

Until I saw the man, his skin dark, hat low over his head, walking steadily down the north road, heading towards the Summer Gate. He knew how to walk; he had a rhythm to him, a confident stride.

I knew what kind of man he was. His hands were tattooed with the circle and the seven lines: a Master's Sun. Made him an auditor, though he was young for one—Rob and Sarah had been much older when they came through, and all the other auditors I'd seen, too.

"Myles has finally done it," I said.

He had been at me all year, worse than any other. The Husklings had taken three of his sheep, an accusation confirmed by the bones I'd found in the Huskling hall. The king hadn't even bothered to deny it. Myles had demanded compensation, but none was forthcoming, so he'd taken it to the council. Five votes had been turned against me because I was known to consort with clever birds and monsters. It didn't matter that I kept far worse things out of the town.

Myles had gathered a few men around him. He'd started stockpiling guns. Now, down below us, was the latest sign of his dissatisfaction.

"Let Jacob deal with it," Nan said, beneath my feet.

"He's not your problem," Bird said.

I was already picking my way down the levee towards the auditor. He was very much my problem.

"You," I shouted, when I was still a little above him, holding my walking stick tight, close enough to see the sweat on his face. "What do you want?"

He looked up at me, eyes slits, face angled to watch the workings of my thoughts. I could tell he was a fella used to reading people like they were books. Well, my pages weren't that legible.

"Miss March?"

I tried not to look surprised; I guess it wasn't so remarkable that he knew of me. Myles wouldn't have neglected to mention the source of his troubles. "Yes."

He cracked a smile that was eight times dangerous, three times charming, though—let's be honest—danger has a charm all itself. "I've walked so long to see you."

"You know my name, but I'm unfamiliar with yours," I said, and poked my stick at him.

"Mark," he said. "I like your watch."

Then, all at once, his eyes rolled up into his head, and he fell backwards. I stood there a moment longer to be certain he

The Stone Road

wasn't faking, noticed the blood staining his shirt, then went down after him.

Bird flew from my shoulder, and made their way to a good observational branch.

I rolled Mark over. He had the shakes in him, and they were getting worse. I could smell the gunshot on him, and I could smell the death in his blood: that was the clearest of all. The earth called him. The dead beneath me roiled.

His eyes snapped open, and he took a deep, gasping breath. "Sorry," he said. "Sorry."

I could tell he wasn't talking to me, and that he was even younger than I'd thought. Maybe two years—four, at a stretch— older than me. His eyes tracked my face as though he was studying it, but I could tell he wasn't really seeing me.

I looked north where he'd come from, hunting for cookfire smoke, or the sense of pursuit. There was something out there, something part calm and part panic. It felt a mile or so distant, and even as I concentrated on it, it backed off, as if I had scared it a little.

I don't like to scare things, particularly things that don't deserve scaring. This one was all fear and determination, so I backed off.

The dead clamoured as I crouched there.

He's an auditor.

Master's child—monster's twisted cloth.

Choke him while you can. Choke him, and send him down, lest he be given a chance to rise.

"Won't be any choking," I said.

Last chance. This one is death. This one is your death. I prophecy that true.

225

I snorted at that, the idea of the dead seeing the future. They were all past, no matter what Dickens might say.

I gave Mark a serious appraisal. He wore guns, and strapped to his belt was a package wrapped in brown paper. The paper had seen better days, and so had he. His shaking steadied, as if it were sinking into him. He looked up at me, and there was a quiet sadness in his eyes. Perhaps it was pain, or perhaps a realisation that death had been sitting on his shoulder all along.

"Sorry," he said again.

"What have you got to be sorry about?"

"Sorry." His teeth chattered.

I knew I wasn't going to get much out of him right now. "You'll be sorry if you can't walk, and I have to drag you. There's more thorns in this earth than soil."

I considered running for help, but I feared he'd be dead by the time I got back. I got him on his feet, felt the heat of him: the sun-sweat and the fever. I gritted my teeth, and we walked, scrambling back the way I'd come. He leant on me, for sure, but still used his strength. I felt the reservoir of it deep within him. What a rarity that is.

Nan grumbled at me, and the dead grumbled, too, but I ignored them.

"You smell of bird," Mark said, his voice not much more than a whisper.

Had to hold my tongue lest I say that he smelled of death. "You think you can make it much further?" I asked. We'd walked into the mostly sleeping town. Those that were up kept their distance. I briefly considered Dr. Williams' surgery, but I'd seen her ride east with one of the Robsons that morning.

Without her, I could do more for him at home. Or maybe I was killing him now, pushing him too hard.

"I didn't think I could make it this far after . . ." he trailed off. "But I walked, and I kept on walking."

That he did, and I swear, as he approached our homestead, with its brick walls, its low circling ridge of verandah, that he sped up.

"You're all surprises," I said to him.

And then, like I'd cut his strings, he toppled onto the dry earth about forty yards from home.

"Where you been, girl?" I knew where *Mum* had been. She was drunk, but inclining towards the rougher edges of sobriety. She had her hands out stiff, gripping the verandah's railing. She looked me up and down, then stared at Mark.

I'd gotten him back onto his feet, but even reservoirs as deep as his have their limits.

My back was bent with the labour of it all. I frowned hard at her, and tried to keep the venom from my tongue. "Doesn't matter where I've been. Can't you *see* what I'm doing?"

She bared her teeth at me, but she came down, and helped me with the boy like it was of no consequence, like this happened every day.

Which it certainly did not.

"He *will not* go in my house." Nan said. "I forbid it. You let an auditor in, and everything ends in gunfire."

Mum must have got a sense of her protests because, despite the sour smell of the grog on her, and the day grown to heat, she smiled at me. "He can sleep in Mum's old room. You'll have to boil some water. After that, straight to Dr. Williams—he's going to need her."

"She won't be pleased. That is, when she gets back from who-knows-where," I said.

We got him in the shade of the house. Mum paused there—I was happy to catch my breath a bit—and gave me a serious look. "Williams took an oath. That grump is all show: How else do you think she gets a moment's peace? She'll do it."

The hardest part came after that: getting Mark up the stairs. He dropped to his knees, and it was all we could do to drag him, one step at a time. Both of us winced at the bumps we inflicted, and the groans that followed.

But we managed to carry him inside and onto the bed.

Mum looked at the wound, and I saw something in her face that made me wish she hadn't done so while I was still there to see it. She shook my arm, made a shooing gesture. "Go, Jean. Go! Dr. Williams will need to attend to this. I'll boil the water."

"He's gonna die," I said.

"Probably."

"No," Mark said, from some groggy place. "I'm not."

"Go," Mum said. "Go."

I ran, hoping Dr. Williams was back.

All the way, Nan moved with me like the earth was water, like she was a wave, a moaning, grumbling, angry wave. "The boy is death. The boy's a *complication.*"

"What would you know? You're dead. Dead. Dead. And this boy is alive. Begone."

Nan was silent, but she didn't leave me, I could feel her disapproval seething beneath the earth. All it did was hurry me.

I banged at Dr. William's door. Locked. Banged again. If it came to it, I could run the length of the town.

If she was out at the Robsons' farm, then it was Alice's baby, Ruth, who had been stricken with the flu. I didn't know how long she might be; I never got sick.

I considered the windows, picked which might be best to break in through. I was more than happy to, if it came to it. I knew enough of death that I might manage to forestall it if I had the tools of her craft. I hovered there, thinking.

"What do you want, Jean?" Dr. Williams asked from behind me, making me jump. I'd never been happier to see a doctor, that's for sure. She looked tired, hollowed out, and I think I knew why. Didn't ask, but she had a sadness about her. Poor Lolly; poor Alice.

"Fella at our place. Wounded. Looks bad."

Dr. Williams nodded like she dealt with this every day. "Who?"

"Not a local."

Dr. Williams considered this. She stabbed a finger at the ground. "And what do your dead say?"

"Say he's an auditor. But they don't need to say it; it's as plain as the tattoos on his hands."

"Myles Preston, calling a fellow like that here. Just for a few sheep." She folded her arms. "There was a reason why I left the Red City, Jean. And that reason had teeth. Probably this fella's turn. You deal out death, and she comes for you sooner than most. A man like that is dangerous."

"Doesn't look dangerous," I lied. "Just looks like he's gonna die."

"We're all going to die, Jean," she said.

"You trying to tell me something I don't know? He's gonna die *soon*, may already be dead. And you start talking philosophically, like we've all the time in the world. You want another death on you today?"

"He's an auditor."

"He's young," I said, ignoring her. "He's got a long life ahead of him, if he survives."

"Long life of trouble," Dr. Williams said, then pursed her lips, unfolded her arms.

"I'll need some things," she said.

To her credit, once she'd made up her mind, she didn't dawdle. I've never seen a person her age run so fast.

Mum opened the door for us.

"Not dead yet."

"That's good, I suppose," the doctor said, catching her breath, wiping her brow.

"Were you thinking of waiting until he dies, Sue?"

She shook her head. "I know my oath, Ella."

"Good."

"Well, let's see him, then."

He was on his belly, his shirt gone. Skin dark, and brutalised. Scars had had their way across him, cuts and gnarls of old disputes. Stories, like the marks on Bird's tree. Either he was violent or he was clumsy, and he didn't look clumsy.

Dr. Williams nodded. "This one's seen some knocks. Sometimes that shows strength; sometimes that hides weakness. The heart's inside; its cage is only half the story. How'd you carry him here?"

"He walked, leaning on me, but I didn't need to carry him."

"What? Up and over the levee?"

I nodded.

She wasn't too happy with that. "You might have walked him to a grave. Might have walked the strength out of him. An auditor dying; now that would bring trouble, even here." Suddenly she was singing a different tune—could have thought of that at the outset. "The Red City and its Council of Teeth don't think on us much, but this might draw their bite."

"Best get to work, then," I said.

"Jean, you know better than that. I *am* working. Have to work with the eyes, first."

She handed me her bag. "Open that. Put it beside the bed."

She approached Mark, slow, all her attention on him, and I knew that she was forgetting me. "That wound's gone septic. Not a good sign, sepsis. Depends how deep." She shook her head, half talking to herself. "Once there were medications and the like for this, magic bullets, almost. I'll need to flush the wound." She looked at me, seemed almost surprised I was still there. "I'll do what I can, but I must have your trust. We trust you to do what you do, so give me a little back, eh?"

"You have it," I said.

"Then leave me here. Go keep your mother company. There's a softness in her today; that's rare. Particularly this day. Let her indulge it."

I wanted to spit at that, but it was true. My mum was not often soft. Not anymore. I'd never told her how Nan had really died, but I think part of her knew, and that part of her had twisted with a deeper self-loathing. I could fight monsters, but I couldn't fight that.

I left Dr. Williams to her work.

Mum was sitting on the verandah, wiping her brow with a handkerchief. "He going to live or die?" she asked, her voice low.

I shrugged, and she patted my arm. "These birthdays of yours . . . this has been the most interesting since—"

"Just a coincidence," I said.

"And we have another visitor. Look," she said, and pointed to the edge of our land.

There was a horse standing there, wanting to come nearer just as much as it wanted to run away. I knew that feeling, and I recognised it here. This was the presence I'd felt a mile out of town.

"Says something of the man you found," Mum said, "that his horse would follow him. Up and over the levee, too."

"How do you know it's his?"

Mum gave her neck a long wipe. The day was beginning to boil. "Who else would it belong to? They're clever creatures. Why don't you go talk to it?"

"Why don't you come with me?"

Mum shook her head, sank lower in her chair. "I want this shade."

I knew what she wanted. I knew she was thinking of the bottle. She was always thinking of it. Some days that made me so angry, others sad. "Okay," I said.

"Hurry now, before it decides to bolt. Plenty of things that would prey on such a lovely creature."

I walked down to the horse. It was standing under the trees, down near the half-dried creek—the river might be flowing, but the creek was a different story. Days too long and hot, and every-thing turning to cracks. Every living thing was hunting shade.

It let me get close, before backing away.

"He's in there," I said to it, jabbing a hand back at the house.

It had scratches along its sides, but none of them were deep. It watched me, steady, but uncertain.

"We're keeping him safe. He'll be okay; you'll see him soon enough. You're welcome here. Both of you are."

I didn't know how to talk to horses. Jacob would have had it eating out the palm of his hand.

It looked at me, and I looked at it. A mare, I could see that, saddled still. Strapped to that saddle were guns, rifles, a knife. All these weapons, as well as the pistols Mark had belted around his waist.

"He must have thought you dead. You'll be a comfort to him. I can tell him you're safe."

She lowered her head.

"How long have you been on his trail?"

I kept asking questions, making gentle chatter. She shivered as I approached, but at last—and it was a long time coming—she let me hold her bridle. I got the sense that it could have turned the other way, if she'd not trusted me. I know nothing of horses, but she knew of people, and it was a knowledge only partway severe. I led her homewards, and she let me lead her.

When we arrived, Dr. Williams stood in the shade, talking to my mum.

There was no smile to her. I listened to the earth. I couldn't hear him there, though it was noisy.

"He'll live?" I asked.

"I expect he will," Dr. Williams said, and nodded at the horse. "Who's this?"

"A visitor."

Dr. Williams frowned. "That horse definitely says auditor to me."

"Or horse thief," Mum said.

Dr. Williams laughed. "Not with the scars he has. Jean's right: He has the marks of Day Boys and the auditors on him. If you get caught with the tattoos of the Sun, and you can't back it up . . . well, punishments are cruel and unusual up north. What these tell me is that he's trouble."

I shrugged. There she was, beating that trouble drum again. "You saw him; he's no trouble to anyone right now."

"Not now, but he'll recover, and the trouble will rise in him. And you should know, Jean, sometimes it isn't the trouble direct. Sometimes it's the things that a fellow like him draws with them. Think about what day it is."

He'd said sorry. I may have argued against the need, but I knew his presence wasn't benign.

"I know," I said. "But that doesn't matter now. My birthday doesn't mean anything. Hasn't since I was thirteen."

Dr. Williams looked at me. "Are you sure? Alice and Lolly lost their child today. This auditor's here, and it's not even midday."

She stopped, realised what she'd said. Poor Alice; poor Lolly.

I looked at her a moment, but only a moment because the town bell started ringing. What else?

"I have to see to this," I said.

"I'm coming, too," she said. I glanced over at Mum.

"I'll stay with him," she said.

"You keep him safe," I said.

Mum grimaced. "What else do you think I would do?"

We hurried out of the house and through the yard.

The bells kept ringing.

When we reached the Summer Gate, Jacob was there. He didn't smile at me; his face was pale. There were others there, too, but none of them could look me in the eye. Except Jacob.

I guess he was thinking it, too. These damn birthdays.

"Jean, you'll want to see this."

Dr. Williams made to follow, and Jacob shook his head. "Just Jean," he said.

We climbed up the levee.

"There," he said,

"Yeah, I can see it." A finger of smoke rose into the sky, dark and angry.

Beneath me, the dead moaned. *The hunter, he'll be hungry! He'll pluck us from the earth. He's dammed the river, and now, he'll have his pick of us!*

"What the hell are we going to do?" Jacob wondered.

"I've no idea," I said.

"Can't you feel it?"

I shook my head. I could see Furnace, but I could never feel it. That call was closed to me. "It's stronger," he said. "Steadier."

"I'm not ready," I said.

Jacob looked at me. "You've kept this town safe for seven years. You're ready."

We stood there a while, and watched the smoke. Didn't matter if I was ready or not: Furnace was burning like it had never stopped. He would be coming.

I went down the levee, towards the Slouches. There it was, stronger than ever, that familiar sickening push. Smoke or not, that hadn't changed. I walked back up to Jacob.

"Happy birthday," Jacob said. As soon as he said it, he looked like he wished he could take it back. Too late.

It had been a very long time since someone had said that to me.

I expected the graceful man to arrive at once, but he didn't. I checked the defences of the town again. Everything was as it was, which meant that Mark's horse had picked her way up and over the levee without disturbing a single marking.

Afterwards, I saw Jacob again down by the butcher's. He called me over. "I'm sorry about what I said before."

I shook my head. "You're saying what we're all thinking." How many times would I repeat that today? "It *is* my birthday."

"Most people just get a cake." He let out a weary breath. "You sure keeping an auditor at your place is a good thing?"

I looked at him. "There's nothing good about this day," I said, thinking of Furnace, thinking of Lolly and Alice's dead child. "But at least I can keep an eye on him."

"He could stay in the barracks," he said.

I laughed. "You mean, the prison?"

"Be safer there."

"He may not live through the night. Besides, he was invited. He's a guest," I said. I looked at Jacob closely. "Did you know he was coming?"

Jacob shook his head. "Who'd have thought that they'd finally listen."

I smiled. "The world's gone mad," I said, and I was only half joking.

"You know Myles is still bitter about those sheep."

"I know, but what he sees as threat isn't. We need the Husklings. And they need us. We're in this together. It's how we live out here."

"You don't have to tell me that," Jacob said. "But be careful. Furnace is burning. Today's events might drive a man like Myles to folly."

"Might drive *me* to it."

"Well, you can't let it. You hear about Lolly and Alice?"

"I heard." Why did everyone keep reminding me? Why did it have to happen on my birthday? I couldn't help feeling responsible.

Jacob must have read that in my face. "Not your fault, Jean," he said. "Sometimes bad things just happen." That he could see such thoughts there made me feel selfish and angry and deeply ashamed.

I wanted to go out there, and see them, but I knew I couldn't offer any comfort. We were hardly friends anymore, and in truth I'd gotten them both into more trouble than I'd ever gotten them out of. Didn't stop me aching for them. There had been few deaths in the town over the last seven years. It wasn't fair that this had happened to them.

"What about Furnace? That's my fault."

"Been seven years," Jacob said. "Town survived Furnace before; we'll survive it again. See to your work as I see to mine. And be careful around that auditor."

So I got on with things. The world hadn't ended. I worked until daylight faded, saw to the town's defences again, spoke to Glade Bettering's dead husband, told her the usual lies and comforts—mixed with enough truth that she would believe it—cut out the anger—no one needed that on this day.

I made my presence known; people needed to see that I wasn't cowed by Furnace. That I was here, that I was ready.

I even walked out to Myles' farm. I couldn't quite face the Robsons' place yet.

He was there, sitting on his verandah, rifle between his legs. There were a dozen men in that yard, setting up cans and stones to shoot at. Bored men with guns never leads to good.

"Here she is," he said.

Bird chose that moment to land on my shoulder.

Myles swung up his rifle.

"You shoot them, and I will never walk the boundaries of your land again."

He took a bead on Bird, then lowered the gun across his thighs. "Maybe you won't be needed," he said.

He'd been drinking; that wasn't hard to see. I didn't bother coming all that close.

"If you're referring to that auditor, he's wounded in bed at my place. Dr. Williams says he may live."

Myles' eyes widened. "What'd you do?"

"Nothing. Saved his life. He got set upon coming down here, I'd say. Nearly died at our doorstep. That the man you want protecting Casement Rise?"

"It's not the town I want protected," Myles said. "When's the town protected mine?"

"We've kept you safe," I said.

"And what about that smoke to the west?"

"I'm here to walk your borders."

"Not wanting to talk about that, eh? How about that poor Robson babe? How about that auditor, then? You know what day it is?"

"I know," I said.

"Must be a hard thing," Myles said. "But you know what's harder? Being anyone else around you. Might have stopped a while, but I knew it would all come back. I never did trust in women and monsters."

"I'll walk your farm," I said.

Myles waved his arm in the air. "Don't bother," he said.

Someone fired a gun. I flinched. There was a clattering of cans. Myles smiled. "I'll see you in town," he said.

It was a hard thing to put my back to him and that rifle. His men leered at me; Bird fluffed on my shoulder. But I walked slow and steady.

"Furnace take you all," I said, once I was clear of the gate.

I could hear them laughing.

When I looked in on Mark, he was sleeping, his breathing steady. I lay one finger across his wrist. He was hot to the touch, but so was I. This was a feverish time. I opened the window, but kept the curtain down. The wind rippled the fabric. The breath of day smelled like dust and smoke and the peppery worn-out scent of a town set upon by summer's full doldrums.

South of here, a storm bruised the sky. Lightning cracked, but it was a distant fury yet. Here, we waited for its beating.

Crows were calling, and a stone-curlew was seeking out his mate, desperation echoing out across the low plains, down towards the trees. I was never lonelier than when I was at home, staring up in bed, making continents and stories out of the shadows and cracks in the ceiling. Here was a world before machines. Here was a world after.

I yanked the sheets around me, letting them wrap me, despite my hot blood. I tossed and turned. Finally, the storm swept in. It broke the heat, and I fell into the roughest sleep. Even a bad sleep is better than nothing.

A town like ours, when it slumbers, slumbers lightly. There are always disturbances. There are jobs to be done, and without them you don't have a town. There's someone who must look after the sheep and the cattle. Someone who must care for the sick. Someone who bakes the bread, or brings those livestock into slaughter, or grinds the grain to flour. Someone who must walk the boundaries of the town, circling and circling, drawing their presence as a shield around the outskirts.

Hoping for the best, preparing for the worst, and knowing which one was more likely.

In the middle of the night, I woke. My sleeping had been crowded with dreams. There was something under my pillow, gripped in my hand. I knew what it was before I even saw it.

The gold coin, warm as blood.

Sure enough, three men had headed west that evening. Furnace was calling, the graceful man was calling, and I couldn't stop him.

Three days of that. Heat then storm, the painful rhythms of the season, and people heading west to Furnace.

When I walked the levee, my feet were coated with white mud. Mark was hardly conscious, though he woke a few times. We made him bone broths, and fed him. He slept the ragged sleep of the sick and the guilty.

One day, I woke to a great thumping. I flung myself from bed, certain it was the graceful man come to claim his revenge. I stalked around the house, and there was Mark's mare, standing on the verandah, gazing through the window at Mark.

I stood there with her, looking at this blasted auditor sleeping. "See," I said, quietly. "See? He's getting better."

The horse let me lead her back down. She wasn't the only one growing impatient.

On the third day, after my circuit, Mum was waiting for me with a coffee. A rare thing, now: We'd not seen traders for months. I wondered if she was trying to charm me.

"Where'd you find this?" I asked.

"Does it matter?"

"I prefer to know whom I owe favours to."

"Alice. She'll see you, maybe today. You've avoided her and Lolly, so she came for you."

"What can I do for her?"

"Be a little gentler. You know why she came."

"I wasn't raised to gentleness."

Mum nodded towards the bedroom where Mark slept. "But you can find it when you need it."

I left her, and went to find Alice, and see what she would have of me.

"This is only trouble," Nan said.

"Quiet."

"We've more to focus on than this."

"Have you not been paying attention?" I asked. "How has your focus helped us?"

"It will."

Alice wasn't at work. I walked to the Robsons' place, and knocked on the door. She must have been waiting because it opened almost at once.

I'd never seen her so pale or lean. The past weeks had eaten at her, brought out the bones. There was no warmth to her, just a desperate resignation that she had to talk to me, that she required what I had.

"I'm here," I said, and resisted the impulse to fold my arms.

"Jean, I have need of you." Oh, how that sentence sickened me.

"Where's Lolly?"

"I don't know. He's been away a lot since it happened."

That made me angry. I gave in to the desire to fold my arms. "Tell me what you need," I said.

And she did. Because that is how these things go.

"Where do you feel the baby strongest?" I asked her. Alice tried not to roll her eyes, but she couldn't quite manage it. Her lip lifted at the edge, curled with a sudden and acute pain.

She put her hand on her chest. "Here. Ruth's here."

I couldn't help but feel a sharper sorrow, then. If that were the case, she wouldn't have come to me. Ruth wasn't there. She could never be there anymore. What Alice was hunting was something to fill that aching space, to smear over the cracks. The dead wound and call, even if you can't hear them.

"You know what I mean: the place she calls you. Where is that?"

Then Alice surprised me. She gripped my hand. Her fingers were dry, and colder than I had expected, rough at the tips. She squeezed. "I'll take you," she said.

We passed into and through Casement Rise. The townsfolk watched us. Alice's face burned red.

"Ignore them," I said. "They all come to me eventually. There's no shame in this."

Nan made a cruel commentary of it all, and I ignored her.

"All I want is to know that she's happy," Alice said. "Can you tell me she's happy?"

I couldn't look her in the eye. They're never happy. The young are the worst.

"When it took her, she was getting stronger. She'd been weak and sick. I'd nearly died with worry, and I wasn't well either. She'd held my finger with her tiny hand. She'd smiled. I let myself relax. And then she died." Alice said this calmly. Not a sob.

I felt such guilt. I'd let all this go on, and ignored it. When had I seen her or Lolly, when had I walked over the levee to check on them?

"Not your fault," I said. "It's not your fault."

She didn't say anything after that, but she didn't let go of my hand, either.

She took me to White Tree.

I wasn't surprised to be here. Furnace was a draw for the living, White Tree called the dead.

I let go of her hand. "Remember when I got you down from here?"

Alice nodded. "I remember. I was so frightened."

"You'll see me hurt," I said. "White Tree won't be gentle."

"You don't know hurt," she said.

I laughed at that, but the sound died on my lips. Looking at her, maybe I didn't.

I approached the tree cautiously. Her spiky presence dominated everything here. I pressed my hands against the bark, and she sensed me directly, a presence stark and swift. White Tree didn't talk: She raged, and burned.

Red ants ran over my fingers, red ants that bit, hard and horrible and stinging. I laid my head against the trunk of the tree. The ants didn't let up, nor would they, as long as I stayed where I was. But I wouldn't move until I was done. They hissed and bit and stung.

The pain focussed me. I sank beneath the earth. Not flesh sinking: I stayed above in body and went below in spirit. Babies are different. I can't just call them up. I have to go to them.

And they fight.

The child came to me. So newly dead. She bit, worse than those ants, for it wasn't flesh she was biting.

I could see where the tree had tangled her.

Her tiny foot was blue. Something had wound around her, a strand as thin and as tough as barbed wine. It would hurt to remove it.

I placed my hand on her leg. She snapped at me like an angry lizard, and I let her bite.

The pain made it easier, gave me focus. I closed my eyes, and reached around the thread. It cut into my fingers. I felt the awful fire of the thread's resistance. My eyes rolled deep into their orbits. Oh, the pain of it!

I tasted blood. But I held on, and I pulled until my bones bent, and muscles burned, and the thread came away at last.

She snapped at me, free and angry, bit a chunk out of the meat of my hand, and was gone. A child isn't bound in the misery that the living cling to. A child will let go.

And then I saw them: the other dead here, wound up in blue.

The dead sniffed at my spraying blood with a chill curiosity. One by one I untangled them. One by one they fell away. Snapping at me when they could, though none of them stayed to be tangled again.

I tried to open my eyes, but couldn't. I tried to pull my hands from the tree, but they wouldn't move. Blue threads wound around and wounded my not-flesh. I pulled. The threads tightened in response, and began to close around me.

I felt White Tree's amusement. The dead are a thin nutrient compared to the living. Here was a naked grab for my power, and my death.

How could I have been so stupid! I should have released Ruth, and fled. I tried to pull away, but I had forgotten which way was up.

Soft and far away, I could hear a voice calling.

There, there. I yanked my limbs free, and it hurt: The threads had cut deep. But I could move again.

I followed the voice.

I fell back from the tree, and landed, hard enough to knock the breath from me.

Ants bit my eyelids. My tongue sat swollen in my mouth. I spat out the ants, but I could still taste the bitterness of their poison.

"She's gone," I said, thickly, not even sure if Alice was there.

"I know," Alice said, and I knew she hated me for it, a little, at least.

People never want me to let the dead go; they want me to bring them back like Orpheus or some trickster king. That's not how it works. I'm no hunter: I cast out, and that is all I can do. I release. And the ones trapped, the ones blind and lost, they would only turn to hate and bitterness. People don't want that, no matter how they might lie to themselves.

Beneath me, I could feel White Tree lashing out, catching the souls of the dead that weren't quick enough in their escape. The tree didn't catch Ruth, though. She was free.

"You saved me," I said. "I was lost."

Trent Jamieson

"I know," Alice said, and she pulled me up. "Let me take you home."

She held my wounded hand gently, and guided me, half-blind, mouth full of blood and bitterness, eyes streaming, nose running. She guided me home. Mark was sleeping. She looked in on him and frowned. Mum was gone.

Alice washed, and soothed me, and I saw the mother that she had become, and wasn't anymore. I wept at the sadness of it.

"Thank you," I said.

Alice hesitated a moment, then kissed my cheek. "You've had a hard life, Jean," she said. "Who cares for you?"

"No one to care for any of us," I said.

"Maybe," Alice said, and kissed my cheek again. "Maybe not."

I would have wept again, but I was all cried out, my body stinging, my eyes sore, though the swelling was going. Alice held me, and I let her hold me, and I realised that sometimes the world isn't so cruel.

I think you don't get much happiness in your life. You could condense it down to minutes out of all those decades. When it comes, you've gotta hold it. You've gotta honour it. Or what's the point?

I must have fallen asleep because when I next opened my eyes, Alice was gone.

A cool wind was blowing through the window, like the memory of spring. I walked outside, and put my feet upon the earth.

"Don't trust her," Nan said.

"You're too long in the ground. You don't trust anyone," I said.

Nan hissed and disappeared, and I stood alone in the soft comfort of the dark.

246

The morning after that was hard, but I rose through my aches and pains, and the dawn itself was glorious. Gilded, like that first time I'd walked the Long Between: almost beautiful enough to make me forget everything but that.

There were fires burning on the Prestons' land. Campfires. I knew he had family in the north. Seems like he'd called more than just an auditor. I watched them for a while, but not long; it wasn't my business. I'd talk to Jacob later.

When I reached the west, I saw someone walking that way, heading to the Slouches and beyond. I squinted, then I growled. I knew that walk. It was Lolly.

He wasn't far along. I followed him. It took just a few steps to feel the push of Furnace, to taste the sickening edges of a migraine.

"This isn't wise," Bird said.

"What do you know of bloody wisdom?"

Bird didn't answer. I ran as fast as I could, hoping that would somehow make it easier. I'd lost enough to this damn road.

"Lolly," I shouted.

His shoulders shuddered.

"Stop."

I was surprised when he did. It still took me a while to reach him, and every step hurt.

"Why are you doing this, Lolly?"

For a moment, Lolly woke from whatever dream Furnace had built. He'd grown a beard, more grey in it than his age deserved. He scratched at it before he spoke. "You know what I'm doing," he said, slowly, the effort of it making him sweat.

"But Alice—"

"She doesn't need me. None of them need me. I already failed her. Failed all of them. Failed my daughter."

"Lolly Robson," I snapped. "You turn on your heel, and you walk back to your farm and your wife."

"No," he said, and he started to walk again. "Just this slowing hurts. You've no idea." I could have punched him right then. "But what's ahead is wonderful; he has a place for us all."

"Not for me."

"Good." He picked up his pace.

I called Lolly's name, pleaded with him using Alice's. He ignored me, so I followed him until I could hardly stand. I stumbled, almost fell. He stopped for a moment, irritation and concern fighting across his face. I bent over, spitting out the sickness in me, or at least trying to. But there was no relief from it; it swept across the land and came crashing into me, wave after terrible wave. I looked up into his face, and saw that concern die, replaced with resigned hatred.

"Go," he said. "Back to that damn town! What have you ever done for me? Filled me with monsters, got me into trouble, hardly got me out of it. And now. Jean. Jean, she died on your birthday."

He may as well have slapped me.

"Please," I said.

"There's no going back for me. And what if he's right? What if things *are* better there? They must be; it feels so true."

I couldn't answer. I could see the hooks of Furnace grow in him. "No. You go home. I'm done; I'm going to see what you can't. Alice will find me, I know she will, and we'll be happy. It calls everyone in the end."

He kept walking, faster and faster, and I couldn't follow. I stood, bent over, my lips bitter with anger and vomit, threads of my sickness staining my shirt. I remembered when Lolly had thrown up at my twelfth birthday party.

"Hey," I said. "Hey."

He ignored me, and I stood there and watched as Furnace took him.

Somewhere along the way, the graceful man joined him, golden eyes glimmering. He looked back at me and waved and bowed, and it was like he had never been gone at all.

Mitcham stopped me at the gate to the Robsons' house. Just like Lolly, he looked older than I remembered him. These days were aging us.

"You need to clean yourself up," he said.

"I have to see Alice."

"I can get you some water. If you stay here. Can you promise me that?"

"No."

"She doesn't want to see you," he said.

I looked past him at the door. We stood there a moment, and he shook his head.

How could I blame her, with her child gone, and now Lolly?

"Please," he said. "Just go."

I walked back to town. I was failing Casement Rise one person at a time.

When I got home, Mark was sleeping, his breathing slow and certain. Mum had gone out somewhere, and I knew she would come back drunk. I sat in the living room, and cried.

I left the house, and put a foot on the ground.

"Don't you give into despair, girl," Nan said.

"You have!" I snapped.

"Of course. I'm dead. I'm in the ground, and there's no peace here, no Stone Road, no way out. But you've still got a beating heart. It isn't your fault, but it's the way it is."

I lifted my foot. When I put it down again, she was gone.

"That you, Miss Jean?"

My little dead boy!

"Where have you been?" I exclaimed. "All this time! I thought you'd been eaten."

"Oh, no! I was lost. That magic that your nan made, it hurled me far away. The light burns so bright here, Miss Jean. And there are so many of us. I tried to find you."

"And you have."

"You sound *so* much older."

"I am," I said. "I feel as ancient as rocks."

"No! You're a babe compared to that! Could you tell me a story?"

"Of course." I hurried to get a book, dreading that he would be gone by the time I got back, but he wasn't. I stood there reading, and it was like the old times. When I was done, he touched the bottom of my foot once, and I couldn't tell if it was a fingertip or a kiss.

"Thank you, Miss Jean," he said.

"Thank *you*," I said, and I meant it, but he was already gone.

Inside, Mark was calling out, but by the time I reached his room, he was sleeping deeply again. Whatever bad dreams that pulled at him had fallen away.

The next morning, the levee was as it always was. Bird and I circled it slower than usual, and more thoroughly. Nothing had pushed against the defences. The land beyond was quiet and still.

It was a beautiful clear morning, but when I reached the western edge of the levee bank, Furnace still sent up its smoke.

There were a couple of people on the road west. The Gibson brothers. The graceful man walked between them, holding their hands like they were children.

I'd find out later that there were five. Five called west in a little less than a day.

When I got home, Mark was sitting up in bed. He still looked sick and frail, but he was lucid. He smiled when he saw me, that dangerous, charming smile.

"You're alive, then," I said.

"Thank you," he said.

"You're welcome. Your horse is here."

"Kala. Her name's Kala."

"She's been looking in on you."

Mark smiled—not that charming smile, but a truthful one, radiant and happy.

"Oh, she has, has she?" He cleared his throat. There was the brown paper package by the bed. He tapped it with one hand. "There's a . . . I mean, I've a present for you, Miss March," he said, gesturing at it.

"Just Jean," I said, picking it up. "Not *Miss* March. What's in it?"

"Why don't you open it and find out . . . Jean."

It was a book. An adventure novel, printed in the Red City. I still liked reading them. "How'd you know?"

"I was told you liked them."

"By whom?"

"By my Masters. They've got their eyes on you. Kinda funny . . . when I was dying, I was more worried about that book than anything. That I wouldn't get it to you. Silly, right?"

This wasn't what I needed to know. "Why are you here?"

"They sent me to protect you."

"From what? Furnace? Monsters? I don't need protection from that."

"There's things you may not know. Things my Masters don't want known. In the last three months, five towns northwest of here have emptied, all of them directly governed by the Red City. Everyone got up and left, taking nothing, the whole town silent. Food left out and rotting on tables, paint tins open by half-painted houses. I've walked through those towns; they're worse than haunted. They're so empty that it eats you, makes your skin crawl from the inside."

I looked at him straight on. I'd not heard even a whisper of this. "What about their Masters?"

"They went, too. Thing is, they came back—not to their towns, but to the Red City. And they came back broken, twisted, and tortured: not wanting blood, scarcely able to speak. Furnace isn't just your problem anymore. When the Masters reached the Red City so damaged, the whole Council of Teeth took notice. Took notice of the south, and special notice of Myles Preston's letters."

"I knew it," I said. "Never thought they'd take him seriously."

"All that was required was for them to be hurt where it mattered." Mark tried to straighten up a little, winced, and hissed. "Your problem turns Masters into men. Not even that. They don't drink or eat. They wither and die."

"But it *is* my problem. Furnace is mine to deal with." I felt affronted. This was my trouble, as Nan had had hers, and my mum must have, too. How dare anyone try and take it from me!

"No. It's mine, too, because the Masters will it," Mark said, then winced again. "Though, look at me. I can hardly sit up."

I nodded at that. "What happened to you?"

"Last town I came through. Knotbridge."

"I know it. Never been there, but I've heard it's a rough place."

"I'm used to rough places. I should have been paying attention. Had a little altercation in the pub. A few men came at me, a day's ride from there. I recognised one from my fight." His eyes took on a hardness. "Of course, they didn't count on me not being so easily killed. I left their ambush still breathing, barely, but you couldn't say the same for them."

He looked ready to sleep again.

"If you want to keep breathing, you better rest," I said.

Seven years I'd been left alone, with nothing to deal with but the simple complexities of monsters. I'd known what I was doing, how to keep my town safe.

Until now. Everything was uncertain again. My trouble was coming, and it wasn't like anything else. Rather than time giving me a full flowering of power to face it, time seemed only to have made my enemy stronger.

I needed something else. Something that had been hidden from me for far too long.

Mum was at Alex's pub. They had a table for her.

Alex met me at the door. "You know she doesn't like seeing you here."

Mum might be belligerent, but at least she was ashamed about it. "She too drunk already?"

Alex shook her head. "Honestly, she hasn't been as bad lately."

I looked around. I hated this place. I hated the smells of liquor, the forced laughter, the hopelessness. I knew I was only seeing it framed through the prism of my mother, but that knowledge didn't soften my feelings. Part of me hated Alex, too, but it wasn't her fault.

She kept the place from chaos, and she kept Mum out of trouble—although no one hassled her much; she'd beaten in too many heads of those who had tried. People needed a place like this. I suppose Mum needed a place like this.

I took a deep breath, then walked over to Mum's table. She sat there facing away from me, a whiskey bottle, an empty glass, and a jug of water before her. She kept tapping them with her fingers.

I cleared my throat.

"I know you're there," Mum said. "What do you want?"

I sat down next to her, and put her silver knife on the table. She looked at it a while.

"It's time we talked, Mum," I said.

Mum shook her head. "Jean, it was so long ago . . ."

"Nan told me her trouble."

"Your nan's turned out much better. You've asked me this before, and let it go."

"But I didn't need to know then," I said. "I need to know now. We might all be dead in a few days."

I told her what Mark had told me. Mum listened, though she didn't seem surprised. I suppose we'd all felt things building, whether we could understand it or not.

She poured herself a glass, didn't water it down. "I won my challenge, Jean, but in the winning, failed. You must know that. I was fully pregnant with you, so you were there for my failure."

"So it *was* my fault?"

Mum laughed. "Despite what I may throw at you sometimes, not *everything* is your fault. I had been with your father for several years. Let me tell you about your father." I'd heard all this before, but I let her speak, as I didn't know where it might lead. "He was a northerner who came down here as a child. Because of that, I think he was always trying to prove himself, but he never did with me. He knew that wouldn't work.

"I suppose I was the same. Nan had taught me since I was four—I have memories of lessons prior, but they may have been imaginings. But I was walking the levee from a very young age, and I was good, better than good. We are born into this, but I was born *for* this! Nan had her ways, and they were wily and cautious, but mine were more direct.

"I know Nan told you that there are fewer monsters now because she has built on the legacy of our family. And there's truth in that. But there is another truth, too: There are fewer monsters because I would hunt.

"Oh, but I loved it. Some folks see what we have as a curse, but I took it as a gift. I didn't argue with the dead; I quieted them. You walk above their grasping hands; around me, they would be still, and if I required them, they would come at my demand. And the monsters! It was as though I called them, and when they came to me, they died." She looked at the knife I had put on the table. "It's such a little thing, but it was so deadly. I see the awkward way you hold it, and it makes me wince."

"Teach me," I said.

Mum shook her head. "I have nothing to teach you. I can't teach a gift, and you do well enough. I did better, that's all. By the time my challenge came, I thought I was above all challenges; that the sun could descend upon the earth, and I'd send it dead back into the sky.

"I had many friends. I didn't shy from them. I wasn't awkward the way you and Nan are; I encouraged friendships. I protected the town, and I wanted people to know that, to celebrate it. Why shouldn't I? I risked my life so that they may sleep safe in their beds.

"One day, I decided it was time to have a party. I took my friends beyond the levee, down to the Prestons' land."

I knew that place. I thought of it now: cold and angry, waiting. I guessed it didn't feel like that then.

"The Prestons owed me. I'd cleared everything but the Husklings from their land, and even they were afraid of me. Your father had prepared a huge bonfire, and we danced in a clearing beneath the moon. I was pregnant, and in love, and I wanted everyone to know. But you know what? I think I was bored, too; I had met everything that the world had thrown at me, and I'd bested it. I think I wanted that challenge. Maybe I was even calling it to me, using my friends as bait. It knew what I wanted, and the world gave it to me: all at once, and in the cruellest way."

"A sudden sickness overtook the party. Everyone there fell into a deep slumber, your father with them. Even you stilled within me. No movement, and you had been such a wriggly thing. I called your name, but you didn't answer—how could you? Even the fire went out: not to embers, but to cold black wood. I stood there, knife out. Then I felt a presence, like a storm, stirring. Footsteps, but made of the churning wind. Nothing that a knife could drive through.

"I could feel the thing's hunger for me. Its whispered voice filled the grove, old and angry. I had brought the challenge to it, I had forced its hand. It told me what would happen as a consequence, that in a few moments everyone would wake, but they would be changed, turned monstrous and dire, as men once had been in the Years of Heat and Sadness. Ten creatures all at once, and I could fight them, or I could destroy them now as they slept, and my husband would survive, and the baby within my belly; its heart would beat again." Mum touched her stomach, her eyes on mine. "I knew this day was coming; I had been waiting all my life. But not for this. Some grand battle, yes, some quest of blood and wildness, but not this cruel, quiet challenge. My dear-heart and my child in the balance. But I knew that voice spoke truly, and I had but one choice to make."

Her eyes flicked to the blade on the table. "I slit my friends' throats one by one. I didn't stop until they were all dead.

"You started to move in my belly again, and your father woke up and looked at me with such horror.

"The town never quite believed me; nor did your nan. I lost the gift I had been given, and she was forced to walk the levee again. Although I know your father believed me when I told him what had happened, our life wasn't the same . . . in fact, I think it was grief that drove him to Furnace as much as anything. All my friends, all of those dearest to me, were dead, and by my hand. I killed Jacob's wife, Agatha, and she was with child. I killed Jacob's wife and his daughter.

"But you were born that day, Jean." Her voice cracked. "I did what I had to do. But I should never have taken my friends there. I should never have risked their lives so."

I reached out, and grabbed her hand, as much to steady myself as her. I looked into her eyes, and saw the ruin of that memory, no matter that she thought she had chosen true.

I was stunned, but at the same time, part of me, that older part, had known all along. "You had to do what you thought was right."

"Yes, and look what it got me."

A *daughter*, I thought, but I didn't say it.

"Look what it got *you*. Not a person in town who doesn't remember that, who isn't frightened of what you may become. Why do you think kids never played with you?"

"I always thought that was my fault."

"Of course it wasn't!" Mum said. She hugged me hard. "You were a good child, but people aren't going to let you have friends. Who'd risk that, after what I did?"

She wiped at her eyes. "Why do you think no one has ever mentioned this? The whole town swore not to let you know. How can a child take that burden? They were scared of you, and, even more, they were scared of your nan. If they let me be, just let me drink . . . well, I didn't care what they were afraid of."

"So what do I do now?" I asked Mum.

"You'll find the right way. You always have. Not a trouble we haven't beaten. Not in the end."

"What kind of answer is that?"

"When it comes to this, when it comes to our troubles, all of us can only do what we think is right, no matter the pain of it, no matter what comes after. Everything we've done, everything we've taught you, is for that reason alone. In the end, you have to decide."

I left Mum there. I knew that whatever we said after that could never make it better. How could it be? And then I went into the Long Between. That thing, that storm of a thing, lay undefeated, waiting.

I let it find me.

It called my name in my mother's voice.

I let it wash over me, seep inside me, and I saw the night of the party, the last night of my mother's power, and the challenge she had faced.

I watched them all die. I owed them that. No wonder I had been so frightened of this hunter. I stood, and honoured their deaths, and mourned them, and my mother, my nan, and our town. Inside me, the storm howled and raged until the last of its winds became silent and still, fading into nothingness.

"Why didn't you ever tell me about Mum?" I asked Nan the next morning, dawn past, my circuit half done. I sounded less angry than I felt.

Mum hadn't come home that night. I wondered if she ever would again. It had been working at me, the shock of it. I'd sit up in bed, hardly slept, my fingers finding that coin, twirling it between them, hot then cold, then hot again, thinking of my poor mother.

The horror of it. The knife drawn across their throats. Poor Jacob's wife and child. I was angry at Nan; I was angry at both of them. Why hadn't they told me?

"It was never my place," Nan said. That answer only made me angrier.

"How come no one did?"

"People knew not to. No one wanted to remember that time, and everyone was afraid. They knew what your mother was capable of; what I was capable of; and, worse, they feared that we might walk away. Both the dead and living feared that. Better that you didn't know."

"But it destroyed her. I might have—"

"What might you have done? You were just a child. You had enough horrors to deal with. She let it destroy her. Jean, you are lucky to be alive. After what happened, all your mother craved was death. You were born in the heart of it . . . How could she not see what she had done when she looked at you? And when your father was pulled to Furnace, all she craved was the bottle. I raised you. I looked after you. Your mother's story didn't matter."

I smacked my walking stick into the ground. Nan hissed. "It did," I said. "One secret of many, but the biggest, the worst!"

"I thought—we thought—it might break you. Make you even more timid. My job, yours, and your mother's, demands that we make decisions, some of them quite cruel. Part of that is knowing that they will be hard, and that they may turn out wrong. Did my child kill monsters, or was she the monster? How could I tell you that? How could I raise you on that knowledge? I fed you what you needed, but I was damned if I was going to feed you that poison. We all make mistakes."

"And look where it left us. No wonder the whole town treated me like they did."

"They needed us."

I stared north, watching those campfires on the Prestons' farm, all that smoke burning like tiny Furnaces. What choices might I have to make? How easy would it be to walk down the levee, to keep walking, to never come back?

"Myles doesn't think so. Maybe he's right."

"Myles is a fool."

"Jacob reckons he might try something."

"He wouldn't dare."

"Furnace is burning again. People are heading west every day. People are scared. Maybe they've had enough."

"Not everyone," Nan said.

I turned my gaze west, then north again, trying to read the smoke. It told me nothing.

"We've a whole town here," Nan said.

"A town I am supposed to be protecting."

"Perhaps it's time they protected you."

I shook my head. "That's how we got here in the first place. Too many people trying to protect me, and me knowing nothing of it!"

This had to stop.

All of this had to stop.

I just didn't know how.

I crossed over the levee, and walked to the Huskling King's hall, careful to keep clear of the Prestons' farm, more for his sake than mine. I didn't know what I would do if I saw that smarmy face.

It had been a while—many years, in fact—since I had come to the king seeking advice. I suppose I'd grown up. The statues in the grove had nearly doubled in number. There was all manner of grotesqueries and beauty. A new one of me, standing tall, one hand gripping my walking stick. My face wasn't happy, but it was strong. And there was Mark, guns on his belt, looking out at the world, all mockery and challenge. That's how auditors were. At least, that's how I imagined them from the books I'd read, and the couple I had met.

"Do you like my work?" The Huskling King asked, startling me. "Or are you just here to complain on that Preston's behalf?"

"Why didn't you tell me?" I demanded.

Bartlett frowned. I could tell that he knew what I was talking about. Perhaps he'd sensed the flurry in the Long Between. "Your nan made me swear an oath. How could I break it? Oaths define my kind."

"You couldn't even give me clues?"

"Oh, I did. There were plenty. Secrets can rot at you. Some things are best left unsaid, but I tried to say those even if I couldn't say it with the clarity it required. I like you, Jean. I didn't think it was fair."

"You say nothing with clarity," I said. The king chuckled.

I peered up at my sculpture. "I look too old here." I said, then I pointed at Mark. "He looks too sweet."

"Allow me a little artistic licence!" He grinned. "It's been a long time between visits."

"I've been busy," I said.

He sighed. "So have I." He gestured at another statue, standing away from all the others. I'd not noticed it before, but now it was all I could see. "I finished that yesterday."

It was my graceful man.

"I felt a hint of him months ago, but I wasn't sure. I kept meaning to contact you, but he seemed so far away. It's a risky thing for us to approach your town these days; all those guns in the Prestons' place. To be honest, I thought I was dreaming him. It's happening a lot; I feel like I am at the edge of something. I sense forces at work. Furnace has been burning longer than we suspect, just hidden. Whatever he has been waiting for has come."

"I've heard that he was busy already, just not here."

"He's a sneaky one, all right. Makes sense, him wanting to avoid you. Things haven't worked out well for him where your family is concerned."

But there was no Nan this time. "The Masters have sent an auditor. They're frightened of him now. Too frightened to send one of their own: He unmakes them." I thought back to Lolly's ceremony and the Master I'd met there. Come to think of it, that Master had been frightened of Furnace even then.

"They should be," the Huskling King said. "But this is your trouble. And you are its match."

"What if I can't handle this?" Panic rushed through me. "What if it's too big for me? Mum may have been able to slit the throats of her friends, but I couldn't. I don't even have friends."

The king laughed, and it was as though the air cleared for a minute. There was nothing mocking to it, just a kindness, and I thought about that man he had been.

"Jean. Jean. You are not your mother. This trouble that's found you is different. And you *have* friends." Bartlett touched my hand. "Most of what the world throws at us, the deepest, hardest things, they're too much for any one person. But you know what?"

I looked at him, confused.

"You're not just one person. You are your town, you are me, you are your nan, and Bird, and wise old Tree, and even your mother. We are you. We are all of us: the air we breathe, and the earth we walk on, and the way we die. We have your back. It will either be enough, or it won't, but don't despair." He paused, gave me a cunning look. "Though I could furnish you with more power, should you require it."

"Like you did with old Jim? No thanks," I said.

The king chortled gleefully. "See? You're wiser than you know."

I visited Tree. Furnace had hidden from her, too. The birds were restless. But now smoke was rising, and thickening in the sky; you could taste it. Something was coming.

Tree's clever birds had stopped flying even as far west as Casement Rise. Furnace was stronger. For the first time, I sensed fear here. Tree had grown blind just when I needed her.

"How did you make it to me?" I asked Bird.

"I look for you," Bird said. "I would fly through storm and thunder for that."

"Does it hurt?"

"Only a little," Bird conceded, though I could tell it was more than that, much more.

I scratched their head. I don't think I cried, but I may have. I looked at Tree's thick white trunk with all those tales scratched upon it by beak and claw.

"Is my mother on there?"

"Yes," Bird said. "We tried to warn her about her challenge, but she never listened to us. I don't think she was capable."

"She was so good at everything."

"Not everything," Bird said.

"Which story is yours?" I asked Bird. They fluffed themselves up on my shoulder.

"I'm still writing it. In my head," they said. "You're in it, a little."

"Do you know how my bit ends?"

"You'll have to wait," Bird said.

"You don't have a clue, do you?" I said, and Bird took off. I stood for a while, staring at all those stories, and wondering where mine would fit, if I earned it, if Bird ever found out how it ended.

When I got home, Mum was waiting for me. She looked rough, but I was surprised by how happy I was to see her.

"Hello," she said.

"Look, I'm—" We both stopped. "You go," I said.

"If you never want to see me again, I'll understand."

I didn't know what to say. I was talked out. So I did what I could: I held her, and she let me, and after a while she held me back. For the first time, we knew whom we were holding, and we did it anyway.

At last I felt ready. Each morning I walked the circuit. Each morning I gazed west and north with my eyes, as well as that gaze beyond sight, but I saw nothing.

A few days later, when I looked in on Mark, he was stronger. He was sitting up in his bed to drink his tea.

"Still here," he said.

"Why'd they send you?"

"You know how auditors are. We have our regions, and we travel the extent of them. There's not too many of us, but there doesn't need to be. I was the auditor furthest south, so they told me to come here directly. And you know what?"

I shook my head.

"I wanted to come here. I've heard of you, Jean. You and your bird, and the monsters you've faced. Word comes from the south as well, you know. Why, there's people that write stories of you."

"No!" I said.

"Why would I lie to you?"

I sat on the foot of his bed. "People have made a habit of twisting truths around me."

"Not me," he said. "I could tell you a couple of stories to see if they're true. Those cold children you saw—"

I shook my head. I didn't want to hear any stories about me. Not right now. "Are there any other auditors coming?"

"The Masters are terrified of leaving the Red City. Auditors are being called back from the margins."

"It won't be long now," I said. "I can feel it."

"Yeah, I can, too. You need me, and I can hardly piss in a bedpan." He put his teacup down, couldn't hide the yawn. His eyes looked at me, unfocused.

"Sleep," I said. "That's what *you* need. Nothing else. I don't mean to make you feel bad, but I think you've made everything worse."

Mark grimaced. "Not the first time someone's said that to me."

Mark was slow to recover, and it vexed him. He pushed against the sleep required, and it pushed back twice as hard. The strong so often forget what it is to be weak that they suffer worse through their obstinacy.

"Force won't heal you faster," I told him.

"I've things that need to be done. I'm here to see you safe."

"I'm safe. I'm not defenceless, either. You're a guest in our house. Let yourself get well."

"I'm a prisoner!" He folded his arms.

I couldn't help but laugh at him. "If you're so set on that, there's the town barracks. Or maybe Myles could see to your well-being. You're a prisoner of your wounds, nothing more." I gestured at the door. "You can walk out at any time. Your horse is waiting."

"Poor Kala," Mark said. "She's had a rough time of it. Let me see her, at least."

Kala had seen him every morning; Mark had just slept through her visitations.

I yielded, and let him walk to his horse. Kala was pleased at his appearance, and the joy it gave him delighted me, too. She was a different creature in his presence, more confident and at ease. He whispered at her, low and calm. She may not talk like Bird, but they communicated just the same. After that, he visited her every day, and the urgency left him for a time.

But it did come back. With health, impatience rises. I'd felt an impatience building in me, too. If something bad must come, let it come.

Mark was waiting in the kitchen one morning after my circuit. No sign of my graceful man, nor a single threat, but people kept leaving. I tried at cheerful, but it was hard. I was in too thin a mood for smiles. Mark had come a long way in his recovery, though his wounds still pulled at him. His desire to see the town, and help with its defences possessed a greater urgency.

"You're up," I said.

"I've been up since dawn," he replied, somewhat pointedly, and poured me a coffee.

I laughed. "That makes two of us, then."

"You promised me a tour of the town."

"You really want to be seen walking with me? I'll taint you with my presence."

"Who knows Casement Rise better? Who has to deal with everyone in it? Maybe Dr. Williams, but she doesn't like me."

"And you think I do?"

"Oh, I know it."

That brought some heat to my cheeks. He was right. But I wasn't ready to give in that easily. Not yet.

I took him to the library, as I had work to attend to.

"This hardly counts as a tour of the town," he said.

"It'll have to do."

When I came back, Mark had set himself up at a desk, piles of books on one side of him, and Dale Preston, the librarian, making him tea, and chatting away like he was some long-lost cousin.

"You're already done?" he asked.

"It's been most of a day."

"This place is a tiny treasure," Mark said. "You've a history of auditors here no more than ten years old. In a town this far south, that's remarkable."

I shrugged. "I've little time for histories."

Mark rolled his eyes. "Well, you should. Histories are important. Why, in the Great Library in the Red City, there's a history of the world that runs to sixty volumes."

"You've read them?"

"Some of them."

"And you are better for it?"

"I'm a better auditor because of it."

I tapped my feet. "I have all the history I need right here."

He laughed. "The role of an auditor is eye, judge, and fist. We are an extension of our Masters' laws. We're here to end the fear. We scare easy, too, because the world's so fragile," he said. "We scare easy. But you don't."

He touched my hand. My heart started to rattle. It beat at my ribs, grown resentful of its captivity.

"I'm a little scared now," I said.

Mark laughed. "You should be."

I didn't pull my hand away. Nor did he, and we sat that way for a while.

Finally, he released his grip. "Will you take me to the levee?"

"Yes," I said. "If it will get you out of here."

We walked past Dale. I grinned at her; she grimaced at me.

"Doesn't anyone like you?" Mark said.

"They don't have to," I said. "There's not a single Preston that will ever like me, and I don't blame them."

"You ever tried a little charm?" he said, radiating it like the sun.

I shrugged my shoulders. "I don't have to like them, either."

After our tour, I took him home. He took a nap, and didn't wake up until midday next.

The next day, I'd had enough of Myles' fires. He still hadn't come into town.

"Bird," I said. "Will you check on that farm? Keep a distance, though. Don't let them see you."

"I can be cunning," Bird said.

I looked at them. "I'm sure you can."

Then they were off.

When the bell rang, I had been home from my circuit for an hour. Mark was sitting in the kitchen; he still moved as though in great pain, and the last few days in the library had taken its toll. His head lifted at the sound.

"I need to see to this," I said.

"I'm coming with you," Mark said. "There's not a ringing bell I've ever liked."

I shook my head. "You're staying here," I said. "If there's trouble, I don't need someone else to look after."

Mark thought about that. He walked slowly, like a man much older than his age—perhaps older than he could ever imagine living—into his room, and came back with a gun.

"Take this," he said.

I shook my head. "That's not how I solve problems."

I hurried to the levee, and I wasn't the only one. I felt a sense of gratification, along with a sickening fear.

Jacob was at the Summer Gate, and I climbed up to him. He faced east. There was a finger of smoke, an odd mirror of Furnace.

I looked around. "Where's Myles?"

I stared at that flame. I knew what it was.

"Tree," I said. I closed my eyes and dived into the Long Between. The space was all chaos, forces crashing around me, laughter and screams coming from the west. But I pushed through. I knew how to shut out distraction.

When I came out the other side, the sky was so bright that I was blinded a little.

"Jean," something called. A familiar voice. My head ached, and my tongue sat thick and dry in my mouth. Smoke stench, and not the smoke of Furnace for once.

"Jean."

"Yes, Bird," I said.

Bird sat puffed up on a nearby branch, their crest raised to a spike above their head. Their feathers were dark with soot.

"You're here," Bird said.

Not far to my left, Tree blazed. Around that fire was scattered the white corpses of the clever birds. Some had been shot, others had just dropped from the sky, killed by the shock of it all.

"They came, crept up when we weren't looking, and burnt us. My tree, my home, let me free of her. I didn't die." Bird said.

"Who came?"

"Prestons, with fire. Must have seen me spying. All the others are dead; they were dead when I arrived. I'm alone."

They fluttered to the earth, and landed clumsily. I bent, and picked them up, held them in my arms. "You're not alone."

They put their head against my neck. "I'm quite mad."

I stroked them gently, looked up, and saw a fire burning to the northwest.

The Husklings! I entered the Long Between for the second time that day, and came out to horror.

Each and every one of them was dead. Gone as Tree was gone. Gone as the clever birds were gone. Attacked in the day; while they were sleeping. Bartlett had put up a fight—his nails torn and bloody—but they had shot him in the head, strung his body up on his throne.

I looked at him, and howled. I felt the earth, and he wasn't there. He was completely and utterly gone.

Jacob hardly even blinked when I appeared next to him.

Mark was standing there, too. "Storm in the Holy Sun," he said, jumping at my arrival.

Bird fluffed up their feathers at him, hissed, then tucked their ash-streaked face behind a wing.

There were a couple of others with them, including Alice's brother Travis, all of them armed.

271

"Tree's gone," I said. Bird moaned at that, and it was all I could do to keep my voice steady. "So are the Husklings."

Jacob nodded, and pointed down. About fifty yards beyond the Summer Gate, a good two dozen men had gathered. Myles was at the front of them, guns belted round his waist.

"You going to let me in, Jacob?" Myles shouted up.

"Not when you're armed, I'm not."

"These are just my men. That witch has ruined this town enough. She and her kin, and those devil birds. It's time we ended it."

"She's kept us safe," Jacob said. "They all have."

"Safe! Tell that to my brother, who Nancy let climb up that rope. Tell that to my sister; throat cut by Ella. Throat cut by the very knife Jean holds now. Tell it to all the head of livestock that I've lost to the Husklings, the grains in my fields I've had devoured by clever birds. All she and her kin have ever brought is trouble.

"My pistols killed those monsters easily enough. We don't need a witch's trickery. Bring her down; let her face justice."

I didn't say anything. There were other folks on that levee, and they were looking at me. I felt then just what Nan had felt and feared: the fragility of my place here. The town that could so easily turn.

Alice's brother was closest to me. He shook his head. Others were frowning, angry, too, and I realised that their anger wasn't directed at me.

"Don't worry, Jean," Travis said. "No one's going to touch you. Not while I'm breathing."

"Bring her down," Myles said, all at once cold and polite.

"No," Jacob said.

Mark's guns were out now, too.

"I thought an auditor would have more sense," Myles said. "I'll be coming up this levee. We've guns enough."

"Shoot him first," Mark said. "Head shot."

Jacob gestured at the folks nearest him, then pointed his rifle at Myles. I wanted to grab their guns from their hands.

Mark lifted his pistols.

I ran out in front of him. A pistol went off; I felt a bullet fly past my head; but I stood there, my hand closed around the gold coin. Where had it come from? When had I put it in my pocket? It burned so hot, I nearly dropped it. I felt for a moment like that twelve-year-old: impetuous, frightened, angry.

The coin had been my secret, but the town had kept a bigger one from me.

I threw my gaze from the levee, from Mark and Travis and Jacob, down to Myles and his crew, all of them armed and aching for death.

"Stop this!" My voice cracked. "Stop this now!"

There was silence. I felt a sudden rush of power from the west, and it had never been so strong. A migraine boiled inside my head. I wanted to vomit. I wanted to close my eyes, close out the sun, and stay that way until the pain was gone. But I did not.

I waited for another shot to come, but no one fired.

Instead, they put down their weapons, Myles' crew and Jacob's, all of them.

They put down their weapons, dropped them to the ground, and turned towards the west.

And then they walked.

"Jacob!" I tried to follow, but Furnace was so strong. I dropped to my knees, sickened by its force.

Jacob glanced at me, worried but distant, as though I were the figment of a dream.

"Sorry, Jean," he said, but he didn't look sorry.

Behind me, there was motion. The whole town was emptying. People were already clambering down the levee, not caring for its markings. What did it matter? There'd be no one to protect.

"This is terrible," Bird said. "This is terrible."

Furnace called, and this time it called everyone, except for me.

I tried to follow them, but I couldn't. There were hundreds of them, and they walked west so easily. I struggled to take even a few steps. I was sick to my guts, and not just with the force of Furnace's resistance.

"Stop, Jean, stop," Nan said.

I ignored her, too distracted by the departure of Mark, and Jacob, my aunties, Alice's brother Travis, and Mum, even Mum.

I called for her, and when she looked back, it was like I wasn't there.

"She can't see you, Jean," Nan said.

I reached the edge of the levee and toppled forward, down into a sickening dark.

When I woke up, I had crawled a ways back towards the levee. Furnace was pushing back, but gentle again.

"Jean," someone said. I looked up, and there was Alice. What was she doing here? Why hadn't she been called with the others?

"They're gone," I said. "All of them are gone."

She shook her head. "I'm here, aren't I?" She bent down, and helped me up.

Together, we walked home.

No one was there, of course. I was too exhausted even to cry. I fell into bed.

"Rest," Alice said. "Rest, now."

I slept, crashed through dreams into the darkest, deepest slumber. When I woke, it was night. My hands were closed around the golden coin, and it burnt so hot that my palms had blistered.

The next morning when I got up, after spending the rest of the night staring at the ceiling, Alice was asleep. I left her there, and walked to the levee to get a look at my troubles.

The dead grumbled beneath me, but I ignored them.

"I've failed," I said to Nan.

"Don't say that," Nan snapped. "You're still breathing."

When I reached the top of the levee, my jaw dropped.

"What is it, girl?" Nan said.

I tried to explain it, but I couldn't.

Beyond the base of the levee there was nothing: not a mist risen from the river, not a hint of road or hill, just an absence that hurt my eyes the longer I looked at it.

The world beyond was gone.

I ran back to the house. Alice was awake, making a cup of tea. The simple normalcy of it almost made me weep.

"What?" she said.

"I can't explain it," I said. "I have to show you."

Alice shook her head. "Not until you've eaten. Not until you've had a cup of tea."

"But—"

"No." Alice said.

So I sat there and ate and drank.

"There's some things we need to talk about," Alice said, "Even if we'll both be dead by tonight."

I looked at her. "If you think that, why do we need to talk?"

Alice rolled her eyes, then took a quick sip of tea. "I'm sorry, Jean. I never meant to hurt you. Not back when we were kids, and not later. I'm sorry that I did."

"I was hardly perfect," I said. "I was horrible."

Alice laughed. "We both were."

There were some things I still wasn't ready to talk about. Not yet. I put my cup down. Truthfully, I felt the better for the meal.

"Now," I said, "I need you to see the levee."

"Storm in the Holy Sun," Alice exclaimed.

"Exactly."

"Where is everything?"

"I have no bloody idea."

The nothing beyond the levee remained just that.

"Can we walk out into it?"

I picked up a stone, and threw it. It broke into a dozen fragments as soon as it passed beyond the levee, and the sound of it breaking was a shrill and horrible thing that echoed, and drilled into our skulls. Bird fell from my shoulder, and thrashed on their back until I righted them, my hands shaking, blood roaring in my skull.

Alice pulled her hands from her ears when the noise had died down. "Don't do that again," she said.

We walked back home.

Bird sat on my shoulder, silent. If only I could ask their advice. I was bereft, of Bird and Tree and the Huskling King.

I stroked Bird's head, and they guided me to the best spots.

"I need you," I said. Bird said nothing.

"Please," I said.

"Tree," they said, once.

"Tree? Tree's gone."

Bird didn't respond.

But I think I had an answer. Bird was bird and tree; their mind was partly made of the stories written on their trunk.

I couldn't get them Tree, but I could do something else. I didn't dare believe that it might work, but what other chance did I have? I closed my eyes, and I could see Tree, the marks scored from root to branch. I couldn't read them, but I could envision them so clearly.

I grabbed the axe by the woodpile, found the biggest tree in our backyard, and began to make gashes in it. I couldn't give Bird Tree back, but I could copy the stories by which the clever birds made themselves.

Bird sat, watching me. At first, they were unchanged, but slowly, with each new marking, their eyes turned sharper, their wings moved with less hesitation. I was drawing them back.

It took most of the day, and when I was done, my fingers blistered, weary as I'd ever been, Bird, my Bird, circled the tree.

"This is Tree," they said.

I let myself have a moment's joy.

"I'm lost," I said. "I can't find my town."

"This is your town," Bird said.

"This isn't my town when there's no one in it. They're gone, and I can't follow."

Bird flew above me, and landed on a branch. They stretched out their wings, thrust their beak amongst their feathers, and watched me with a glittering eye. "You can't follow because you're using the wrong gate. South to winter, west to autumn."

I knew what I had to do.

I ran into my room, felt under my pillow.

When I came back into the kitchen holding the coin with what I am sure was a look of mad triumph, Alice nearly dropped her tea. "What have you got there?"

I waved it in her face. "You mean, you can see it?"

"Of course I can!"

I told her everything. It flooded out of me, about the coin, about the night after we fought, and I'd wished her mother and Mrs. Paige away, and by the end, despite it all, she was hugging me, when I'd expected her to be shouting, or worse.

"Don't you dare blame yourself, Jean. You didn't make my mother walk to Furnace, just like you didn't call them all there now. That was the graceful man's doing. You were a kid—we were both stupid kids. You don't think I didn't wish you gone that night, or dead? I wished harder than you would believe. Whatever that coin is, it's magic, and some of that's impossible to fight. Magic and madness, we've all got our limits against them. If you think it will help. A coin has two sides, after all."

"It does," I said. "It does!"

I got ready, slipped on my belt, and sheathed the bone needle and the silver knife in it.

Down we went to the Autumn Gate. I stood there studying its patterns. Autumn sat between the heat and the cold; it was as variable as any of that rusted ironwork. You could wake up any day during autumn, and not know if you were moving away from heat or towards it. And yet, as the days passed, the change was certain and obvious.

"This gate's never been opened," Alice said. "I don't even think it's a gate."

I shook my head. "It's just been waiting."

"I think you're right," Nan said beneath me. "Clever, clever."

I studied that door. It wasn't easy, but I found it: a tiny dimple in the art, a circle the size of the coin. When I pushed the coin against the door, it slotted in neatly.

A door unlocked can change everything.

The world jolted, shifted counter to the earth.

The coin fell back into my hand, and I slipped it into my pocket.

I put my hands against the ancient metal, and I pushed. It wasn't easy, at first, but Alice came, and leant against it with me, and the door swung out, and behind it there was an opening through the levee to the road. The absence that had surrounded the town had fallen inwards, and become the world again.

Somewhere in the west, I sensed a great disappointment, and then he was there, standing beside me. He waved a hand through the opening, pulled it back as though it burnt.

"You don't need to do this," the graceful man said. "Don't you like your quiet town? Isn't it what you wanted?"

"Begone," Alice shouted.

The graceful man blinked at her. "How did I forget you? But then, you were never really of consequence." He turned to me. "Look, I'll even give her to you. She can keep you company."

"Keep her company? Give me to her?" Alice flung herself at him. "You stole my Lolly!"

The graceful man ducked away from her, grinned. "Ah, that's what you want! He's not gone. He's patiently waiting."

"Go!" Alice said.

"I'm not even here," he said, and then he wasn't.

"Let's do this," Alice said. "Before he comes back."

I gripped her hand. "Yes." We walked through the doorway together.

For the first time in my life, I saw the road to Furnace as it truly was. No dust, no smoke, a land as verdant as any in the region. For the first time in my life, Furnace's call had me. It was bone-deep, the purest, most painful of longings, and it could not be denied.

"Can't you feel it?" I said. "Everything's changed."

"No. It's just the same."

"Good," I said. "Because I'm not."

I felt like I'd found the edges of the world, and curled my fingers around them.

I took another step, then another, and tumbled onto my knees. I'd been tugged forward, harder than my exhausted legs could manage.

I landed hard.

"Careful," Nan said. "Careful." I could feel her beneath me, feel the others, too. So many, just beneath the surface. They may not have been able to cross the Winter Gate to the Stone Road, but they could come this way.

"Are you all coming with me?"

"Where else can we go?" Nan said. "You're all we can see."

Alice pulled me up. "Are you all right?"

I shook my head, then I nodded. She squeezed my hand, and it was like Nan all over again. I nearly cried then and there.

Furnace called, a desperate, powerful force, and it pulled at me from the back of my throat. My mouth began to salivate. My legs were itchy, desperate to run, but I was too weak.

For the first time I used that walking stick the way it was meant to be used. Me bent over it, limbs shaking, sweat streaking down my face, my legs, my back. It wasn't a hot sweat, either: It was cold, as cold as a crisp autumn evening.

"You're shaking," Alice said.

I couldn't help but laugh, no matter how mad it might look: Here I was, ready to face my enemy, the great challenge of my life, and I was so weak I could hardly stand. The dead whispered caution, but none of them demanded that I run away. They were frightened—I could sense that in the rolling heave of them—but they knew it was time for something new.

The road was prettier than I expected: There were wildflowers blooming, kangaroos mobbing. I saw a goshawk in a tree, and Bird stiffened, and crawled under my hair until the goshawk lifted itself up, like it was pushing down the world, not pushing up from it, and flew north.

The whole walk was an enchantment, even with the dead boiling beneath me, and though I was pulled along, almost frantic with desire to reach Furnace, I was steadied by Alice's hand in mine.

I could see the land that we passed through. It was little different to the east, farmland and forest. You could almost imagine it being a part of the Robsons' farm. "Beautiful," I said. "It's beautiful."

Alice shook her head. "Not what I'm seeing. There's death and dust here."

I didn't believe her. I was used to strangeness and horrors; Alice had only fled from them. We'd both had different reactions to our world, and both made sense. If anything, hers more than mine.

But I'd been raised peculiar, and it was peculiar that was needed now.

We walked to the Slouches, and I admired the trees that grew thick upon their slopes. To the north, there was a small homestead where people were working on a stone fence. I wondered if we had ever known the people who lived here.

By late morning, we were over the hill, and heading down into a valley, and below us was a town built beside a creek. Both of us stopped, shocked. We knew this place.

"What is this place?" Alice said. We both knew what it was.

It was home, and not home.

It was Casement Rise, only there wasn't any levee. There were houses and roads leading right to the edge of town, around which were dotted farms and orchards. No smoke: The air smelled sweet.

"We have to hurry," I said, repeating Furnace's demands, its chorus singing in my bones.

"Is it true? What I'm seeing?" Alice said.

"I don't know. Just hurry!"

We almost ran into town. Past the barracks—though they weren't barracks, but shops—past the town hall, and onto the town's gardens. Everything was flowering, the earth dark and rich and perfect.

There they were, my people, working and gardening. I saw Mum, and she stood with my father, and they were both laughing. I saw, in the biggest surprise of all, Jim. He and his crew were harvesting, and sorting wheat, his cart already half full with bags of grain. Lolly was there, too, chatting with one of my aunties, like it was any other day. There was Jacob, leading a cart of fence posts out to the edge of a farm. None of them registered my presence.

Not Jacob, not Mark, nor Myles, who was helping dig a new garden bed. I turned to Alice. "What do you see?" I asked her.

She frowned. "I don't know. It's home, but not. It's perfect, but something's burning, Jean. Can't you smell the smoke?"

I shook my head. The air smelled pure and clean.

"She can't, little Alice," the graceful man said behind us. "There's no smoke for those who are ready, those whom I call. And now you can't smell it either, can you?"

His lips turned to wickedness, and he clicked his fingers, and Alice shot past me, straight to Lolly, and he kissed her, hard, as though this wasn't some madness.

"Not good," Bird said on my shoulder. I stroked their back to calm them.

"I've been busy this morning," the graceful man said. "Each day I visit everyone in town, making my circuit, and I tell them that they are safe and loved. And you know what? They are. Even those I called last. They were full of such hatred. Now it is only love."

"You called them here to stop the fighting?"

"It's what you wanted, wasn't it? You had them all to yourself, once. A whole town, and I had nothing. Until one by one they came to me. I've been lost all these years, Jean, but now you've come here. Now I have the full set."

"They should be home," I said.

"This is home! When I was born—as a man, grown whole and strong," the graceful man said, "it was to the sounds of a child crying in the east, and here I was. I knew nothing, had no mother's breast to sup from. Just me, and this place, springing up as you cried, and bit that doctor's hand. You should have seen it: each house blooming, each street stretching out its limbs. I would have laughed, but I was so scared. You were such a fierce one, Jean. It filled me with such dread. I could see that blood; I could taste it on your lips."

He gripped my hand, and I felt the strength leach from my limbs. "Stop with your worries," he said.

He led me to a place I knew well: home, but with so many rose bushes in the garden, fresh paint on the walls. In the front yard was a chair I recognised, the one that had horrified me as a child.

"All I wanted was for you to shut up. Then those men came—the ones your nan sent—and I whispered to them, and they bowed towards me, and they said they would keep me company. I was so awfully lonely, Jean.

"I wanted more, so I sent them away. They came back with others, and it felt a little better, but not enough, so I went off myself, and started gathering my town. I still find it funny that it was your nan that started it, sending those fellows here. I would have just stayed here, alone, seething, building my power to craft your destruction because that is what we do. Instead, I built a community."

He made me sit down, then. "I'm sure you recognise this."

It was the cord Nan had thrown over his shoulders near a decade ago, all the knots untied. He looped it around my arms, and tied me to the chair.

"You'll have to agree that it's only fitting. We're the shadow of your family, me and my kin—those things you call trouble. Can you imagine what it's like, being called to fight something, being dragged into a conflict for no reason? Who knows why or when it started? As time passed, and you grew, I came upon all sorts of recollections, right back to those days of steel and glass, and heat and sadness. I saw evils and lightning, great crawling terrors, and silent stealthy deaths.

"But I wasn't any of those things; I was just alone, and I knew I could make it otherwise. I dammed the path of the dead, blinded them, and they fed me, yet they still gathered around you. How is that fair? I made myself a special life, but you were always there, a beacon calling.

"All of this could have been fixed earlier, except your nan meddled again. Summoned me, brought everything to a head, then hurled me into confusion. It was all I could do to keep this town alive. But I managed it, even without my Furnace. And then I unpicked those knots, one by one.

"Now, look at us, all grown up."

He pulled the silver knife from my belt. Bird snapped at him, and he flicked them away. They flew back, and he knocked them to the earth, and there they shuddered, and squawked.

"Still, Bird," I hissed. "Be still."

The graceful man hushed at me. "This knife's been so much trouble: for you, for me, for your mother. It makes sense that it would be your undoing, too."

He threw it in the air. It disappeared, then he snatched it from behind my ear.

"You've never really learnt to dance with a knife," he said. "I'm sure if I asked Jacob or your mother to speak true, they would tell me how much that disappoints them. It's a shame you must die for want of such a skill. I did tell you to stay home. One of us must walk away from the mirror in the end."

He tossed the knife up in the air again, and reached out to catch it, but missed. He'd fallen forwards.

Hands gripped his ankles, like those first hands that had gripped me.

"What?" he said.

The dead held him, grabbed his legs, pulled him down. He stumbled, beat at them, but they remained steadfast, and rageful.

I yanked at the cord, but it had no give in it. A hand grabbed my ankle. "Do you trust me?" Nan asked.

"Always," I said.

"Then let yourself fall."

I pushed back against the chair, let it topple. I was on the ground, the cord tight around me.

Nan pressed the knife into my hand. "Hurry."

I was already cutting away. The cord was strong, but the knife was sharp, and that wretched confinement fell from me. I kicked the chair away, and tried to get to my feet. It was a struggle, for the dead in their excitement were confusing me with him, and pulling me down among them.

"Get away from her," Nan yelled. "Get away."

Bird was stirring, shaking out their feathers.

For the first time, the knife felt like it lived in my hand, belonged there, and I wondered if this was how it had been for Mum, when she'd fought monsters, when she'd slid the blade across her friends' throats.

"You brought them here!" the graceful man said. "How did you bring them here? They're scared of me." He shook one leg free, then the other, and he loomed up over me, his hands become claw-like. He was my graceful man, but he was also a beast of fire and fury, a voice that whispered in the dark.

But I didn't step back.

I barely even moved my wrist, and the fingers of his reaching hand tumbled to the earth, to be snatched up by the dead. And they were fingers, not leaves, bugs, or the rude workings of the earth. Flesh, like my flesh.

He looked at his hand with dismay, and I looked at the blood-stained knife with horror.

Then the dead surged up from the earth, and they grabbed, and dragged, and pulled him down.

He'd not walked barefoot amongst them. He'd only ever had to deal with their terror, not their rage. He'd been too busy hunting them, too busy haunting me.

But here it was now: anger, such fierce anger. It was hard not to let it wash over me. Hard not to drown in it. That anger had tricked me into wanting murder when I fought Alice, but I'd learnt so much since then.

For the first time, I saw the fear in his eyes. I knew that look; I recognised it as a face I made, like a frightened, lonely child. He pulled a leg free, and they grabbed it at once, pulled him back to the earth.

He was sinking, breathing hard, his chest bellowing, his arms flailing. He struck at the dead, but they were so many. The gate had been closed for so long.

"You can't do this!" he said. "Isn't everything perfect?"

I shook my head. The knife had its own imperatives. It yearned for an ending. And—for the first time, despite all of Jacob's lessons—I knew what to do with it.

But instead, I stopped.

What if everything I had been taught was wrong? What if the battle wasn't what we thought it was? What if the troubles that I'd been taught to face were more complex, and the solution was less obvious than death? I thought of my mum, and that whispering storm, and the grief of all those lives lost.

"Quick," Nan snapped. "You must be quick."

"No," I said, and looked down at the knife. "Every challenge, every darkness that our family has faced, we've destroyed: thoroughly, and completely. And the next challenge has come back, reborn even stronger. Where has that gotten us?"

I dropped the blade, felt in my pockets for the coin.

The graceful man was sinking so fast. He reached out towards me. "Isn't everything perfect?" he asked again.

"It's all a lie. How can a lie be perfect?"

"Jean, Jean. Only a lie can be perfect. Real life is too raw for perfection!"

He was right.

I held the coin up before him. He'd told me once that he was the giver of keys, and that had proven true. I thought of the Huskling King, who had said that I wasn't just one person. I think I understood what he meant now.

I looked around me, out at the perfect town, where, even now, people were living their lives, everyone oblivious and happy, and I knew I'd wanted this, too. But what I'd wanted, my graceful man had *craved*. We weren't so different because we weren't different at all.

"Here," I said. "This is yours."

He took it from me because I wanted him to. Because he wanted it, too, even if he didn't realise it.

"It feels so warm," he said.

I reached out, held his face in my hands, and pulled. The dead gave way. Their grip released, and we stood there, face to face. Eye to eye.

"What are you doing, Jean?" he asked, his breath warm and smokey. But I didn't let go. He stood there unmoving, shocked to stillness.

"What are you doing?" Nan hissed.

"I'm sorry," I said. "I'm sorry for your suffering. I'm sorry for these wars, and the wild rebirths. I'm sorry about it all. But we can make it better. I hope. I think. I know. Graceful man, I have need of you."

Then I kissed him on the lips. His eyes widened. He struggled, but only for a moment, and then he held me, not as a monster, not as my challenge or my death, but as another living being.

And, in that embrace, we became one.

Memories crashed at us, new and old, distorted and remixed. I was a crying babe, so frightened I burned the darkness with my fear, and all I wanted was to not be alone. A flood, a hand snapping out to hold its reflection. A nest of leaves and bugs and shadows. A town. A town. A town.

I dropped to the ground. My limbs felt foreign, but with every heartbeat, they seemed more familiar, until they became mine.

The dead snatched at me. *That you, Jean? That you?*

"Of course it is," I said. And it was.

I smelled the smoke again, but it didn't sicken me. It was a memory.

I lifted my head, and this town, this lie, desperate for truth, undid itself. There was no sudden tumultuous ending to Furnace; it just fell away, burned out all at once.

A wind came in from the west. It was hot and dry, and it caught the smoke of Furnace, and carried it, dispersed it. The gardens died, and the too-perfect mirror of Casement Rise was gone.

All the people of Casement Rise and beyond were gathered where the square would have been, those I had last seen yesterday, or ten years ago, or longer. One by one, they woke. With them were others who had been called from towns distant. It was more people in one place than I had ever known. There was one I had to see at once.

"Jean," Mum said, when I found her. "Was I dreaming?"

"A little," I said. "But we all were. Look, though," I said, pointing at my father. "He's still here."

Mum was staring at me. "Your eyes."

"What?"

"They've turned golden." She held my shoulders, looked deep into them. She didn't ask me if I was still in there, though. She didn't have to. I was there, all right.

All of me.

I heard a commotion to the right of us and turned, just as Mark was hitting Myles in the head with shovel.

"Still work to be done," I said.

"Never stops," Nan said beneath me.

"Of course it doesn't," I said. "We're only just beginning."

So much happened, then. Believe me when I say I don't remember it all. Getting home, seeing to the town's defences, filling houses that had been empty for so long. None of it was easy.

We had to deal with Myles. I'd never banished anyone before—never thought anyone deserved it—but I wanted him gone. In truth, Myles couldn't face the town anymore. I could see the shame in him.

As much as I seethed, I wasn't cruel. How could more deaths solve anything? I just let Myles and his men go, but not before they helped me bury the Husklings, and the clever birds, and gave them proper monuments.

I made them see the pain of what they had done. They saw me weep, and I made them watch. I think Myles was a changed man, and I wondered how much Furnace had had to do with his rage.

After that, Myles and his men went north. There were plenty of people returning to towns they had been taken from, and his northern cousins could have him.

Jim made his peace with my nan. It was an embarrassing conversation to relay, but I let them have it. I'd never known quite the extent of their love.

"Sad the way the world turns," Jim said to me after. "That she is gone, and I remain."

"When's the world ever been fair?"

Jim shook his head. "Sometimes the right thing happens though. Look at you."

Jim took his crew back north. "We'll keep to the roads as long as we can," he said when I saw him off, "And I'll be back, my granddaughter. I hope you don't mind me calling you that?"

How could I mind? A person needs as many grandparents as they can get.

I hugged him goodbye.

Mark took a long time healing—that walk into Furnace did even more damage—but he did get better. When he was almost ready to leave, I took him to see the Husklings' sculptures. The statues could be instructive if you let them.

"There you are," I said.

He winced to see himself so starkly drawn, but he was also pleased. Not many get to see themselves as a Huskling has seen them.

"You really need to go back to the Red City?" I asked him.

He nodded. "For a little while, at least," he said. "I've promises to keep. Besides you'll need a voice there."

"And when you're done?"

"I might come visiting, eh?"

"I might be here," I said. "Who knows, though."

He seemed downcast at that. "That's more than I dare hope."

I knew he hoped for more than that! Maybe I did, too. But I wasn't going to hurry anything.

I smiled at him, then kissed him quick. "More than you deserve."

Never seen anyone look happier.

I missed Mark, and Kala. But the town relied on me to make its rhythms anew, just like those stones on the levee, their pulse constant like they had never stopped. There were still monsters, of course, and I was there to redirect them, to protect my town from their hungers.

There was one more thing I had to see to. The dead blinded by Furnace still waited beneath me.

"The door remains locked to us, Jean," Nan said. "You'll need to lead us, but start by preparing the mycota broth. It's a long process, but it must be done. And if there's anything the dead have, it's time."

So I did. Nan took me through each step: the last of her lessons. The dead had lost their fury. They were waiting, and I guess I was, too.

"Do you think the troubles will return?"

"Something always does," she said. "There'll always be shadows, as long as the sun shines."

My twenty-first birthday was a new experience. We ate cake, told family stories, people came and visited, and I even got some new books, brought down from the Red City, Mark's name scrawled in the card that came with them.

And when the night was at its deepest, a little cold—unseasonal, but welcome—I drank the mycota broth.

Mum kissed me goodbye. Dad, too. It was hard getting used to having a father, but I think we both liked it.

"We'll be waiting," Mum said.

"You better be," I said, and kissed them both again. Even then, just a few minutes after taking the broth, they were thinner, less real. I wondered if it wasn't the other way around, that the world was shedding me.

I walked to the Winter Gate, Bird hunched on my shoulder. They didn't speak much now. I think their cleverness was slipping away from them, despite my carvings, but they were still Bird. The day before, they had scratched their own markings in the tree.

"What does it mean?" I'd asked them.

"You," they said. "You and me."

They had made their own story, at last.

The dead moved beneath me, but didn't grab or grumble. We passed White Tree, and more joined us. I felt White Tree release them, and there was no bitterness in her. She shone in the moonlight, and Bird made a low, beautiful exclamation in their throat. I felt a momentary sadness, but I didn't stop, not until I reached the Winter Gate.

Nan joined me in the song she had taught me. Above and below, we sang.

I turned the key in its lock, and the world shifted with it, holding its breath.

The door opened easily. It wasn't just my will at work behind it: This was a dam I was breaking, a river set free.

The Stone Road shone bone-pale and, as soon as I stepped upon it, the dead started flowing around me. They rose up, no longer in the earth, no more snarling mouths or grasping hands.

So many! Some rushed past, some held back, and there were those that stayed and walked with me.

"Will you take us all the way?" my dead boy asked, and I saw him for the first time. His eyes were warm and curious, his lips ready to curl into a smile. He was no taller than my shoulder; he'd never grown up.

"Yes," I said. "How else can I say goodbye?"

We walked together down the Stone Road, a grand carnival of death. There was singing, and it was sweet and sad, but the bitterness had gone.

Ahead of us, clever birds flew, and Bird called out to them.

"You can follow," I said to Bird, but they nestled deeper into my shoulder.

This time, the journey didn't take long. We reached the statues carved by the Husklings after what felt like hours, and discovered new ones. There was Nan, and Mum, and me as well; Bird upon my shoulder, ready to fly. Looking at them, I saw not rage nor anger, just a quiet reflection, a strength that existed without violence.

"I like these," Nan said. "I think he's getting better."

When we reached the Mumbling City, it was lit up, ready for the influx. I paused at the edge of town, and let the dead go on, down towards the buildings and beyond them, down the rest of the Road, down the many paths that led to sleep, to silence, to secrets that the living couldn't know.

The little boy hesitated. He was still so young, but he didn't look frightened. "Thank you for the stories," he said.

And, with that, he was gone.

Nan stayed a little longer.

"We made it," I said.

"Of course we did," she said, and smiled, as though there had never been even a hint of doubt. "Ah, there he is. I think he's been waiting long enough, don't you?"

I looked up. My grandfather stood near us on the edge of the road.

"Thank you," she said, and I couldn't tell if she was talking to him or me.

He dipped his head, reached out his hand, and Nan took it.

"I love you," I said.

Her face was as mild and happy as I had ever seen it. He said something to her, and she laughed, and they walked into town. That was the last I heard or saw of them.

Beyond the city, the clever birds called.

Bird stretched out their wings, and tilted their head to appraise the sky.

"It's okay," I said.

They pressed their beak against my jaw for just a moment, then they flew, crying out, joyous and shrill, their wings beating furiously, chasing their kin across those strange heavens. The flock turned back to greet them, and I don't think I had ever felt as happy or as sad as I did right then.

I stood upon the silent earth, and watched the birds fly until I couldn't tell them from the dust that floated yellow in the south. Then I put my back to the city of the dead, and followed the Stone Road home.

Acknowledgments

A book is at once a solitary endeavour and a work of community, and it is for that community that I am truly grateful. I could fill a book with thank yous and it wouldn't be enough.

I'd like to thank Mandy Brett for stringing logic and urgency to this world. Thanks also to Rochelle Fernandez. Thanks, too, to Brio and David Henley for giving it a home in Australia. It means so much to me.

For the American edition, thank you to Liz Gorinsky, whose wise and thoughtful edits were a delight, and steadied a rocking boat. Thank you, too, to the rest of the team at Erewhon who have made this book a beautiful thing. I'd particularly like to thank Martin Cahill, Cassandra Farrin, Viengsamai Fetters, Lakshna Mehta, and Sarah Guan. Qistina Khalidah's cover, along with the type design by Samira Iravani and art direction by Dana Li, is truly divine.

Alisa Krasnostein published the first and very different bit of this story.

Grace Dugan got me focused again.

Genevieve Kruyssen read an earlier draft and made me think it wasn't too terrible.

Thanks, and thanks, and thanks to my agent, Alex Adsett, whose faith and determination found this book a home—a dear friend without whom many of my dreams would have seemed impossible.

This book was written in part with a Qld Writer's Fellowship, and the patience of my employers at Avid Reader: thank you Fiona Stager and Kevin Guy.

Thanks to my writer compatriot, Krissy Kneen, and to Helen Bernhagen, my Sunday stalwart, and dear friend, who put up with a lot while I was writing this book.

This is a book about family, and I would like to thank my parents, siblings, and grandparents.

Thanks to my daughter, Essie, who has taught me about babies and toddlers, and their wild and wonderful ways, and who I sometimes feel was almost summoned into being by this book, and was already a presence in its later drafts: even before we met her. And welcome to the world, my son, Charlie. May it treat both of you well, my children.

Finally, thanks to Fiona Jean MacDonald, my heart, who gave this book serious study and helped me guide it back along the Stone Road. I love you, my darling.

This book was written on Turrbal and Jagera land—always was, always will be. It is beyond time that we had a treaty in this country.

Thank you for reading this title from Erewhon Books, publishing books that embrace the liminal and unclassifiable and championing the unusual, the uncanny, and the hard-to-define.

We are proud of the team behind *The Stone Road* by Trent Jamieson:

Sarah Guan, Publisher
Diana Pho, Executive Editor
Viengsamai Fetters, Assistant Editor

Martin Cahill, Marketing and Publicity Manager
Kasie Griffitts, Sales Associate

Cassandra Farrin, Director
Leah Marsh, Production Editor
Kelsy Thompson, Production Editor

Alice Moye-Honeyman, Junior Designer

and the whole publishing team at Kensington Books!

Learn more about Erewhon Books and our authors at erewhonbooks.com.

X: @erewhonbooks
Instagram: @erewhonbooks
Facebook: @ErewhonBooks

Reading Guide

EREWHON

✳ About the Author ✳

TRENT JAMIESON is a multi-award winning Australian novelist and short story writer. He is the author of *Day Boy*, the Death Works series, and the Nightbound Land duology. His picture book *The Giant and the Sea* won the 2021 Environment Award for Children's Literature. When he's not writing, Trent works as a bookseller at Avid Reader in Brisbane.

✳ Book Discussion Questions ✳

These suggested questions are to spark conversation and enhance your reading of *The Stone Road*.

1. *The Stone Road* starts with Jean's birthday party and a visit from the mysterious Graceful Man. Jean isn't surprised that something terrible happens on her birthday. How would you feel if your birthdays were constantly beset with troubles? And how would you feel if you were one of the townsfolk of Casement Rise?

2. Jean realizes quickly that there are secrets being kept from her, and that her grandmother, Nancy, has been protecting her by telling her nothing about her family's past. Do you feel this was the right strategy? What would you have done in Nancy's place?

3. The Clever Birds in the book derive their name from the phrase "Who's a clever bird?". They are based on corellas, a type of cockatoo. Could you have stood still like Jean through the gyre of wings? What do you think they were looking for in Jean? Would they have found it in you?

4. The Husklings are monstrous creatures, bat-like and squabbling, but also capable of great sensitivity and art. What do you think the writer is saying about the nature of art, and the monstrous? Do you agree?

5. Jean's best friend is Lolly Robson. They are both outsiders and see that reflected in the other. Did you expect the trajectory that their relationship took? Have you experienced friendships like Jean and Lolly's? How did reading about their friendship make you feel?

6. Jean and Nancy walk the Stone Road, the path of the dead, by taking mycota broth. Mycota is another word for fungi, and in the book, its ingestion distorts and clarifies the landscape through which the characters walk. What were you expecting to see in the Mumbling City? How would you have dealt with facing one of the angry dead?

7. *The Stone Road* was a novel drawn in part from the Aurealis Award-winning short story "Cracks," but there is also another character drawn from the author's earliest published story "Threnody," Sal the Threnodist. They'd always wanted to return to that character and in the writing of *The Stone Road*, Sal unexpectedly appeared. What do you think might be the challenges of creating a novel out of the seeds of a short story?

8. The dead grumble and complain, but for Jean and Nancy, the dead are very physical presences grabbing and clawing at their feet. Jean must learn to face their power or forever be cowed by them. How do you carry the weight of your past, and how have the dead shaped your world?

9. This book is set in the same world as *Day Boy*, but the worldbuilding is deliberately loose, using slightly different terms for locations and concepts. How do you think this world may have come about? Why might the author have avoided telling readers exactly what happened?

10. Furnace is a constant presence in the book through the smell of its smoke and the visitations of its master, the Graceful Man. What were you expecting Furnace to be?

11.   The citizens of Casement Rise live a long way
      from the Red City, a region ruled by vam-
      pires. It's a hard life so far from the Red City,
      in a region that even the vampires tend to
      avoid. What could be the benefits of living in
      Casement Rise?

12.   *The Stone Road* is filled with clocks and mir-
      rors and magical doors, and deliberately
      plays with reflections and echoes. What ele-
      ments did you notice were reflected? Bear-
      ing that in mind, what were your feelings
      about the ending of the book? Have those
      feelings changed since you finished reading?

✳ More from Trent Jamieson ✳

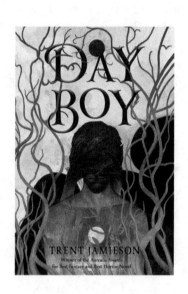

Check Out Erewhon's Recent Titles

EREWHON

More from Erewhon Books ✳

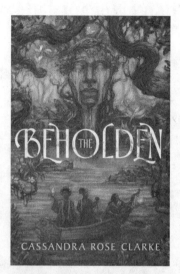

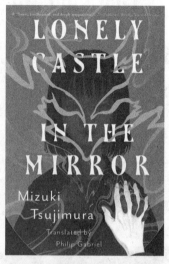

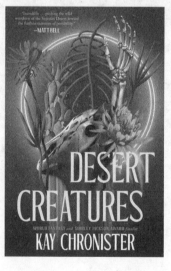